AMY COLE
IS ZEN
AS F*CK

Elizabeth McGivern

PERNICKETY PUBLISHING

ISBN 978-1-9996403-2-3 (eBook)
ISBN 978-1-9996403-3-0 (paperback)

Cover Design: Maire-Clare Doran
Photo Credit: Jess Lowe

To Conor,

Always remember that night:

"It doesn't matter" – The Rock

Yes, I'm trolling you in a book dedication. Like a fox.

Let's just keep turning the bathroom lights off x

Prologue

For as long as I live, I will never forget the sound of the body hitting my windscreen.

The gut wrenching thud, the screech of the brakes, and how our ragged breathing hung in the air for, what seemed like, an eternity.

"What have you done?" cried Elle.

"I..I…I didn't see him," I stammered.

"Don't just sit there! Phone an ambulance! Now!"

I frantically searched for my phone while she struggled to undo her seatbelt and get out of the car.

Tears sprung from my eyes and my hands shook as I tried to dial the three numbers no one ever wants to call.

The emergency operator answered within seconds and I didn't have time to compose myself before I tried to speak.

"Please hurry. I've just hit a man with my car and he needs help," I choked.

The rest of the conversation went by in a blur. I answered the operator's questions like a robot and after she reassured me help was on the way, I hung up and sat in the car, immobile. I looked at the kidney-shaped crack on the windscreen trying to process what had just happened.

I watched Elle as she frantically tried to call to the stranger and rouse him. She looked up to the car and saw me sitting like a statue, staring at the scene unfolding in front of me.

"Get the fuck out here!" she screamed.

I slowly unbuckled my belt and got out of the car to walk towards the motionless man. I was aware that Elle was saying something in the distance but I kept looking at the blood that trickled from his ear.

"Amy? Amy? Don't you go into fucking shock here," she said, as she grabbed both my arms and physically shook me back into the present moment.

"Did you hear what I said?" she asked.

"No," was all the reply I could manage.

"Amy, I can't find a pulse. I think he's dead."

One week earlier

Chapter 1

Ding Dong the bitch is dead.

The inner bitch, that is.

After 51 long sessions of sitting in a cramped, stuffy office with Dr Jeremy Kelly I have been officially declared 'sane'.

Well technically I haven't - he refused to use that term or indulge me in a small graduation ceremony involving a certificate I printed out at home which read: 'Amy Cole is perfectly sane'.

I did manage to convince Elle to make me a little paper graduation cap and hand the certificate to me afterwards at Joseph's café.

My final therapy session had arrived and I was being discharged with all the tools I needed to keep me from throwing myself into a lake again.

Huzzah.

I wasn't going to miss my time with Dr Kelly but I was grateful for everything he'd taught me. Cognitive Behavioural Therapy had worked wonders on my mental health and after working through several significant psychological barriers he thought it was time for me to go it on my own.

I excelled at school. I was the epitome of a teacher's pet and I was no different in my approach to therapy. In order to prepare for my imminent discharge from his care I had bought every book that dealt with preventing depressive episodes, printed hundreds of thought records and achievement charts in order to keep me on the straight and narrow.

If I'd known keeping myself on the right side of sanity would involve new stationery I would have gone to therapy sooner.

This journey of self-discovery, learning to love myself and effectively murdering that wretched inner voice who caused me years of unhappiness was a slow one. It took Dr 'Just call me Jez' Kelly six months to get me to talk about the miscarriage and another six for me to compromise and call him Jeremy (I will never call another human Jez, I just don't care).

After eighteen months and 51 sessions I was a free woman. I just had to get through one more hour with him to be officially discharged and so I could close this chapter once and for all.

The relief that the day had finally arrived was palpable. It practically radiated from my husband, Ben, whenever I stood close to him, but I couldn't blame him. He'd been the main catalyst in getting me to therapy in the first place but his 'I told you so' attitude about how effective it would be was excessively irritating.

When I came home after every session he would sit on the edge of the sofa wanting to hear how it went and handed me print outs of new articles he'd found on CBT. I don't think I ever read any of them, but I did put them in a folder (neatly categorized with my new label maker, of course).

Sexy, sexy stationery

He offered to drive me to the last session but I declined. I reasoned that I shouldn't make a big deal out of it; that now was when the real work began, but in reality, I just wanted him to look after the kids so I could escape to Joseph's for a coffee after, undisturbed.

It worked out well for us both, he thought I was stoic and committed to my new life post-therapy and I got to drink a coffee at the temperature God intended without hearing the word 'mummy' 576 times.

Win, win

It wouldn't come as a surprise to him that my first port of call would be to the café. It was the base of operations for Elle and I. We didn't have an official name for our business – despite Elle's best attempts at trying to convince me of 'Bad-Ass Consultants' – but we were officially a company.

After the successful launch night of *Joseph's*, business owners from all over town (and further afield) began to call in and ask to speak with us about their own troubles in commerce. To begin with we just gave general advice, but when we realised we could make a legitimate business out of things we hassled Joseph into letting us rent one of the unused rooms above the café as our office. After nearly two years in operation we were ticking along nicely, but we could be doing better. On more than one occasion I had to sit Elle down and explain that our retainer fee could not be paid in cake. Neither of us particularly liked to charge an already struggling business, but we also had bills to pay and we made ourselves feel better by justifying that our fee was a small percentage of all the money they would make thanks to our work.

It was sometimes trying to work with my free-spirited best friend, but she really was the most creative and inspiring person to work with. Her PR campaigns alone would rival that of any of our big city competitors and her rapport with the clients was like no other. She instantly made them feel at ease, listened to their problems and spoke with such confidence about our abilities that by the time they left, they looked like they no longer carried the weight of the world on their shoulders.

She had officially separated from her husband, Keith, and was counting down the final weeks until her divorce could be finalised. For the first few months of their break-up she felt 'compelled' to paint nothing but ominous dark paintings so she could 'work through the pain'. I indulged her and let the office be cluttered with half-finished canvasses of depressing, barren landscapes. I finally convinced her to clear them out because it was making potential clients sad.

One day I came into work and they were all gone. In their stead there were flowers everywhere – and I mean everywhere. The majority were fake and hung off every possible place she could affix them to. Long gone was the simple cream carpet and instead she had taken inspiration from the café and installed artificial grass.

"This way it fits in with the atmosphere of the rest of the building and I get to walk around bare foot," she said, "You know I get so much more creative when I'm connected to nature."

"But you're not connected to nature," I countered, "It's plastic. If anything, you're connected to the hardware store."

She waved her hand dismissively and flatly ignored my protests about the impromptu makeover.

"Our clients are in pain. They are worried about the future and their livelihood," she continued, "With an office like this we are welcoming them into a healing environment and they're going to love it."

We lost two potential new clients that week.

Eventually I grew to like the grass and the flowers. It was like working in a forest without the hay fever or the insects and sometimes I liked to pretend I was a woodland nymph. This wasn't something I ever said out loud or at therapy, for fear that I would earn myself more time in the good doctor's couch.

As I arrived at my destination I looked at myself in the mirror and gave the most convincing smile I could manage.

"Ok, Amy, you look sane enough and all you have to do is get through the next sixty minutes and we are free. You get to book a holiday as a celebration and you won't ever have to sit on that itchy, uncomfortable chair ever again," I said.

It was a warm Spring day and my favourite time of year. The beginning of a new season brought out the optimist in me and I strode, with purpose, into the dingy little cupboard-sized room which passed for an office.

"Amy," he said, warmly.

"Jeremy." I reciprocated his smile, but wanted to keep all expressions muted in case they could be misconstrued as manic.

"We don't have much to do in this session," he continued as he gestured towards my usual chair, "It's more of a questionnaire and I will give you a chance to bring up any issues you'd like to discuss before we finish."

I tried to hide my excitement at the word 'finish' but a little squeak escaped my mouth. I quickly bit my lip and went back to looking completely zen-like.

"It's ok to be excited, Amy," he said, "You've worked hard and have come a long way from our first session."

He handed me the questionnaire and I awkwardly balanced the sheet on my knee as I tried to tick the appropriate answers.

I loved multiple choice questions there was no way even I could mess up on multiple choice. All I had to do was to not tick the answers a raving lunatic would choose.

Easy.

The answer options I had were:

- Always
- Mostly
- Occasionally
- Seldom
- Never

Q1: When was the most recent time you thought negative or harmful thoughts about yourself?

I was already stumped by the first question. None of the answers made sense to the phrasing of the question and I couldn't answer it.

I should just point this out to him. Wait. What if this is a trick question and if I bring up that it doesn't make any sense, he'll take that to mean that I need specific dates to answer because I'm still thinking shitty things about myself?

My face betrayed my inner dialogue and Jeremy peered over his glasses to see why I looked like I was trying to solve a complex mathematic equation.

"Is there something wrong, Amy?"

"No…Yes…I don't think so. Is this a trick question?"

"There are no trick questions, Amy, it's just a simple exit questionnaire that I get all my patients to fill out for their files. Is there something you'd like to discuss in more detail?"

"No," I said a little too loudly, "It's fine. I'm fine. Everything is perfectly fine."

"It doesn't seem to be fine. Can you tell me the question that is giving you difficulty?"

I showed him the question and explained my problem. He chuckled and said: "I've been handing this out for years and no one has ever noticed. You're right it doesn't make any sense."

I breathed a sigh of relief.

"It should read: 'How often do you think negative or harmful thoughts about yourself?' Would you like me to print out a new copy?"

"No, it's fiii- sorry, no it's good. I can just answer 'never' because that's the truth and I'm sane now." I said with a fake giggle that sounded more disturbing, than comforting.

Jeremy went back to reading his notes and I scribbled the updated version of the question onto the sheet. As I went to tick the 'Always' box I realised too late that I was meant to say 'Never' and ended up ripping a hole in the sheet with the pen right into my thigh.

"FUCK!" I screamed.

The loud cursing shocked Jeremy out of his work and he jumped onto his feet.

"I'm sorry, I'm so unbelievably sorry," I said as I furiously rubbed my thigh, "I stupidly decided to wear a poxy dress and now I've stabbed myself with a pen because of this bolloxing, secretly sneaky, test.

"No bloody way does this count as self-harm. I'll sue if you put that down in your notes."

"Amy," he soothed, "Please sit down."

I didn't realise I was standing up and pointing my pen in his face like a crazed accuser. I quickly sat the pen down on the coffee table in front of me and sat, cross-legged, on the chair trying to pretend I was in control of my emotions once more.

"There seems to be a bit of tension coming from you, today," he continued, "Is there something bothering you?"

I weighed up if I should continue the farce of nonchalance or if I should just come clean and hope for the best. I opted for honesty, simply because I'm a dreadful actress.

"I guess I'm feeling a bit overwhelmed," I said, "I've been waiting for this day from the very second I first walked into this office and now that it's here I'm beginning to feel like a bit of a fraud."

I could feel the lump in my throat continue to rise and no amount of gulping would push it back down.

"A fraud?" he asked.

"Yes. What if I leave here and all it takes is one bad day for me to be back to square one. What if the depression has just been biding its time and comes back worse than before? I'm scared to feel this well, to feel in control. I think I'm scared to be happy."

The tears fell silently and I looked at the ground in shame.

11

You will never be free from this

"Amy," he began, "What you are feeling is perfectly normal."

The relief at hearing those words was indescribable.

"You have spent a large portion of your life thinking and feeling a certain way and now you have been taught to view things completely differently. It's perfectly natural to feel overwhelmed at ending this part of your journey and going out to the world. Many people view this office as a safety net – it's not something I like to encourage, which is why I put so much focus on your work at home – but I understand that 'cutting the chord' with these sessions is daunting."

He smiled, kindly, and asked: "What have I told you in every session since you first came tumbling into this office?"

"Just because you think it, doesn't make it so," I replied, like the obedient student I was.

"You are going to be just fine. You are in control of your life and you have all the know-how to deal with a bad day. I am very proud of the woman I see in front of me."

I decided to forgo my usual standoffish nature and hug Jeremy. I stopped short of calling him 'Jez', even though I had a sinking suspicion that he's been waiting his whole life for someone to call him that.

The rest of the session went by uneventfully and by the end I felt much more relaxed about going back into the world and leaving the bitch, the lake and my past right there in that room.

With that chapter closing I just had one final thing to get through: the rest of my life.

Simple.

Chapter 2

I walked into the café and was immediately blinded by an unsettling amount of confetti thrown into my eye.

"SURPRISE!" they wailed when I was finally able to dislodge the paper from my pupil.

I was met with blurry versions of my nearest and dearest, all gathered at the entrance of Joseph's café.

I tried to reach out for a table to keep my footing but it was misconstrued as an attempt to hug the blurry figure beside me – thankfully, it was Ben.

"I'm sorry, you know what she's like I couldn't rein her in," he whispered as he hugged me close.

I managed to adjust my eyesight and take in the scene properly.

Elle had managed to rope all the staff, including a very grumpy Joseph, into wearing tiny party hats and were each holding pom-poms so they all looked like really pissed off cheerleaders.

My parents, Eloise and James, were behind Ben and my two sons stood at their side looking very pleased with themselves for successfully keeping this party a secret.

Elle was next to come towards me, with a glass of champagne and my homemade graduation cap.

"You did it!" she bellowed, "You're no longer fucking mental."

Ben winced at her phrasing but I was used to it. She gave me a kiss on the cheek, turned to the rest of the party and said: "Alright, you glum-looking bastards let's get pissed!"

It wasn't a request and everyone there knew as much so they all slapped panicky smiles on their faces and grabbed champagne glasses in order to pretend they were instantly having a good time.

My saintly father came up to speak with me. I was always comforted by his presence, he always had the ability to make me feel safe no matter how fast the earth was spinning.

"I read in the paper the other day that drinking champagne can kill you," he said.

Christ. Thanks, dad.

I subdued my reflex to spit out my drink and just decided to indulge him by asking about this latest conspiracy theory. He had recently discovered online and had been obsessively looking at videos which 'proved' that 9/11 was an inside job so I was quite relieved at the change of topic.

"I'm going to need more information than that, dad."

"Don't look at me like that, Amy. I know you think I'm just a doddering old fool but I'm telling you it's what I read. You wouldn't catch me drinking that swill. It said in the article that there's something in the bubbles that cause cancer."

"So what are you drinking? Water?"

"God, no. That stuff is even worse."

"Water? Are you actually telling me water is also going to kill me?"

"Yes! The Government has been putting these experimental chemicals into the water supply little-by-little over the years and that's why people don't know about it until it's too late."

"What's too late?"

"It makes you sterile."

"Water?"

"Yes, Amy. I'm not making this up, it's all over the internet you just have to read the truth."

"Why do they want to make us sterile?"

"To keep the population down. Amy, you really need to pick up a newspaper once in a while, in fact I'll send you a link to the site I swear by. It's going to blow your mind."

"So what is the tipple of choice for the man in the know?"

"I stopped at the supermarket on the way here and bought a multipack a those *Face Blitz* energy drinks, they're great."

The irony, and my eye-rolling, was lost on my father so I left him talking with an unsuspecting waitress while I tried to track down some more killer alcohol.

I can only hope it does the job so I don't have to be at this party anymore.

My mother was next to find me. As she enveloped me into a one-armed hug, followed by a brief kiss on the cheek, I was surprised to find that she wasn't as stiff as she normally is during our infrequent shows of affection. To her credit she had gotten a lot better since my breakdown and was always interested in my recovery, as well as wanting to hear about what the 'quack' doctor was telling me that week (her words, not mine).

"Don't let your father see you drinking that stuff," she whispered as she let me go.

"Too late, I've already been informed I'm either going to die or become sterile."

"He's driving me mad, Amy. I've had to start turning the wifi off in the evenings and telling him it's broken when he gets too wound up with whatever the latest fake disaster is."

"Does he not just go and check the box?"

"Don't be ridiculous he doesn't even know where the box is. Once when he walked past it in the hallway he thought it was an air defuser.

"Anyway, enough about that silly old man, what are you going to do now that you're 'sane'? Finally go back to work?"

I tried not to get annoyed by the obvious air quotes around 'sane' and opted to taking an extra-long swig of the champagne until my blood stopped boiling.

See? More zen by the second. Thank you, killer alcohol

"I do work, mother," I said as calmly as I could manage.

"You do? No, I'm not talking about that little side hobby you and that maniacal Australian do; I mean a real job."

Nope, there's not enough alcohol in the world to talk to my mother.

I searched the crowd for Ben, he was the one I needed to calm things down and I also needed to murder him for making me go through this. I found him trying to coax Arthur away from the tray bakes behind the counter. As I looked at him I felt a wave of affection for the ridiculous man that is my husband.

"I was coming over here to shout at you," I smiled, "but fortunately for you, fatherhood makes you look rather cute."

I rubbed my nose along his jawline and gave him a soft kiss on the neck while Arthur took advance of the distraction and shovelled another cupcake into his mouth.

"Short stack," I called, "stop trying to give yourself Type 2 Diabetes and go annoy your granny."

"How?" asked Arthur, barely disguising the excitement in his voice.

"Tell her she looks marvellously menopausal."

"Ok."

Cruel? Maybe. Worth it? Absolutely.

"You're a terrible daughter, Amy Cole," said Ben, in a nervous tone.

"Yes, but that's why you married me."

"I married you because you promised me sex and chocolate, woman."

"Well I delivered. Those two sons of yours didn't appear via stork – I have the ravaged midriff to prove it – and judging by the dad-bod you're sporting you've had a steady supply of chocolate for years."

"Hey! Now, you're just being mean to everyone."

"I'm kidding, you know I'm kidding. You're as gorgeous and gullible as the day I met you."

I left him with a perplexed look on this face, as if he was trying to figure out if he had been insulted again without realising it.

I watched as the owner of this miraculous place, Joseph, bickered with his son-in-law, cook and all-round good guy: Michael. It didn't matter what the argument was about, they would always be on opposing ends of any conversation. Although Michael had managed to find his voice and not let himself be pushed around quite so much, I still hadn't witnessed him actually win an argument against his boss.

"My Amy," said Joseph, as he crushed me into his familiar bear-hug.

"We talked about you not doing that, remember?" I said as the air was slowly being drained from my lungs.

"Don't be silly, I'm an old man you should just humour me."

"She's accepting hugs now?" called an incredulous Elle from the other side of the room.

"No!" I replied, as firmly as I could.

I watched as she picked up two more glasses of cheap fizzy wine – I doubted that Joseph splashed out on the real stuff, even if I was his favourite.

"Not bad, eh?" said Elle, as she handed me a glass and surveyed the chaos in front of her.

While I grimaced at the noise, mess and generally being in such close proximity to my parents, Elle was proud of her party and for that I loved her. The divorce was taking its toll on her but the infectious optimism she had was still as bold and bright as ever.

"I got you a present," she said with a mischievous grin.

I don't like the sound of this

"Don't look so scared! When have I ever given you a rubbish present?"

"Well, there was my birthday that you bought me that really expensive face cream which turned out to be a knock-off from your dodgy friend, Damo, that had inexplicable traces of ammonia in it."

"Didn't your skin look amazing though?"

18

"I was quarantined in hospital for three days, Elle."

"But your skin –"

"Stop talking. What's the present?"

"It's up in the office and you're going to love it."

I seriously doubt that

I reluctantly followed my over-excited friend upstairs to our office until she suddenly stopped in front of our door and demanded that I close my eyes. She decided to put her hands over them for good measure.

"You know I can feel you rolling your eyes under there," she warned, "just once, can you stop overthinking and go with the flow, you might even enjoy it. I'm giving you a present, not sending you to a face a firing squad. When have I ever given you a terrible surprise?"

"Well there was the time at Christmas that –"

"You know sometimes, Amy, you could just lie to spare my feelings instead of remembering every little thing. Surely that's better, especially when I have you blindfolded at the top of a very steep set of stairs."

She ignored my audible gulp and marched me into the room. As she removed her hands and my eyes adjusted to the light again I heard her shout: "Ta-dah!"

I blinked several more times trying to see what was obviously in front of me but I was still at a loss as to what I was meant to be looking at.

"What is it?" I said, cautiously.

"It's the chair!" she squealed, excitedly.

My grubby office chair was as crappy as it always looked, although it had been moved away from my desk. I tentatively went over to sit on it to see if getting closer was the key to figuring out this particular present.

"Not that piece of shit," cried Elle, "I bought you a brand-spanking new one!"

My head whipped round to spot the beautiful cream leather finish of an unmistakable new chair, nestled behind my desk.

"I love it!" I said, with genuine enthusiasm, "It's just beautiful."

"I told you! When have I ever got things like this wrong?"

"Well... you know what? I'm not even going to say it because this is bloody brilliant. It's exactly what I needed; my back has been killing me on that other one."

"What are you waiting for? Take it for a test drive!"

I felt giddy as I kicked off my shoes and nestled my backside onto the leather.

This could rival hotness for stationery

"Hold on to your ass!" called Elle from the other side of the desk, as she bent down to switch on a plug.

What the?

As soon as she flicked the switch my seat began to rotate. The circles became wider as the speed increased and I could feel the familiar sense of panic gripping me. The nervous look on Elle' face as she ran towards me, did nothing to help alleviate my fears.

"Just relax, princess!" she called out over the deafening sound of the whirring chair.

"RELAX? What the fuck is going on, Elle?"

"It's one of those hula hoop chairs. It's to help you exercise while you work!"

It was hard to concentrate on what she was saying over the noise and growing pain in my side with each passing rotation.

"TURN IT OFF!" I cried.

"No! It just takes a second to get used to. I've seen the adverts and everyone loves them on the shopping channel. You're never going to be able to sit at a normal chair again!"

"THAT'S WHAT I'M WORRIED ABOUT! I'M GOING TO BE SICK."

She started digging out the instructions and reading aloud: " 'Just five minutes a day on the hula hooper will banish those unsightly love handles for good, blast that bulge and realign the spine' see? It's a really good chair."

Why can I smell burning?

"TURN THE CHAIR OFF!" I called.

"Maybe it's something to do with the settings? Hang on, it even comes with a remote control so you can change the speed. I saw it around here somewhere," she continued.

"ELLE, LISTEN TO ME: I'M GOING TO THROW MYSELF OFF THE CHAIR, YOU NEED TO BREAK MY FALL. I'M GOING TO COUNT TO THREE."

"You'd think the red button would mean 'stop'? I'm thinking it's something to do with a heating option."

"1..."

Christ my ass is really hot

"Ah, here's the bugger. It's the green button. Who would make the stop button green? That makes no sense."

"2..."

"Hey! Amy can you hear me? There's a weird burning smell coming from it, probably nothing to worry about but the 'stop' button isn't working so I'm going to just switch it off from the plug. Hang on to something."

"3!"

I launched myself at my unsuspecting friend and she crumpled instantly at the impact of my weight.

"What the fuck are you doing? Christ, my arse," she wailed.

"What do you mean? I was trying to save MY arse from being burnt alive! Why would you give me that death trap?"

I could tell she was gearing herself up for an argument about how she was a fantastic gift-giver but her train of thought was derailed when the chair caught fire.

"FUCK! FUCK! AMY! WHAT DO WE DO?!"

I ran around the room trying to find some sort of blanket to smother the growing flames but all I could see were fake flowers everywhere.

If those catch fire we are doomed. Throw it out the window? It would never fit. I can do this, I can figure this out.

Despite my internal reassurance of my capabilities in a panicked situation, my brain neglected to tell my fight or flight instincts to kick in and actually do something so I stood beside Elle, crying and looking helplessly at my new chair. We held hands and watched as the fake leather melted onto the ground and singed the plastic grass underneath it. It didn't take long for the sprinkler system to kick in and come to our rescue, however, it went on downstairs too – judging by the sound of screaming coming through the floor.

Once I was confident that the flames were dying down, I took off my soggy cardigan and sat it over the seat to extinguish the last of the fire and make sure it didn't decide to spontaneously combust again. Ben burst through the door to find two drenched, sobbing women, staring at a smouldering chair.

"I'm not even going to ask," he said as he retreated back to the chaos below.

Chapter 3

It took well over a week for the office to dry out. Thankfully, because of our unconventional flooring, we just had to pull up the sheets of 'grass' and let them dry off in the sunshine instead of ripping up soggy carpets – a pro that Elle didn't tire of mentioning to me several times a day.

An electrician had to come and make sure there was no water damage (there wasn't) but did charge an extortionate rate to tell us this good news. Elle offered to take him out to dinner if he gave us a discounted rate (he didn't) and she spent the rest of the day looking at herself in the mirror and mumbling about how her ex-husband sucked away her youth. That was a long day.

I went back to my boring, stationary, desk chair and decided that I would never complain about it, or my waistline again in front of Elle, however, I did come across a new slimming group that I thought I should try. The unsettling thing about this decision was I only happened to mention it once, in passing, to Ben over dinner and then my phone kept bringing up sponsored adverts about the new class opening this week. It made me more convinced than ever that my phone is spying on me and I've now taken to turning it off several times a day just to ease my paranoia.

"Are you staying much longer?" asked Elle, from behind her computer.

"No, I'm going to that slimming group I was telling you about. It's just up the road, are you coming with me? Moral support and all that?"

"Fuck, no. That sounds awful. Why would I want to give someone money to tell me not to eat everything I want to eat? Why don't you just visit your mother, she'll do that for you for free."

"It's about support and camaraderie and basically I need the pressure of standing in front of a room of people on scales to scare the biscuits out of my hand. Besides, no one is going to tell you to stop eating, it's about educating and support."

"Are you reading from their website or something, because you sound like you're full of shit."

I silently clicked the window closed on my computer and went back to pretending to file invoices.

"Right, princess, that's me done. I've sent you that pitch idea for the pet groomers and I'm going to stuff my face full of complex carbohydrates and watch trashy television. The excitement doesn't stop around these parts."

"You can always come to ours for dinner after I go to this thing?"

"No, you'll try and covert me into your weird diet cult. I like cheese, just fuck off. See you tomorrow."

I hated the evenings when Elle's twin girls, Hannah and Louise, spent the night with their father. She was always a little bit darker in her demeanour and usually wanted to be alone. I don't think she wanted to spend time with a family while hers was a broken shell of what it used to be.

I closed up the office and decided to head straight to the new club, before I chickened out. It was unfortunate that it was being held in the community centre down the street from the café – home to Elle and I's mortal enemy: Margaret Clunting. She was the formidable and downright unhinged leader of the parent and toddler group: Special Mums United in Growth, or Smug Club as we affectionately called to. We had come to an uneasy truce last year after our pranks to get back at each other escalated into a neighbourhood turf war. However, it wasn't until the community centre found out that Margaret was behind a particularly nasty smear campaign focusing on Elle, that she finally backed down and apologised to us both. It was graciously accepted by Elle, and by 'graciously' I mean 'not at all'. I believe her reply included the phrase: 'suck my dick'.

Since then we've all just avoided each other and if an unfortunate meeting does happen we do the adult thing and pretend we don't see each other. It's working. Two years ago I would never have dreamt of walking back into that community centre on my own, to talk about my weight in front of a room of strangers but Amy 2.0 had this shit all figured out and was ready to take a leap. I just wished that the leap was into a bucket of butter.

I reached the entrance without balking and making a run for the Chinese take-away and came face-to-face with a huge cardboard cut-out of a slim woman wearing a pair of jeans that were several sizes too big for her. I assumed this was meant to be inspirational as a before and after picture but it just seemed like she was a clown out of makeup waiting for someone to stuff cream pies into the trouser legs.

"Inspirational isn't it?" said the voice behind me.

I jumped at the intrusion into my internal monologue and turned to face the real life version of the cardboard woman, now wearing jeans that fit her.

"This may surprise you to know," she continued, "but that woman in the picture, is me."

"I…"

"It's ok, don't worry people often don't recognise me. I have completely transformed to this hot tamale in front of you."

Probably best not to contradict her

"My name is Melanie," she said with a smile so genuine I felt completely mesmerised.

"I'm eh an Amy," I stuttered.

"What an unusual name Anamy. Is that from your Scandinavian roots?" her American accent was delightful and the tone of her voice was like honey. She had a very comforting air about her.

"What?"

"I'm very intuitive, Anamy. I can tell you're not from these parts. Come on in and you can meet the rest of the gang and don't worry if your English isn't great I can SHOW YOU PICTURES."

Why is she shouting and enunciating so wildly? What the hell is going on here?

Before I could get answers to either of those questions, Melanie put her hand on the small of my back and led me into the main hall where a small crowd of nervous-looking people were standing. Their expressions mirrored my own but I didn't look quite as hungry as them. I was glad that I ordered an extra-large portion at lunch because I had a feeling this new food education was going to be a lot more gruelling than I had planned.

Melanie disappeared into the crowd and I found myself in front of a sign-in desk. The woman handed me a clipboard asking me for medical and bank details most of which I didn't know the answer to. I decided this was a case for my personal assistant: Ben.

Amy: Hi love, by any chance do you know my weight, height, blood type, most recent vaccinations, account number and sort code?

Ben: Are you joining a cult and are you giving them all our money?

Amy: I don't think so. They are going to make me skinny but they also think I'm a Viking.

Ben: I'm not sure what to say to that. Go on the banking app for your money stuff and make the medical crap up – no one checks that.

Bolstered by Ben's confidence I decided just to make things up as I went along in order to make the horrible form-filling stop.

Height? What's average height for a woman? Like 6ft 2"? Fuck it, that will do. Blood type? I think it's like Type K positive or something, that sounds familiar.

I dutifully handed in my membership form and after close examination the woman behind the desk asked: "Is any of this true?"

"What do you mean?" I asked in mock indignation.

"Well you're about a foot shorter than what you have written here and I don't think they vaccinate against 'goat gonorrhoea'?"

"I liked the alliteration…" I said, sheepishly.

"Of course you did," she replied, with a bored smile.

"My name and the bank details are correct," I continued, hopefully.

I really don't want to get kicked out of this group before I've even got started

"Well then, that's all I care about."

She gave my sheet a stamp of approval and gave me a membership card.

"All the new guys get weighed at the end, you'll have to sit through Melanie's sales pitch until then."

"But I'm already sold, I've given you my details."

"I don't make the rules, I'm just here to take the money. Next!"

I was pushed aside by a large man, who looked at me like I was getting on his last nerve. It probably didn't help that I stepped on his toe on the way past.

I settled down in my seat and decided to switch off my phone in case it picked up where I was and started putting sponsored ads for tummy tucks and religious cults in my timeline.

I wonder who does marketing for cults? Do they need marketing? Isn't it meant to be a secret?

My trip down that pointless rabbit hole was halted by Melanie as she took to the stage dragging her 'inspirational' cut-out with her.

"Hi, guys!" she said as she waved warmly to a crowd who looked like they didn't want to be there.

"I know what you're thinking: 'who is this woman I'm holding?' Right?"

There was a slight mummer of agreement but I was still confused as to why she kept expecting us not to recognise her. I wanted to keep on the right side of my fellow cult members and decided to nod along with them.

"What would you say, if I told you this was the night your life is going to change FOREVER? WOOHOOOOOOO!"

Do we clap? Do we 'woohoo'?

There was an uncomfortable silence in the hall broken only by someone coughing at the back. I felt that this woman's planned pitch was more suited for a conference in Vegas and not for a small town in Ireland. I began to cringe internally and I had a feeling things would be getting much worse before I escaped.

"Ok, guys. I know you fat, lazy swines are used to not exerting any energy, but that's because you're eating yourselves to death and I'm here to put a stop to this now."

Wait, what?

"I am going to make you wake up and see what vile, disgusting, drains on humanity you really are. Welcome to 'Fat Shame, Life Gain'."

I am in hell

My mind started racing back to all the adverts and information leaflets I'd seen on this place and realised that not once had it ever said the name of the programme. I could feel myself wanting to shrink slowly onto the floor and crawl out the back door without anyone seeing me. I had a feeling that it was going to be impossible, under the watchful eye of Melanie. The warm smile she flashed to me at the entrance was still plastered on her face but now she represented everything I hated. I just wanted to lose a couple of pounds and maybe learn how to cook without having butter in every meal. I didn't want to loathe myself into an eating disorder.

I can't sit here, I can't give money to something as perverse as this

I tried to get my nerve together and walk out with my head held high, I would not be party to fat-shaming of any kind by an over-enthusiastic American. My seat betrayed me as it loudly scraped along the floor as I stood up.

"Anamy! My friend from outside, it's great to see you get involved so early," she beamed, "Ladies and gentlemen this Scandinavian goddess has decided to take control of her disgusting obesity and is going to change her life this very second. Get up here, Anamy, I want people to see just how brave you are about changing your hideous self."

What's going on here? Why am I walking? Amy? AMY! STOP WALKING TOWARDS THE ENEMY.

"Anamy, tell us about how you let yourself go so much?" she said, with overzealous compassion.

"Eh, I guess it was when I had the children," I replied in – what I hoped – was a Norwegian accent.

I give up, you're on your own you absolute moron

"Ahuh, ahuh, I hear ya, sister. Kids are hard and it's also a lazy, no-good, lie you've given yourself so you could eat cake and let yourself get this huge."

"I don't think I *am* huge. A couple of pairs of trousers are getting a bit tight so I thought - "

"You thought: 'man, I am a wildebeest and it's time I got this sorted out before I take up more of the NHS' precious resources for my laziness? Isn't that right?"

"No, I -"

"You see, ladies and gentlemen if our foreign friend has the courage to come and make a new life for herself in this country and also transform herself from this fugly

31

mess, then you should be brave like Anamy. You can sit down, Anamy, we can talk properly at the scales after all this."

I mutely went back to my seat and decided that there was no point in making more of a scene. I could easily slip out the back after it finished, it couldn't last forever after all.

The next hour seemed like the slowest in creation. I listened to her talk about her struggle with her weight and how it was the root cause of everything that had gone wrong in her life. I tried not to let my newly-found therapy knowledge make me scoff, but some of the things she was saying were just downright lies.

"The facts don't lie, people," she shouted from her pulpit, "It is a certified fact that 98% of people hate themselves and I can tell you here and now the singular reason for this worldwide hatred, is because we are all falling victim to the silent assassin: fatness. It is a pandemic, people, and we need to wake the hell up and make sure we become part of the solution."

I felt like somewhere in the Middle East, Taliban leaders probably weren't sobbing in the mirror as they looked at themselves in a bikini nor was it because of their middle-age spread that they would conduct a terrorist attack. I felt that even if I did object to her ridiculous, and obviously made-up, facts that she would somehow twist my words and blame my disbelief on a sugar dependency.

I also noticed that her once honey-like American accent had become more southern as the time went on. By the end of her speech I was waiting for her to put on her Stetson and start wrangling us like cattle if we tried to leave without getting on the scales.

"Y'all, it's like this: do you want to be good people, living your best life or do you want to keep being useless, fat, leeches on this beautiful world that our Almighty Jesus Christ has provided for us? He gave his life for y'all, not just so you could waste it by eating your weight in fried foods. Now, you disgust me, you disgust yourself and now you disgust Jesus.

"If you are ready to make a change like our obese foreign friend, Anamy, then get your asses over to those scales and praise Jesus for this chance at redemption."

I braced myself for the deluge of abuse that was obviously going to come from everyone sitting in the room. She was an evangelical, fat-shaming, maniac – I decided that I earned the right to remark on her mental health because I recognised a kindred spirit. Instead people started to clap, not just clap – clap with actual enthusiasm. I heard cheers, whoops and I was even sure I heard someone shout 'praise Jesus'.

What the actual fuck is happening?

I picked up my bag and made my way through the crowd congregating at the scales but was nabbed by Melanie.

"Now, you wouldn't be trying to make a getaway without facing your real truth would you?" she asked in a voice that didn't seem altogether pleasant, "Your fellow fatty will make room for you and let you skip the line. We are all in this together and we are going to stop this epidemic in its path."

She pushed me in front of the man waiting in line. Obviously it was the man I had stepped on earlier and I managed to step on his foot once more, for good measure. I felt like an apology wasn't going to be well received so I decided just to drop my belongings and step on the scales. Melanie asked her minion to move aside while she took the reading.

"I'm not going to tell you what you weigh right now, Anamy, it's an irrelevant number. Fat is fat and you are fat. No one is going to know exactly what they weigh but they will be told if they have lost and have pleased God or if they have taken another pound towards the devil."

"Actually, Melanie, I'm an atheist so this probably isn't for me. I think I'll just head on home."

"Do y'all hear that?" Melanie shouted to the large queue formed behind me, "Our dear friend Anamy is planning on leaving here to resume her fat, lazy life. Are we going to let her do that?"

"No!" they shouted, in unison.

Have they practised this?

"Anamy, give this book a read and give this programme two weeks to change the way you think about yourself. I can guarantee you that you will not regret it and I can't in good faith let one of my followers go back into this world without being protected against the evil of carbohydrates."

"Is this a Bible?"

"No, darlin' it's your meal plan for the next week and some motivational quotes to keep you on the straight and narrow and then soon enough you'll be straight and narrow too. You are going to be my special project."

She laughed at her own bad joke and then turned her attention to the next person in line. I left feeling even more confused about what I had just paid money for. By the time I got back to the house I had already thought about just trying a few of the recipes and pretending the rest of the horrible programme didn't exist, but even that felt like a betrayal against my principles.

"Hi, sweety," called Ben as I closed the front door.

"Hi, you."

"How was your new club?" he asked.

"I think I've become a poster child for an evil weight-loss guru."

"That's nice, dear, always good to have hobbies outside of the home."

Chapter 4

"Have you ever been sent a dick pic?" asked Elle.

I managed to cover my mouth before coffee came spluttering out.

"What?"

"A dick pic," she repeated, as if saying it again would make this question any less bizarre.

"I bet you've got a whole host of them stashed away somewhere. Ben seems like the type."

"You're saying my husband 'seems like the type' to take pictures of his penis and send them to me?"

"Don't make it sound seedy, it's quite fun – here look at this one."

She shoved her phone into my face and there it was: a rather flaccid-looking penis.

"Why are you showing me this," I said, as I tried to shield my eyes, "That image is now burned into my retinas. I feel like that constitutes as some sort of assault."

"Stop being dramatic, Amy, I just wanted your opinion on it. I haven't seen anyone's penis – other than my scumbag ex's – in a very long time. It doesn't look like Keith's. Does it look like Ben's? Should I show it to Michael and Joseph and see if they think it's normal looking?"

I grabbed her hand to stop her from leaving the table and showing the picture to any other unsuspecting bystanders.

"It looks a bit sad," I said.

"Yeah, doesn't it? I know I'm new to this internet dating malarkey, but surely he could have taken a better picture than that? Or maybe that *was* the good picture, that's a depressing thought."

Going against my better judgement, I picked up the phone and looked at the picture again.

"Do you think he's used a filter, or is it really that purple?"

"I hope it's a filter, or else I should just reply now and tell him to go get it checked out."

She sighed as she flopped back on her seat.

"I'm bored of being single, Amy. I just want to meet a nice guy, who likes me and the girls and possibly has a normal-coloured penis. All I'm getting are these idiot 'lads' in their twenties, who just want to meet up for a quick fumble. I hate that I'm not happy on my own – I really never thought I would need a relationship to feel whole, but here I am. It's pathetic."

I tried not to have a sympathetic look on my face but I was caught out and told to 'stop it, immediately'.

"You'll meet someone, the right someone, but I doubt you'll get much success on that app you're using by the sounds of it."

"No, I was told this was the one you needed to download if you wanted to find your soul mate. I'm sticking with it. Especially because it cost me £1.99 to download," she added.

"Let me see it then, maybe it's something you're exuding on your profile which is making all these undesirables flock to you. A bit of an edit could make all the difference."

She reluctantly handed over her mobile and I clicked on her profile.

Her username was Elle's Bells and the bio read:

Hi to all you sexy guys out there. My name is Elle and I'm a 29-year-old, fun-loving MILF who knows how to party hard and fuck even harder.

I stared at her incredulously.

"Seriously, Elle? You think that profile is sending out a 'I'm looking for a relationship' vibe?"

"Look, I know I said 29 but I figure the picture I'm using is a few years old and if we met at a dimly lit restaurant I could probably get away with it," she replied.

"I'm not talking about the age lie - although I think we should circle back to that – I'm talking about the party-girl persona who sounds like she's here for the ride."

"Do you really think it reads that way? Honestly?"

"How can you not think that? Of course these morons are sending you dick pics."

"Well, that's really given me some food for thought. I figured if I'm up against real 29-year-olds I should have a catchy bio to reel them in."

"Look, if you want to screw around and have some uncomplicated casual sex, then go right ahead. I support you 100%, but don't complain that you're not being matched with Mr Right when you have 'no gag reflex' listened under the *Special Skills* section."

I could see that she was mulling things over and weighing up the advantages of just having a few one night stands, compared to getting involved in a new relationship.

"What do you think I should write then?"

"Just be yourself; your awesome, 35-year-old self," I smiled.

"What should I do about purple penis?"

"Delete the photo and maybe never say those words to me ever again,"

"You're no fun now that you're not mental," she said, sulkily.

She eventually deleted the photo and then we spent an unproductive half hour thinking of all the words for 'penis' that we could think of. My personal favourite was 'Mr Wong' but it was later stricken from the official record for being deemed too racist by our adjudicator, Michael.

"I feel like we're not going to get anything productive done, today." I mused.

"What are you talking about? We made a huge list of penis words, that's definitely going to come in handy when I start sending dirty messages to the next guy I meet on my app."

"It's good to know you're taking my advice so seriously."

"I am, I am, I'm just bored of this online shite. Can't we go out? I'll get a group of us together and we can paint the town red. We can pretend we don't get hangovers or have any type of responsibilities. Please, princess, I'm desperate."

"But we don't have any friends, we literally have each other."

"Speak for yourself, I know plenty of women who want to go out on the lash with me. You just get Benny boy on board for having the sprogs to himself all night and I will take care of the rest."

She always used that as some sort of selling point when she was trying to convince me to do things, but all it did was make me very, very nervous.

"Fine, this Friday night; that way I don't have enough time to think my way out of how this is a terrible idea."

"Yes, yes, yes! You are not going to regret this."

"We both know I am."

***

I sat in Elle's kitchen sipping on a pink concoction that I was told was gin of some sort and closed my eyes as she did my make-up. This was one of the conditions I had negotiated in order to agree to a night out which included a club, with music and dancing.

There was no word on who was going to come out with us so I decided not to rub the 'I told you we were loners' in her face but I felt fine about going out with the two of us. Elle had enough energy for three people and this way I wouldn't have to make awkward small talk.

"There," she said, as she stepped back to observe her handy work, "you are a work of art, so don't get pissed and rub your eyes or you're going to look like a racoon."

As I surveyed my makeup there was a tap at the door and Elle jumped out of her seat, clapping her hands as she did.

"It's official, our first girls' night guests have arrived, there's no going back now!"

She ran off down the hallway to open the door and squealed with delight at whoever was standing at the other side of the door. The girlish cry wasn't reciprocated and I internally thanked the universe for not sticking me with two screaming women on a night out.

I instantly regretted being too thankful when my mother walked into the kitchen holding a bottle of Merlot.

Fuck my life

"Hello, Amy. What's all that muck on your face, you look like a lady of the night."

I sat, dumfounded, at the fact my best friend thought that a fun night out for me would involve my overcritical mother.

"Elle, a word," I said through clenched teeth.

I dragged her into the living room and struggled to remember a time I didn't feel this angry.

"What is she doing here?" I hissed.

"What do you mean? She's awesome and she complimented you as soon as she walked in, she called you a 'lady'. That's some proper girls night shit right off the bat."

"She called me a hooker!"

"Relax, I thought it was time we got to know each other so she would stop referring to me as a crazy Australian and she's bound to have some inclination to have fun otherwise she wouldn't have decided to come."

"All you had to do was explain that you're not a crazy Australian, you're a crazy South African, and we could have saved me a whole evening of increasing criticism fuelled by alcohol."

"Trust me, when have I ever let you down?"

I bit my tongue to stop me listing off the ream of times she has, in fact, let me down and decided just to pretend that Eloise Galbraith was not my mother and simply a woman - an irritating, overbearing, battle-axe of a woman.

We returned to the kitchen and found Eloise struggling to locate a corkscrew while turning her nose up at the mess in the room. I never minded the mess around Elle's house, mostly because I didn't have to live in it, but to an outsider it would look like she was allergic to closing cupboards and putting things away. It was superficial mess, but irritating none-the-less.

The doorbell went again and I wondered what fresh hell it would bring. I decided it was the perfect opportunity to set up some ground rules with my mother so I could try and salvage some part of the night.

"Mum-"

"Let me stop you there, Amy," she said as the cork finally popped out of the bottle, "I would prefer it if you didn't call me 'mum' tonight. I'm here to enjoy myself and get out of the house. Unfortunately my friend Deirdre is a nightmare to convince to get out of the house at the weekend – always gardening – so when the maniac rang I thought 'why not?' I know she's your friend and I'm on your territory or something but just let me enjoy myself. I don't want my night spoiled by your constant criticisms."

"Perhaps you could start by calling her Elle and not 'maniac' then?" I said, not quite believing what I was listening to.

"You see? Always criticising. Tonight I am Eloise, no one's mother just a classy, mature woman ready for a night out on the town. Got it?"

"Got it."

We sipped our drinks in silence and waited for Elle to return to help break the ever-increasing awkwardness between us.

"Next up we have: Donna!" announced our hostess as she dragged a shy-looking woman into the kitchen to face a cool reception.

"Fuck, who died in here?" Elle asked, "Donna ignore these two they're old rivals. Fell out years ago over the same fella but tonight it's all about mending fences and sisterhood."

"I thought it was about getting drunk and meeting men that aren't on the internet?" asked Donna.

"That too, babe, that fucking too."

Our group was complete and what an odd group we were. Thankfully, Donna was actually very nice to talk to, but was more interested in getting 'out on the prowl', as she called it, than spending time getting to know her new sisterhood.

"I've been divorced for two years, we are still on great terms and he's been with his girlfriend for about a year. I wasn't really interested in dating because I've just been focusing on the kids and trying to figure out the new family setup," she explained.

"That was until his 'save the date' card came in the post about three weeks ago and now I refuse to attend that damn wedding without a date. It's too sad."

"Why don't you just not go?"

"But then he wins."

"Wins what?"

"The 'I'm completely fine with this break-up' battle we've been doing for two years."

"Divorce is war," chimed in Elle, "Amy is still with her husband so she doesn't get why there's all these rules and games you still have to play even after you've broken up. It's all about the power."

Donna nodded sagely in agreement.

"So is your husband the one you two fell out over?" she asked.

"No, Amy settled for him after the better woman won *my* husband, James. He made his choice, bitch, get over it," said Eloise.

That's it, I'm making dad cancel whatever channel the Jerry Springer reruns are on.

"Let's all keep things civilised for the evening, shall we, Eloise?" I said, with a sickly, sweet smile.

She didn't answer and opted to take a long sip of her drink.

"Don't we make a fun group," said Elle, to break the silence – and probably reassure Donna that I wasn't about to jump across the table and attack my mother.

The world's most awkward foursome continued to make sporadic small talk and sip, rather sensibly, on our tipples of choice. I could tell that mum and I were both conscious of drinking too much in front of each other, but I had a feeling Donna and Elle would be making the most of their freedom by the time they got to the bar.

All too soon, the taxi arrived to take us into the one decent bar that played, somewhat passable, music on a Friday night. The entrance already had a queue at the door and almost instantly Elle sensed my reluctance to stand in line for anything other than food.

"It will move really quickly and then you can stand at opposite sides of the bar from your mother for the rest of the night, I promise," she said, with a look so desperate I could do little else but nod in agreement. So far this wasn't exactly the night of my life but I didn't want to ruin it for Elle, and subsequently Donna, just because I didn't want to hang out with my mum for the evening.

I know other people can do that: enjoy their parents' company as if they were best friends, but I've always felt perpetually awkward around her. These days we were definitely closer than we'd ever been but there's never going to be a time when either of us seek each other out for company, we're just not those kind of people.

To my surprise, Eloise unexpectedly hooked her arm into mine as we stood in the queue and rested her head on my shoulder.

"You are my favourite daughter, Amy," she slurred.

Ah bollox, she's already pissed

"I'm your only daughter, mum."

"I know that, I just mean I wouldn't swap you for another one."

I smiled, despite myself. This was probably the nicest thing she's ever said to me, I didn't care if she was pissed.

"I think I should get you home, mum, and let these young ones have fun without us."

"Not a bit of it," she said, straightening up and blinking furiously to stop her eyes from glazing over further, "I'm just as young and fun as those two. Even more so, I'd bet."

"Ok, ok, you're plenty fun; but I think it might be time to call it a night."

Donna overheard my plea to my mother and pulled Elle towards us.

"These two are fading," she said, accusingly.

Jesus. She's getting intense.

"NO! You're not going anywhere," Elle pleaded.

"Mum is pissed, I need to take her home," I explained.

"No, I'm not," protested Eloise, as she swayed side-to-side.

"See? No, she's not."

"Wait? She's your mum? Does that mean you fancied your dad? That's messed up," said Donna.

I didn't have the patience to explain the truth of the situation as I struggled to help mum keep her balance so instead I handed over her arm to Elle while I skipped out of the queue to hail a taxi. I reckoned this early on a Friday night it wasn't likely to take long.

I was wrong.

After 15 minutes of waving like a desperate woman stranded on the side of the road, a car finally took pity on me and stopped.

"Where to, love?" he asked through the window.

"Adelaide Close? It's not far, it's for my elderly mother," I added to really play the stranded female card.

"Where is she?"

I suddenly realised the queue had moved on exponentially since I'd been standing here and as I looked round I could find none of my new sisterhood.

Bunch of bitches

The taxi man rolled up the window and sped off without waiting for an explanation. I didn't blame him too much, I'd say Friday nights, surrounded by a lot of drunken morons would be a trying time. After years of listening to my father's tales of weekend runs I always had a mountain of patience for all taxi drivers.

I walked to the top of the queue and pushed my way through the crowd of groaning people who were disgusted at my line cutting, but they must have sensed my aura of irritation because none of them vocalised it loud enough for me to hear or react. I wouldn't normally have the nerve to cut in line but I felt like I was under pressure to stop my mother from agreeing to dance on a bar or get tequila sucked out of her belly button in an attempt to prove that she was still young and fun.

I could be at home in my pyjamas right now, but instead I'm babysitting my 72-year-old mother and her two sidekicks with lowered inhibitions and on the prowl for men.

I braced myself for the crush of the packed bar as well as the rolling of eyes and tutting I would receive from everyone I was pushing past in order to find my group. I was pleasantly surprised to find that it wasn't as full as the queue made it out to be and I assumed that was the point. Make people think it's such a desirable place to be because of the people willing to queue.

Clever move, bouncers

Unfortunately, the music was still too loud - and there were more people than I cared to stand close to as a rule - but needs must and I definitely needed to find my mother before she did something that would result in divorce proceedings.

I came across Donna first, she was trying (and failing) to get a barman's attention. I think it had something to do with the obnoxious way she was waving her money in one hand and clicking her fingers with the other.

Good luck, Donna.

"Have you seen my mum?" I shouted over the music of the live band.

"Yeah, her and Elle went to the bathroom."

She went back to her clicking routine and I fought my way through the growing crowd to the bathrooms where I found Eloise Galbraith comforting a sobbing 20-something-year-old woman.

"There, there, no man is worth crying over," she cooed.

I couldn't help but feel a pang of jealousy at how nice she was being to this complete stranger but it took two breakdowns for her to come close to showing me motherly affection.

"He…said…I…was…the…ONE," wailed the young woman between hiccups of emotion.

"Yes, well that tends to happen. He probably meant you were the one for right now."

Her nugget of wisdom didn't seem to be comforting her new friend as much as she hoped so I thought it was the perfect time to swoop in and try to convince my mother to get into a taxi.

"Amy!" she cried, with genuine warmth.

She really is drunk

"This is my daughter, everyone."

I'm not sure who she was talking to as there was only the three of us in the room.

"Now, you should take her as an example for waiting for the right man," she continued, "She had a whole string of unsuitable bastards before she settled with Ben. I mean, she could do a whole lot better – and I mean a whole lot better – but he's nice and he's nice to her and that's all you need, isn't that right, Amy?"

It took all my energy not to let my impulse to walk out and leave her to her own devices for talking absolute rubbish about my marriage, but I managed it.

"Don't let people tell you settling for someone is bad, it could work out completely satisfactorily, just look at my daughter," she continued.

"Ok, mum, time to go."

"It couldn't be, I've only got here and I haven't even danced yet."

"You have, you've been dancing all night and had three cocktails," I lied, "You only came into the bathroom to cool down a bit because you're so warm from all the dancing."

She looked at me suspiciously but decided I was either too honest or too stupid to lie about this and agreed to come with me. I had to throw in a pit-stop at the chippie on the way home just for her to agree to get into the car.

As we staggered out of the bathroom I managed to catch a glimpse of Elle talking with a man at least two foot taller than her. I didn't like the way she was eyeing him up but what right, or hope, did I have from stopping her.

I off-loaded my mum to an infuriated looking Donna while I tried to have a quick word with Elle. I tugged at her arm and asked to speak with her quickly.

"I'm bringing mum home, she's pissed," I said, "I promise I'll leave her with dad then I'll be straight back."

"No, it's ok," she said, with a sideways look at the man she had been speaking with, "I think I'll be fine with Max."

Who the hell is called Max anyway? Serial killers, that's who

"Please don't leave with him," I said, trying not to sound like I was being a prude.

"Are you slut-shaming me, Amy? I'm a grown woman with a healthy libido."

"I'm not, I'm really not. I just don't think it's wise to bring a stranger home, you don't know anything about him."

"I knew Keith for over ten years and I didn't know anything about him either. I might as well get laid."

"Just wait, let me get my mum home and then I will come back and give him a quick interview. If you still like him after that and I don't get any murder-y vibes from him then you can do whatever you want. I won't be long. Please?"

"Fine. I won't have hot sex with the stranger, I'll get to know him," she said, rolling her eyes.

I breathed a sigh of relief and went to collect my mother, who had fallen asleep at the bar and was running the risk of getting thrown out. Thankfully, it was a lot easier to hail a taxi this time around, mostly due to the older woman falling asleep on my shoulder.

I had to pay extra to convince the driver to stay for a few minutes as I handed over my charge to my very-shocked looking dad so I could make it back to the bar.

"She's fine, she needs water and sleep," I called from over my shoulder while jogging back to the taxi.

As the car drove off I looked out the back window to see Eloise plant a very large and sloppy-looking kiss on my father.

Gross

It didn't take long for me to be back at the bar and I managed to walk to the top of the queue once again. I had a feeling the bouncer was beginning to get sick of the sight of me continuously running in and out all evening. I gave him a nod of appreciation, which was reciprocated and I instantly felt like one of the cool kids.

I scanned the bar to try and find the giant serial killer and my best friend. They were nowhere to be found but I did manage to spot Donna playing tonsil tennis with a man who was about 5 years younger than her.

Good woman, Donna

I knew she wouldn't be happy if I interrupted this obviously romantic - and not at all drunken moment - but I was concerned that there was a man preparing to wear Elle's skin as an overcoat. I nervously tapped at her shoulder but she wasn't coming up for air. I tried again, more deliberately and for longer.

She turned to glare at whoever was ruining the story she was going to tell her grandchildren.

"WHAT?! Oh, Amy, sorry. No, not sorry: WHAT?!"

"I'm looking for Elle, have you seen her?"

"She left about ten minutes ago with that tree-trunk."

"You didn't try and stop her?"

"I've been a bit busy, Amy."

"Do you know where she's gone?"

"Probably home and far away from her cock-block best friend – now, kindly FUCK OFF."

I'm beginning to feel like this sisterhood craic isn't for me

I took a deep breath, pulled out my phone and started to call her number frantically.

Please answer, please answer, please answer

My calls rang out time and time again so I decided I would just have to go there in person and perhaps try to stop a 7 foot axe-murderer. I had to admit: I've had better Friday nights.

There was no hope in getting a taxi by now so I would just have to pretend I wasn't in heels or woefully unfit and get there by foot. At a brisk pace I could make it there in less than 15 minutes, probably closer to 20 if you factored in my non-existent fitness level and the rather large hill leading up to her estate.

I thought about phoning Ben but he was likely to be sound asleep on the sofa after three beers (the usual Friday night position) and there wasn't much he could do without having to pack up our sleeping children in the car and drive them, whilst over the drink-driving limit, to try and help me prevent a murder.

He could just be a nice guy?

I clung to that hope and cursed myself for continuously reading the trashy magazines that always had at least one murdered woman story in them every week. I huffed and puffed my way up the final hill and collapsed at her door, using the last of my energy to bang on it. It was a pathetic attempt so instead I took off one of my shoes and used it as a knocker.

It was a lot louder than I expected and caused two of the neighbours to twitch at their curtains to see what the commotion was about.

It didn't take long for Elle to answer the door in an oversized t-shirt and damp hair.

"Amy? What are you doing here? I thought you were going home."

"You…promised…to…stay…at…the…bar."

Keep the sentences shorter, Amy, you're about to have a heart attack. I really need to go to a gym

"I tried to text you but my phone died. I just decided to head home when you left and Donna had hooked up. I just thought it was a bit depressing to be there on my own."

"What about Max?" I asked as I held my hand at the stitch on my side and tried not to dry-heave.

"He was nice but you're right, it would be silly to bring a complete stranger home. I just walked home and got into my sweats."

"Did you have a shower?"

The blush that appeared at her cheeks was instant.

"Eh, yeah I was just feeling a bit gross from the sweaty bar."

"I need to phone a taxi, are you going to let me in?"

"Of course, sorry, I don't know why we're standing out here giving the neighbours a show. They probably think you're my booty call."

I collapsed, head first, into the sofa and tried to collect my breath.

"I'll phone you one now," she offered as she picked up her mobile.

"I thought you said your phone was dead."

Another blush betrayed her.

"It was, I charged it when I came in."

"What's going, Elle? You're lying and you're doing it badly."

"I'm not," she protested, half-heartedly.

At that moment I heard a creak of the floorboard from above my head.

"Who's upstairs, Elle?"

"No one, this is an old house, there are creaks from history."

"Your house was built in 2006."

I could see the clogs in her brain trying to churn out another weak lie so I took my chance and bolted from the room and straight up the stairs. So far, this fun girls' night out had involved more cardio than I had done in five years.

I knew Elle was hot on my heels so I threw myself into her bedroom door and twisted the handle but I wasn't quick enough to prevent her grabbing one of my heels, sending me tumbling through the doorway and landing on my knees.

When I blinked open my eyes I came face-to-face with a neon pink bra barely covering the crotch of a very tall and very naked man. He used his free hand to help me onto my feet while his other firmly kept the bra in place to conceal the last remaining part of his dignity.

"Eh, Max, this is my best friend, Amy; Amy, this is Max, the guy from the bar," said Elle as she lay on the ground, trying to figure out if she should explain why she had just rugby-tackled a woman into her bedroom.

"Hi, Amy, I've heard lots about you," he said, brightly, as he offered to shake my hand.

I refused the offer and did a limp wave instead.

"I see you guys have been busy in the hour that you've known each other," I said, hoping that it sounded like a joke and not a judgement. As I looked in Elle's direction I realised I had failed in my attempt.

"No, no, we haven't done it yet," he said, "Not that I'm expecting to do 'it' or anything; I mean we've done stuff and -"

"Max, I'm begging you to stop talking," said Elle, as she put her face into her hands.

"Max, are you a serial killer?" I asked.

"What? No! I'm a vegetarian."

That's kinda comforting

"Are you going to murder my friend and use her skin as an overcoat?"

"No..."

"You seem unsure."

"I'm a little scared," he replied, flatly.

"Amy, it's time for you to leave," interrupted Elle as she physically removed me from the bedroom and marched me down the stairs.

"I have ordered you a taxi, it will be here in 15 minutes and in the meantime you are going to sit in my living room and wait quietly while I go upstairs and have sex with the beautiful man – that's if he hasn't climbed out the window in fear."

"I was just -"

"I know you were 'just' being you, but I need this night and I can't think of a better person to pop my getting-over-Keith cherry with than that beautiful, bearded giant."

I didn't know what else to say to her about it, so instead I hugged her, told her to have fun and text me in the morning. I was warned not to show up at the crack of dawn to see if she was alive and that she promised to text me as soon as she woke up and would sleep with a knife under her bed 'just in case'.

I knew I was defeated so I opted to sit on her front step and wait for my ride. I figured it would be better than listening to those two have sex.

When the taxi eventually arrived I realised that I had spent all my money on various cars and absolutely none in the bar. I tried to make myself feel better by reminding myself that at least I wouldn't have a hangover to contend with in the morning and I promised myself that I would never wear heels on a night out again. I don't care if this meant I was short and unfashionable, I was finally ready to embrace the fact I cannot teeter about in stilettos.

I watched the blur of the streetlights glide by the window and tried to stay awake until I got back to the house but it was proving difficult. Thankfully my phone buzzed loudly enough to shake me back to consciousness.

Elle: Thank you for being so worried about me, you're a brilliant friend. I'm lucky to have you in my life.

P.S Max's dick is huge, he's in the bathroom washing his balls and arsehole for me AND THEN I'm going to ride him like there's no tomorrow. Love ya!

As I finished reading her message I felt like I definitely didn't need 50% of that message and yet I knew I would be getting a lot of unnecessary information about her intimate evening with this man in the coming days. One of the most frequent conversations I had with this woman was about where we should draw a line about oversharing. A line she refused to acknowledge even existed. As far as she was concerned we should know every intimate detail about each other's lives and sometimes that was really sweet, but there was one thing that really concerned me about all this:

Why was he washing his bum?

Chapter 5

Ben was unusually chipper for this early on a Saturday but I knew it was because he was eager to hear about my evening.

"You're letting the family name down, Cole," he said, before I'd even opened my eyes.

"How? I'm home in my own bed and I don't smell, or feel, like I've spent the night in a brewery."

"Exactly! You're getting old and sensible."

I didn't bother with a reply but instead, opted for a swift kick to his shin, under the blankets.

"Oww! Sorry, sorry. I mean, how are you my love? Have you gotten younger?"

"Better. Make me tea and I'll fill you in on all my juicy gossip."

Ben had never been able to resist gossip, even if he didn't know the people. It was exactly how I managed to get him to do most things around the house. He threw on a t-shirt and padded down the stairs in search of caffeine for me as I blindly reached for my phone to see if there was anything more from Elle – there wasn't.

I half expected to have a message or two from my confused father but judging the way Eloise launched herself at him when she got home I didn't think they would be coming up for air until this afternoon.

Horny parents are gross

When Ben returned with two mugs of tea I sat up and recalled my disastrous evening and waited on him to give me his verdict. I knew he would be disappointed that I'd left Elle to her own devices and I was prepared for the lecture about leaving her vulnerable with a stranger.

"I can't believe you almost cock-blocked your best friend," he said, as he shook his head.

"What?! You're on her side? And what is with this 'cock-block' nonsense that everyone keeps saying to me."

"Well, it means -"

"I know what it means, Ben, I mean have you all taken a vote and decided to put it in our regular vocabulary rotation, because it's a horrible phrase and I want you to quit using it."

"I know your heart was in the right place but you really need to loosen the apron strings a bit."

"I was trying to make sure she wasn't going to be murdered by a stranger."

"I understand, I just think that she really needed to carve a different name into her bedpost to get the whole Keith thing out of her system. She's still hung up on him and he's more than moved on."

"She is? He has?"

How does my husband know more about this situation that me?

"She talks to me sometimes, just when she's over for dinner and you're sorting the boys. I think she just wanted a male perspective on some things and it's harder for her to tell you that she's struggling with getting over him. She's worried that you'll think she's taking too long so she asked me what would a guy do."

"I would never, I can't believe, what is going on?" my confusion caused by this revelation made it impossible for me to get a complete sentence out.

"I told her to go have a fling," he added, matter-of-factly.

"That is genuinely terrible advice."

"We don't know that, maybe it's the best advice known to man."

"And if she's murdered?"

"Then you can say I told you so."

"Deal."

I spent the morning in a bit of a daze, constantly checking my phone to see if I'd heard from her. I resisted my natural urge to phone incessantly and see if she would pick up in case I made things worse. My state of anxiety wasn't helped by Ben's hovering.

"Any word yet?" he asked.

"For the fifth time, no. Max, is probably selling her organs on the dark web as we speak."

He decided it was safer to retreat to the front room with the children instead of trying to speak to me. I didn't blame him. I couldn't figure out if I was madder at him for his terrible advice or at me for not seeing how bad she was still feeling. I worked with her every day and we spent most of our free time together, yet she was worried about telling me something so important. I thought we were past all that secretive behaviour; I hated having to drag the truth from her when she was too embarrassed or upset to speak.

She can't tell me about her lingering feelings for her ex but can tell me about the size of her one-night-stand's penis. Standard, Elle.

My thoughts were interrupted by a knock at the door and I ran out to see if it was the police wanting me to identify a de-capitated head.

It was Elle.

I wanted to squeeze her into a bear hug out of sheer relief but I soon discovered that she was accompanied by Max and they were holding hands.

"Hi," she said, nervously.

Ben had reached the door before me and was awkwardly standing in the hallway waiting to see if the visitors were going to come in.

The silence continued until Max stuck out that helpful hand again and introduced himself to Ben. After the unusually formal introductions had been made they were welcomed into the kitchen.

"You guys are up early," said Ben, "Not that I assumed you were together all night or anything, you might have met this morning."

"You can stop that terrible lying, Ben, I know Amy has filled you in by now. I'm not remotely ashamed of what I did with Max, we are just here to set Amy's mind to rest."

"You could have just sent a text," I said, sounding more annoyed than I had planned to.

"So you could convince yourself that it was Max texting for me and I was locked in a dungeon somewhere?"

I hadn't thought of that…

"What are you guys up to today?" she continued.

"Nothing much, might go for a walk with the kids to pry them away from the television." Even as I said it I knew I would be fighting a war of resistance with Adam and Arthur, as well as Ben. I just had to look at his scrunched up nose at the sound of the word 'walk' to realise my prediction was correct.

"We'll tag along," Elle offered.

"You hate walking," I reminded her.

She replied with a high-pitched giggle and said: "Amy likes to kid around, like I'm not the one who whipped your arse into shape after you had those two darling boys."

"But you -"

"Amy? A word," she said in a terse voice, "I need to discuss work matters before I forget."

She gave a smile to Max and left him in the increasingly awkward presence of Ben while I was ushered out to the hall.

"I've told him I'm a personal trainer," she whispered, "I kinda am."

"You were a boogie bounce instructor over two years ago, how does that make you a personal trainer?"

"It makes me one because I said it does."

Sound logic if ever I heard it

"He's this big outdoorsy freak and I just started agreeing with all his hobbies and before I knew it I said 'me too' when he said what he did. He got all excited and I couldn't back down on the lie."

"It doesn't explain why you're here; I knew you weren't that concerned about my worrying."

"He suggested we go for a run to 'clear out our hangovers' and there's no way I could handle that shit so I said we should come here to check on you. I didn't actually think you'd be going to do fucking exercise. At least this way, with the kids in tow, he won't expect me to run."

"I'm basically a pawn in your lies to get laid?"

"Yeah, but I'd do the same for you. It's not going to be for long, I figure I can get a couple more rides on that particular stallion before he realises that I'm full of shit and then we're back to normality."

"Fine," I said, defeated.

At that moment, Ben came out to the hallway and asked: "Do we have any turmeric?"

"I don't know, possibly, why?"

"Max is making me a smoothie, he says it will revitalise my 'T' zone. I'm not sure where that is, but I'm excited."

Christ

"If there's any it will be at the back of the cupboard, just use your damn eyes."

I knew he wouldn't find it, no male in this house can ever find anything unless it's sat two feet in front of them and even then it can be hit and miss. We returned to the kitchen to find Ben pulling out the contents of the freezer.

"How is that a cupboard?"

"Didn't you say freezer?"

"Put that stuff back and get out of my kitchen."

I watched as Max deftly chopped and diced various fruits and vegetables. I had never been more thankful for having done groceries the day before. In an attempt to kick-start my healthy eating regime I raided the local green grocers (which I had to find on Google because I'd never bothered setting foot in one before). I was pleased that it must seem that I'm actually a really healthy person just to have all this stuff to hand and also that it was being used. Ben had predicted that the whole lot would go off before a single blueberry was eaten by anyone in the house.

Suck it, Ben

"This will be perfect to get us energised for a great family hike too," said Max, without stopping his prep work.

"I said 'walk' no one mentioned 'hike', Max," I replied, trying to gain control of this health train.

"Walk, hike, what does it matter as long as we're getting our heart rate pumping; isn't that right, Elle?"

"It is indeedy."

Since when does she say 'indeedy' and when is she ever this chipper? Apparently stallion penis will do a lot to someone's personality.

I decided that my obvious eye-rolling and generally prickly demeanour was not going to be well received in the kitchen and my time was better spent wrestling my half-naked children into clothes and away from technology.

Predictably enough, I was told that I was ruining their day (it was usually their 'life' so I was feeling hopeful on the downgrade) by taking them into the outside world and away from the cartoon channel. I left the smoothie drinkers downstairs and tried to track down some suitable clothing for me to go walking in. Searching through the bottom of my wardrobe, where clothes go to die, I found my neon yellow active wear I wore to my first outing with Elle.

Thinking back on the person I was then, it felt like a world away. There were still touches of the ridiculous about me, but I felt healed from all the hurt that made up who I was on the inside. I smiled to myself feeling proud of the progress but it didn't bring me any closer to finding what I was going to wear now.

Elle appeared at the door of my bedroom and I braced myself for the inevitable overshare of her night. For once she was surprisingly coy.

"He's nice, isn't he?" she asked, avoiding my eyes.

Is she embarrassed?

"I mean he's gorgeous and the sex was fan-fucking-tastic but he's also nice."

"Should I be sitting down for the next part?"

"Next part?"

"The part where you tell me shocking details about everything that went on with him, including the length, girth and colour of his penis?"

"Not at all, I can be secretive sometimes; unless you're trying to live vicariously through me?"

Am I actually feeling disappointed?

"Well, look at you; you're all grown up," I said, proudly.

"But I don't mind telling you he could crush a walnut with his arse."

Nope, I'm relieved. That's a visual I could have done without.

***

Our merry party set off towards the towpath on the outskirts of the city. It was the type of place nice families spent their Saturday morning. The ones you see with little dogs with tiny coats on them, children cycling happily or people strolling along hand-in-hand.

Our group was a little bit more haphazard than that. Max looked the part (despite sporting his clothes from last night), he was followed closely behind by Ben, who was experiencing some sort of man crush on this fitness Adonis. Elle and I straggled behind – each of us dragging a small child, both of whom were crying and asking about going back home, three strides into the walk.

Max was definitely trying to set the pace of a much faster experience than any of us were willing to commit to but Elle tried her best to keep up in order to play the fitness guru part she'd written for herself.

Eventually the boys – Ben included – settled down and accepted that they weren't getting back to the car any time soon. We strolled along, making the most of our peaceful surroundings until I heard an almighty scream coming from my youngest son.

"MUMMY!" HELP ME!" cried Arthur.

I don't think I ever ran so quickly to get to my child and find out what on earth was wrong.

"LOOK!" he yelled.

His chubby little finger pointed to an injured bird that lay at the side of the path. It looked as if it had come in contact with a cat, or something similar. Its little heart was thumping wildly through its chest and although it was still blinking the head and wing was contorted in a weird position.

"Help it, mummy," he said, with tears in his eyes.

Ah, fuck.

The rest of my party all gathered round to see what the screaming was about and all the adults had the same grim look on their face as they tried to find a way to get Arthur and Adam out of the area without having to tell them this bird was a goner.

I had managed to avoid the whole 'death' conversation with the children up until this moment and I wanted to keep it that way.

"You're in luck, Artie," said Elle, "Your mum is a wizz at looking after animals and she will have this sorted in a jiffy."

What the fuck is she doing to me?

"She once mended a robin's broken wing at the café by making a little napkin sling."

Why is she still talking?

"Did you really?" asked Ben.

"Is that a serious question, Ben? Why don't you take the children up to that bench over there so Elle and I can assess the patient?" I replied, tersely.

He dutifully dragged the children ten feet away and tried to distract them while I tried to figure what the hell I was going to do with the bird.

"You don't really need me do you? I'm terrified of birds," said Elle.

"Are you fucking kidding me? You've just told my children I'm Snow fucking White so you'd better believe you're going to stay here and help me figure out how to euthanize a bird."

"You can't do that!"

"What the hell am I meant to? I don't have my handy bird-healing knapsack with me at present. Look, I'm just going to move it over to those bushes over there and then tell the kids it flew off."

"Good idea, but how are you going to move it?"

"Give me your jacket."

"Fuck off! I like this jacket, you're not getting bird guts on it."

"Would you prefer if I take off my t-shirt in public?"

She reluctantly handed over her jacket and we positioned ourselves either side of the dying bird in order to move it into the bush, while simultaneously trying to block the children's view of the operation.

"Oh, fuck, it stinks," said Elle, as she gagged on the smell, "Are we even sure it's still alive?"

"It's blinking, it's still alive. Hang on, let me just get a closer look."

I knelt down closer to the injured animal, marvelling at the beautiful colours of the feathers. Had I just been walking by I would have thought it was an average brown bird but getting this close to it I could see the flecks of yellow and orange sprinkled throughout the brown. It was rather beautiful. I was just about to tell Elle my observations on this little creature when it unexpectedly jumped onto its feet and flew straight into my face.

The wings hit my eyes while its tiny little feet clawed at my nose and cheek. I couldn't tell if the high-pitched shrieking was coming from me or it but it was deafening. I could feel parts of it getting tangled up in my hair and I genuinely felt that I was in a living nightmare.

This is how I'm going to die

Just when I thought things couldn't possibly get more traumatising I felt the unmistakable thump of a closed fist making contact with my right cheek and I landed flat on my back trying to figure out if I was being mugged by some type of bird-robber tag-team.

When I managed to open my eyes, Elle, was standing over me saying something I couldn't quite make out.

"Amy? Amy? Are you ok?" she repeated.

Ben, Max and the kids came rushing over and encircled me, all of them talking at the same time as I lay on the tarmac wondering how I had managed to get here in my life. I eventually sat up on my elbows and glared in Elle's general direction.

"Can someone explain why I ended up on my ass?"

"I was saving you from the flying rat trying to scratch out your eyes," Elle offered, as if this was a reasonable explanation for punching me in the face, "I almost got the fucker, too."

Is that pride in her voice?

"He flew off over there before I could get a second swing."

"Oh, I'm sorry that my face got in the way of your fist. Ouch." I winced. I knew I wasn't lucky enough to escape without getting a black eye from this experience.

"I've had enough of nature for the day," I announced to the group, as I ran my hand over my cheek, "I'd like to go back to the car."

The kids and Ben gave a quiet 'whoop' of excitement about getting away from the outdoors and I ignored the defeated shoulders of Max.

"You did great at saving that bird, mum," said Arthur.

"Thanks, kid. Next time though, the foxes can have it."

We trundled back towards the car and I tried not to feel paranoid that my eye was slowly getting puffier by the second. The happy couple walked slightly ahead and I could hear Elle doing her flirty giggle which still sounded unnatural to me. It was good to hear none-the-less.

As we walked along the path I was lost in a daydream of double dates and figuring out how Elle would be able to explain her way out of the personal trainer lie if things started to get more serious with him.

Not great to start things off with a lie...

Just as we were about to round the corner a woman pushing a buggy came into view and almost simultaneously to this, Max dropped Elle's hand and forcefully pushed her into the ditch by the roadside.

Max stopped and bent down to the child in the pram while speaking brightly to, presumably, the mother. I watched as Elle scrambled up the ditch in order to find out what on earth was going on.

I don't like the look of this

"Did you just see that?" said Ben, "Was that a stork?"

"What are you talking about?"

"That bird that just went by; was it a stork? I don't think we get storks. I think they're called cranes or something," he rambled on.

"Did you not just see Elle being pushed into a ditch?"

"No I was looking at the stork, I mean, crane – I think…"

"Come on, we have to catch up and see what's happening."

I pulled at his arm to try and get closer to hear what was going on.

Elle looked ashen-faced as Max was talking at speed to the woman with the buggy.

"Here are my other clients now! Amy, Ben, I'd like to introduce you both to my wife: Danielle."

How ironic: his arse may be able to crack nuts, but his nuts are definitely about to be cracked

69

Chapter 6

"Hi," said Danielle. Her tone was confused but she did well to stop her face betraying her. I glanced at Elle to find her staring at the ground, silently.

"I'm just finishing up with this group session, they're getting the whole family involved – kids and all," he said, pointing to Arthur and Adam. They were busy fighting over a stick to care what kind of hideous confrontation was unfolding.

"Well, it was a great first session, guys," he continued, "I'll get talking to you during the week, Ben, and we can organise our next outing – and hey, thanks for letting me crash on your sofa after our poker night. I owe you!"

He flashed us all a huge smile and practically pulled his wife and buggy in the opposite of our dumbfounded gang. None of us spoke for a few seconds but Ben and I looked at Elle wondering how she was going to handle this turn of events.

"Elle?" I asked, tentatively.

She simply raised her hand up to stop me saying anything further.

Her shoulders shuddered and my heart was breaking at the sight of my poor, damaged, friend having her heart broken by yet another unworthy liar. Her hair was covering her face and the sobs, which had started in a ragged noise, began to get louder. As I went closer to embrace her, she flipped her hair back and I found that she wasn't crying at all, she was laughing.

"Did he seriously just throw me into a ditch?" she said, in between breaths.

"Eh yeah..."

"Well that one is definitely going in the book."

What book? Was she writing a book? Should I add this to the list of things she's keeping from me?

"Are you ok?" Ben asked.

"Ah Benny, don't worry about me. This is one of the pitfalls of dating at my age – you're bound to come across a couple of gobshites like Max there, or indeed my ex-husband. It's not exactly a surprise that the first man I sleep with after my philandering, arsehole of a husband was a man exactly like him."

"But you didn't say anything? Why didn't you call him out?" I asked.

"In front of his little one? Even if the kid is in a pushchair and can't understand what the fuck is going on I don't think one of the early memories I'd like to ingrain on him is of his mother taking chunks out of his father."

"That's noble of you...I think."

"So you're going to let him get away with it?" said Ben.

"Away with what? We had a fling, that's as far as my role in his story goes. Whatever happens in his life after that is his own doing. Stupid fucker."

Ben and I shot each other a knowing look but neither of us had the courage to say anything further about the situation.

"Right then, who's for going to Joe's and getting a big fry up because I'm fucking hanging and this exercise thing is complete bullshit."

Ben heartily agreed, clearly his smoothie had done little to curb his hunger. We all got into our cars and headed to our haven in order to stuff our faces and forget all about our run in with Mr and Mrs Nut Cracker.

***

When we arrived, the place was its usual busy self for that time on a Saturday. People recovering from their nights out had managed to drag themselves out of bed in search of sustenance but they all still wore the same grey-faces of people who needed IV fluids and a week's worth of sleep.

I was glad I got to feel smug about not being one of the walking dead and strutted behind the counter to place our orders with Michael.

"How's the head after your big night out?" he asked, expecting to see me hiding behind sunglasses and complaining that sound was too bright.

"I took it easy, Michael, it's best not to over indulge when you're my age," I replied, whilst imagining my halo glistening above my head.

"No need to look so surprised," I continued, "We'll have three full frys and pancake stacks for my boys."

"I thought you were on a diet?"

"Shut up, Michael."

My halo had received a bit of a dent but I decided it was the weekend and I should be able to let loose a little, besides I hadn't decided if I was even going back to that nutter's diet cult. I hadn't managed to finish weighing up my principles against my desire to fit into a two-piece on a sun holiday. I know there were other ones I could join but maybe this tough love approach would work. Or maybe it would put me into a pit of despair and self-loathing.

Our threesome chatted about inconsequential nonsense until the food arrived, allowing us all to lapse into comfortable silence and inhale our grease-laden carbs. I had never been a slow, conscious, eater. I was more of a blink-and-you'll-miss-me-inhale-this-entire-plate kind of person. Thankfully I had married someone similar and Elle was actually faster than the two of us combined. Ben went over to the boy's table and began his negotiations to try and get them to stop playing with the toys and eat some of their brunch.

"I meant to ask you about the book you're writing," I said, nonchalantly, in the hope that if I appeared casual enough she would be tricked into thinking she'd already told me all about it and spill some further information.

"I'm not writing a book," she replied, looking genuinely confused.

"You said back at the towpath you were going to put Max in the book."

"Oh, *the* book."

Well that clears up exactly nothing

"Should I know what book you're referring to."

"It's the 'Book of Hate'," she said.

Well I did ask

"I started it back in school," she continued, "Basically I used to just write in it about all the horrible arseholes I came across. I figured I could learn something about men along the way and I'd know exactly who to avoid when I was older. Clearly it's an experiment that failed miserably."

"You still have this?"

"Of course I do, some of the stuff in there is hilarious and when all that shit with Keith happened it was kind of like a therapy."

"Have you ever shown anyone?"

"For a time, in my late teens, I used to just write about them on scraps of paper and made like a big collage of stories on my wall. I thought it would be like this edgy, modern art installation, but really it just looked a bit psychotic so I copied them all into the book."

"You're going to have to show me this, you know that?"

She took a second to think about this, then simply shrugged.

"Fuck it, yeah that's fine. It's up in the office, will I go get it?"

"YES!"

My enthusiastic reply disturbed several of the hungover patrons still trying to shove their breakfast down their throats.

She returned to our table a few minutes later brandishing a tattered jotter. It was blue and red with the words 'Book of Hate' scrawled at the front in blue biro.

"Well there's no denying what's in here then," I said with a chuckle.

The first page was a type of introduction that was so filled with teenage angst I couldn't help but imagine Elle as a young emo, lying on her bed, trying to write this out with some chuff pop rockers playing on the CD player behind her.

"Now, you can't just laugh at all my disasters. There's some pretty emotional stuff in there I'll have you know," she said.

"I swear," I replied, with my hand on my heart and a mock-solemn expression.

She joined me at my side of the table where she could see exactly who I was reading about. I could tell she was going to enjoy reminiscing with this book, despite her protestations that she was emotionally scarred by all these males.

The first few pages were mostly about school crushes who didn't notice her or didn't reciprocate her feelings – nothing too out of the ordinary for every school girl at one time or another.

"Ah, this one was a right piece of work," she began, "He was the first real nut-job I had a relationship with."

I feel like that implies there was more than one 'nut-job' in her dating history

"His name was Rory and he started off as such a nice bloke," she continued, "We really hit it off and I connected with him really well after my mum died. His parents had died too so we kind of bonded over the grief. I felt like an orphan and he was one so we just sort of fell into a relationship.

"We worked in the same bar together and he convinced me to go to Spain for the summer and work in a bar over there. I thought it might be a bit of an adventure so I figured I'd go for the craic."

"Did he leave you stranded at the airport?"

"No, nothing like that. I should probably tell you that his parents were murdered."

"He murdered them?"

"What? No. Just let me tell you my story, Amy."

"Sorry."

I resisted my natural urge to try and guess the end of the tale and settled for biting my lip instead.

"He told me when he was younger, his parents were taken out the back of the garden and murdered by paramilitaries. It was really fucking traumatising and he was raised by his grandmother since then."

That poor boy; I'm sure whatever imagined slight he had done to cause this particular breakup could be traced back to the trauma of this.

"We went to Spain, he didn't get a job and I spent all my time working to support us both so it wasn't quite the adventure that I thought it would be," she continued.

"On one of the days at the bar the phone went and when I picked it up it was Rory's grandmother on the line because she hadn't been able to get through to him. I reassured her that he was fine and was probably just asleep. This was the first time I'd actually spoken to her so I thought I'd get a bit of info from her to see if I could get him off his arse and start pulling his weight.

"Thing was, it wasn't his grandmother. I just assumed this woman at the other end of the phone was her but it was his mum."

"What?"

"He'd only gone and made up the whole fucking story. His parents were alive and well."

"What did you do?"

"I did what any normal person would do, I went back to our shitty little apartment and threw the entire contents of our kitchen cupboards at him."

As you do

"Apparently, it was a chat up line he'd been using for years and it always worked. Women would feel instant sympathy for him and more often than not he'd manage to get them into bed."

"I mean as far as chat-up lines go it's…original?" I said, not quite sure what else I could say about it.

"I got the next flight out of there back home and left him stranded without money for his own flight. For all I know, he could still be out there but I'm sure his dear old parents helped him back."

"That's wild," was all I could manage.

"I'm not even sure that's the worst one," she mused.

"Really?"

"Yeah, I mean the Keith stuff is pretty bad."

"How are things going with that?" I tried to tread lightly but I didn't want the moment to pass without asking her. If she confided in my husband she should be able to confide in me.

"I've bored you enough with all that, I'm onto the next chapter of my life."

"It's not about boring me. You're never boring me, I don't think it's possible for you to do that," I said.

She smiled but I knew she wasn't going to give anything more away.

Our moment was interrupted by the wail of Adam accusing his brother of stealing one of his pancakes – despite neither of them eating, or wanting, what they had on their plates.

"Another successful mealtime with the Coles," I remarked.

"I'd better head, I want to make sure there's no sex stuff lying around before Keith leaves the girls home."

Do I want to know what 'sex stuff' entails? Nope, keep that Pandora's Box sealed.

"Ok, love," I said, as I gave her a kiss on the cheek, "Text me later and we can bitch about horrible men. I've a few entries for this book if I can apply to be a co-author?"

"Really? Yeah, that might be fun. We can compare tragic love lives, although yours is pretty picturesque from where I'm standing."

She did a heavy sigh as she looked at Ben play with the kids and I couldn't help but feel relieved that they were all still mine and I wasn't going through the same hell that she was. I instantly felt guilty at the thought.

She waved her good-byes to everyone and Ben came back to our table to join me.

"All ok?" he asked

"Yes, she just wanted to get back to the house before the girls were due."

"She's a tough cookie, don't be worrying too much about her," he said with his usual reassuring squeeze of my hand, "Besides you won't have time to worry."

"I won't? Why is that?"

"Because I have big plans for us, Mrs Cole."

His knowing smile gave me butterflies in my stomach and I instinctively sat closer to him to hear what raunchy plans my wonderful, romantic husband had in store for the weekend.

"Do tell, Mr Cole."

"Well I thought we could get home and have a lovely relaxing afternoon curled up on the sofa."

"Yes, and?"

"Well then…"

Surprise babysitter? Dinner in that new fancy restaurant I've been hinting about? Finally trying that weird sex position I emailed him about the other week? Tell me, man!

"Well then we are going to have a special visitor."

78

"That's a weird name to call your penis," I said.

"What? What are you talking about?"

"What are *you* talking about?"

"I'm talking about my mother. She's coming over this evening to stay for a few days. Surprise!"

Fuck

Chapter 7

It's truly amazing how much cleaning one can get done when both angry at your husband and dealing with the imminent arrival of your mother-in-law. Every so often, Ben would come into whichever room I was manically scrubbing to ask if I was 'ok'. This question was never well received.

"Am I ok? Are you a seriously asking if I'm ok? In which universe would you think I would be ok with knowing, three hours ahead of time, that my mother-in-law – who hates me – is arriving and staying for a holiday for the next 'few' days?"

"This universe?"

"No, Ben. It is not this universe, nor any universe conceivable to the human brain."

He stopped asking after that particular outburst.

I had managed to make it to the bathroom with an hour to spare, but I knew it would take more than a mere mortal to sort the gunge that lived in the crevices of this particular hell hole of a room.

I know she will be checking the skirting boards, she did that the last time, but I'm ahead of the game this time. It's just the grout in here that needs bleached within an inch of its life.

I looked at my ever-dissolving sponge and I knew it wasn't going to get the job done. A flash of inspiration hit and I realised that Ben's toothbrush would be perfect for really getting into those hard-to-reach places that Mrs Cole Sr. would be checking and it would definitely help me work out some unresolved anger towards my idiot husband.

I scrubbed until my knuckles turned white and Ben came in to open the windows to make sure the room was ventilated.

"You really should go easy on the bleach, love," he said, matter-of-factly.

"You should really tell me a week in advance when you mother is coming to stay so I can book a spa break instead."

"I don't know why you get like this when she's calling."

"She hates me."

"She doesn't!"

"Oh, really? Let's consult the list, shall we?"

"Not the list..."

"First up: she keeps bringing up your ex-girlfriend, 'Kate the saint', she talks about our marriage as if it's on its last legs, she wore black to our wedding, complete with fucking veil, she groans at my cooking, she makes comments about my weight and she calls me: Aimsy."

"I know she can be a bit difficult, but she's my mother. Am I going to just cut her out of my life because she gets your name wrong once in a while? You've got to remember, she's getting on."

"She's 57, Ben."

The doorbell rang and I could feel my stomach fall through the floor.

"It's too late, she's here," I moaned.

81

I handed him his bleach-covered toothbrush and ran into the bedroom to get changed. It didn't matter what I wore, it was always going to get her 'look'. A look like there was a bad smell under her nose, and that smell was wearing a creased t-shirt and poorly fitted jeans.

I could hear the chatter of a happy reunion between her and the males of the house. I decided that if I bothered to put on make-up now she would think I was trying too hard, but if I didn't she would think I wasn't bothered about her being there at all. I couldn't win. There were a lot of chess moves to consider and this was the first one. If I got this right then I would off to a good start, but if I mess up I'll be on the back foot for the next few days.

Who am I kidding? I can't even win Connect Four against my three-year-old – no make-up it is.

I plodded down the stairs and found her smothering the two boys in kisses, leaving stains of a peachy lipstick all over their faces. She always had a full face of make-up on. I have never seen that woman without blue eyeliner and bright pink blush on her face. Even when we would stay overnight at their home, she would look immaculately made up by the time we were down for breakfast. Her hair was bleached blonde and she towered over the rest of us in her six-inch heels. Her idea of casual wear still involved some height in her footwear. I don't think she owned a pair of flats.

I always felt that women who mastered the art of walking in heels, making it look effortless, were miraculous. I don't feel that way towards my mother-in-law, I just felt like she must have sort of weird hooves that meant she could only walk in heels permanently. I knew she also used her height as a physical way to look down on me, when she couldn't use her words.

We did our usual greeting. It involved air kisses on each cheek. I started this tradition. She thought it was me trying to me 'continental', whereas I just didn't want any of her nasty lipstick on my face.

"There's the woman of the house," she said, "Let me take a look at you."

She pushed me away from her to get a good gawp at how I was presenting myself this time.

"Just lovely," she said, with a look that made it seem like she was inhaling pure sulphur.

"Althea, it's such a lovely surprise that you're here; it's been too long."

Don't smirk, Amy

"Surprise? Ben has been suggesting I come down for months, I've just not found the time but I didn't want to offend so I've juggled things around to fit you all in. Have to keep the family sweet."

Ben gave me a nervous glance and offered to take his mother's bags up to the spare room before I had the chance to gauge his eyes out with my bare hands.

I'm going to smother that man in his sleep

"Lead the way, boys, take your nana to her seat."

I decided to retreat to the kitchen and make some tea. There were no biscuits and this would be completely unacceptable to Althea Cole. A hostess should never be without biscuits. Ben came tip-toeing into the room in order to salvage our marriage.

"When she said 'suggesting it for months' she means -"

"You were suggesting it for months?"

"No, I wasn't. I mentioned it when we were on the phone a few times, just in the way you end a telephone call like 'it would be good to see you' and all that but I didn't mean to come up and stay for a few days. I swear I didn't."

"Go be with your mother, these may be your final hours on this earth; make the most of them. Also, there are no biscuits."

"There aren't? Oh no, she'll crack up. I'd better go get some."

"Don't you dare leave me here with her!"

"Keep your voice down, I'll be back in two minutes."

He grabbed his keys and ran out the door without saying a word to his mother. I stood in the kitchen hoping that I would manage to remain out here until he came back. Unfortunately, the closing of the door alerted the houseguest from hell and she soon found me rummaging in the cupboard, trying to find three matching mugs.

"Where has my son run off to? Finally seen the light and left, has he?" she did her irritating giggle and clapped her hands, as if she'd just told the world's funniest joke.

"Ha. Yes, yes he has. Shall I give you the address of the hotel he's going to and you can stay there?"

"Oh, Aimsy, you're always so sensitive."

I wonder if I shove the handle of that spatula into my ears would I be able to get some time away in the A&E Department? I could bring a good book.

"He's just going to get a few things at the shop; I didn't get time before you arrived."

"Tisk, tisk! Failure to prepare, is preparing to fail. Actually, you should get one of those big noticeboard things for the kitchen so you can keep track of things. I would be so mortified if people came to the house and I wasn't prepared to greet them. That would just be awful."

Maybe I should just put a fork in my eye

"Why don't you go, sit down and relax while I get the tea ready. Ben will be back any minute," I said, in a tone which conveyed more than a suggestion but less than a threat.

I stood at the sink, waiting for the kettle to boil and tried to breathe deeply. I looked at my neglected 'Action Sheets' that I had planned to fill out, throughout the day so I wouldn't feel overwhelmed. I realised I hadn't done any CBT work since finishing my last session. I wondered if the noticeboard suggestion wasn't such a bad idea. I could really use the safety net of having a decent grip on my mental health when faced with spending the next few days with the human embodiment of pure evil. Ben burst into the kitchen, out of breath and wielding three different packets of biscuits.

"This should have us covered," he gasped, holding onto the countertop to try and get his breath back.

"The jig is up, she knows we weren't prepared."

"Ah damn, I shouldn't have bothered running then."

I made up the underwhelming tray of tea and biscuits and presented them to Althea. The look was out in force, as she surveyed the offering of biscuits on display. She settled for a custard cream and sniffed her cup to make sure the milk wasn't off before taking a sip.

I hate this woman

"Ben, you'll never guess who I had the most splendid lunch with the other week."

I bet I can guess

"Who?" he asked, already knowing the answer, and feeling his cheeks blush under my glare.

"Kate!"

What a shock

"Oh, she's looking ever so well and doing great at her nursing. Why don't you give her a ring and go out sometime?"

"Because he's married?" I said, offering my unwelcome input to this highly insulting and inappropriate conversation.

"Aimsy! I mean just to catch up as old friends, I would never suggest he would see another woman while he was still married to you."

Still married?

"Mum, how's dad?" interrupted Ben.

"He's wonderful," she replied, wistfully, "Always so busy and travelling with work but these things have to be done. He'll retire in six short years and then we can be sick of the sight of each other like you two."

She had only been here for a half hour and the sound of her giggle was, by far, the most obnoxious sound I'd heard in years.

"I thought we could go out for dinner, Ben, it might give Aimsy a bit of a break from the hassle of trying to cook," she continued, "I found this lovely little bistro just out of the city and booked us a table for 8.30."

"That's a bit late for the boys to be eating, mum. There's a pizza place around the corner that's great and has family deal."

"Pizza? What nonsense. I suppose you're right about the boys though. Have to keep everyone happy. Aimsy, why don't you stay here with *your* princes and I'll take

86

my prince out for a meal. It's about time he gets some good food into him and you can have pizza here?"

"Of course, Althea. You spend all the time you want with *your* little prince."

"Excellent!" she shrieked.

I have a feeling that particular little prince will be making his own dinner for quite some time after this evening

Chapter 8

Ben was busy trying to find a shirt that would suit for his date with his mother. It was funny to watch him fuss over what to wear, as I lay on the bed purposely not helping.

"You don't seem to panic when you're getting ready for our dates," I said.

"You don't judge everything I do."

"Yes I do, you just stopped noticing."

There was a light tap on the door and Althea came in before I could answer, to see what we were up to.

"Taking it easy, Aimsy?" she said, with a sneer.

I resisted the urge to throw a pillow at the door and just nodded back.

I'm not sure how many days of this I can take

"I'll be down in a few minutes, mum, just trying to find a shirt," he called, with his head still buried in the back of his wardrobe.

How deep is that thing?

"Don't forget a tie, Benjamin."

"A tie?" he said, as he thumped his head off one of the shelves.

"Yes, a tie. You might as well make the most of the occasion. You don't always have to dress like you live in squalor, we can pretend for the night."

Ben and I shared a knowing glance, but I refused to take the bait. Usually I would have kicked off by now; after all, there's only so much bear-baiting this particular grizzly can put up with but not this time. This time I was going to be so damn zen-like her stupid, blonde head would explode.

"I'm sorry," Ben whispered, when she finally left.

"You will be."

I smiled, sweetly, at my husband and tried to figure out my revenge for putting us through this hell. I didn't mind the dinner thing – I could do with the break from her – it was the fact that after all these years Ben never stood up for me in front of her. He never stood up for himself in front of her. At the beginning of our relationship I would call her up for all the little sly digs but somehow her passive-aggressive explanations always ended up making me seem like the bad guy, overreacting to her 'meaningless' comments.

I stopped reacting a few years back and it's gotten steadily worse since then. After each visit, she would gain new ground and chip away at my self-worth; but this time I was prepared. With the help of Dr Jeremy Kelly I was able to see her problems with me were not a reflection of my worth but more of a statement on herself.

God, I'm so fucking wise

I waved the two of them off on their date and allowed Ben to give me a kiss on the cheek before he left. I sat with the remote in one hand and the pizza delivery app on my phone ready to go. Just as I hit 'order' on my double cheese pizza feast, the doorbell went.

Of course someone is here

I heaved myself off the sofa and answered the door to be faced with Elle and her two daughters. On the one hand, I was happy of the company but on the other, I'd have to share my pizza.

"Sorry, princess, it's an emergency," she said, as she pushed into the hallway.

I stood out of the way and watched as they all piled into my living room leaving a trail of shoes, socks, bags and coats in their wake.

At least they feel at home

I shut the door behind them and followed the tornado of mess that led into my living room. The boys were delighted with the surprise visitors and instantly dragged them up to their bedroom to show them their toys. The girls reluctantly followed, they knew by now it was impossible to avoid my children's overzealous friendship.

"What's going on?" I asked.

"I have a date!" she said, with a little excited jig, "I need a babysitter…"

"Ah, the penny drops. It's not with Max is it?"

"Fuck, no. He's text a few times offering some lame explanation but this is from the app."

"Purple penis?"

"No, he's also been blocked from my life."

"Ok, then who?"

"His name is Alexander. He sounds like a Russian aristocrat, doesn't he?"

"I don't really know what to say about that."

"Can you please have the girls?"

"I can't have them overnight. Althea is here, her and Ben are out for dinner so she has the spare room."

"FUCK."

I jumped at the increase of volume in her voice.

"I'm sorry, there's no room at the inn."

"They could sleep in my bed?" offered Adam, "And I can share with Arthur, if he promises not to kick me."

"Where did you come from?"

"Arthur bit me," was all he offered, as way of explanation.

"Did he break skin?"

"No."

"You'll live, go back and play and stop listening to adult conversations."

I turned to find a hopeful Elle staring back at me. I found that there was no point in trying to reason with her when she was this excited about something.

"Fine, they can all bunk in with each other but I'm feeding them a shit-tonne of sugar in the morning and sending them home early so you can deal with that."

"Deal, I swear, I will never ask again."

Well, that's a lie

"Get out before I change my mind," I said, with a dismissive wave.

She kissed my cheek and added: "We're meeting at that horrible bar in town, the one that uses leopard print without irony."

"*Cheetahs.*"

"That's the one, hopefully that's not an indication of his taste."

"It must be, he was matched with you."

"Bitch!" she laughed.

"Text me at least ten times to make sure you're alive and ring me when you're home. If there's a big emergency and you think he's going to murder you, text me a random word so I know it's you and I'll come there."

"What word?"

"I dunno - pineapple."

"Pineapple, it is."

She was soon running out the door before I changed my mind and called 'good-bye' to her kids before they too changed their mind about their cramped sleeping arrangements at aunty Amy's.

The pizza arrived shortly afterwards and the five of us sat on the carpet in the middle of the floor watching mindless television with canned laughter. The girls were pleasant to talk to, although they were only a couple of months older than Arthur, it could have been years. They seemed mature and thoughtful whereas he was still a baby to me. As my youngest, I suppose he always would seem that way.

I let them stay up later than I normally would. The company was nice, they were all getting along and it seemed pointless to put them up to bed when I knew the last thing on their mind was sleeping.

I realised I'd left my phone in the kitchen when I was dishing out the food. If Elle had been frantically texting 'pineapple' to me, she definitely would be chopped into bite-size chunks by now.

There were two messages: one from each of my abandoners.

Ben: Hi love, this place is really fancy. You'd hate it xxx

What the hell does that mean? I could do fancy. He's actually buying into his mother's crap about him slumming it with me all this time. Jerk.

Elle: Hi! He was late but his shirt has tiny llamas on it, which I like. Going good so far – you're a saint!
I preferred her message.

Eventually the peace in the living room was starting to fracture. There were a few arguments over blocks so I thought it was time to get them to bed. I noticed the girls had an overnight bag with them. I'd like to think she packed them for the girls on the off chance that I would be free, but I knew it was because she was never going to be taking 'no' for answer.

I'd spent time in therapy discussing about the feeling of being taken for granted. At one of the sessions it was discovered I would continue to feel like this because I allowed the behaviour to carry on – something I was still doing by the looks of things. I could have stood up for myself this evening and told Althea she was being a bitch but what was the point? It wouldn't have shortened her stay, it would have made the atmosphere around here awful and caused a fight between Ben and I. I also could have told Elle to sling her hook, it was a terrible time for me and I was already stressed with an unwelcome visitor but again, what was the point? The girls were no trouble, all four were asleep (or pretending to be) and she got to meet a new guy she was excited about; someone who may, or may not be, a murderer.

Everyone's a winner. Except Elle, if she's murdered.
I picked up a spare bit of paper to see if I could write out a thought record and determine if I was *really* ok with all of this or if I was being a martyr for the sake of avoiding an argument. Before I'd even started my phone beeped and I was relieved to see that it was Elle again.

Elle: He's very different from his profile. How are the girls?

Amy: Girls are injecting heroin into their eyeballs, but other than that they're great. In what way different?
Elle: Like he said he was an environmentalist and a strict vegan but he's chomping down the complimentary mozzarella balls like there's no tomorrow.
Amy: It's not exactly a crime against humanity.
Elle: No, just against the cows he's meant to love.

I decided she was nit-pinking out of nerves and left her to it. I threw the paper to one side and decided not to turn my Saturday night into a therapy session. Instead, I chose a movie I'd seen at least three times before and decided I would wait until the first ad break before I cleaned up the mess left over from the various pizza boxes and sides.

I woke with a start and the distinct feeling that I was being watched. I didn't remember falling asleep or anything after the first ten minutes of the movie.

As I blinked more I realised Ben and Althea were both standing over me looking concerned.

"Oh, you're back. That was quick," I said, rubbing my eyes and feeling nervous under her obvious scrutiny.

"It's nearly midnight," replied Ben.

"I must have dosed off. Did you have a nice evening?"

"What happened here, Aimsy? Were you eating your feelings?" said Althea, as she gestured to all the empty boxes around the room.

"What? No it's that meal deal thing it comes with lots of extras." I left off 'you judgemental prick' in my reply.

"We don't normally finish everything," said Ben.

Ah Ben, you stupid, stupid fool. You're going to pay for that

"Well, Ben, Elle's children are here for a sleepover so we polished everything off. If that's ok? Or would you prefer to fat shame me some more?"

He let out an audible gulp.

"I'll clean up in the morning," I said with a sigh and picked up my phone to go to bed.

"Aimsy, you should never go to bed with a heavy heart like that. I'm sure Ben didn't mean to 'fat-shame' you or whatever, but I feel like a good dose of reality when it comes to one's poor eating habits is a good thing in a relationship. You wouldn't want him to leave it too late would you?"

That's it. I can try to be zen tomorrow, but tonight she's fucking asking for it

I took a deep breath and turned round to give her a piece of my mind. Her sanctimonious bullshit was about to be stuffed down her throat along with her romantic meal with my husband. My phone suddenly vibrated in my hand and I noticed that I had missed a call from Elle. Actually, I had missed 3 calls from Elle and five messages all saying the same thing:

Elle: Pineapple!!!!

Chapter 8

I pushed my way past Ben and the mother-in-law from hell when I read the messages. My eyes scanned the room for my car keys and, for once, they were sitting somewhere handy.

"What's going on? Where are you going at this time of night?" asked Ben.

"Elle needs my help," was all the explanation I had time for.

"What's wrong?"

I managed to shout "pineapple" over my shoulder before the front door slammed behind me and I ran to the car to start the engine. I rang her number, over and over, but there was no answer.

If she's alive and ok I'm going to kill her

I sped through the town trying not to clip any awkwardly parked cars or tipsy pedestrians, who were starting to fall out of the pubs. One good thing about the dive that is *Cheetahs* was that it had a decent car park, meaning I didn't have to waste time trying to wake up the grey matter in my brain which was specifically linked to the memory of parallel parking.

That shit can stay dormant for a while longer

I jumped out of the car, not checking to see if I'd locked it, and ran into the bar to see if she was there. She was. Chatting happily to a man wearing a shirt covered in tiny llamas.

She's going to wish he'd murdered her by the time I'm finished with her

"Amy!" she said, with a shocked look on her face, "this isn't what it looks like."

"That you're having a drink with a man?"

"No, I mean, it is but it's not what you think."

Why do I have the feeling I'm being used in a 'get out of terrible date' scenario. Best play along then.

"Tell me, what do I think?"

"I'm sorry, I'm just a weak woman. When the dick comes a-calling I have got to answer that ring, you know?"

"Not really," I replied, genuinely, as I scanned up this Alexander from the internet.

"Alex, my man, this is my girlfriend. I promised I would give up the cock for her and now she's caught me. I think you'd better scarper."

"Let's not be so hasty, ladies," he said, with a smirk.

"Let me stop you there, Alex," I replied, "I am not like my girlfriend. I like lady parts, exclusively. Even if I did like your kind of anatomy I would not be interested in your llama-wearing arse. Get lost."

He shot a look at Elle, who simply shrugged so he admitted defeat and left the bar.

"Amy, you're savage," she said, once the coast was clear.

"You're about to find out exactly how savage I am. You were meant to send me that word in a life or death situation, not just to get a lift home!"

"It was life or death. I nearly died of boredom."

"Not the same, Elle, not the same."

She recalled the evening and apart from his name, it seemed that the person that Elle had matched with on his profile was a complete fraud.

"I kept catching him out on these really obvious lies. The vegan thing, a bit weird but not sinister, his children – he said he had none but within the hour he mentioned three of them and his ex-wife – again, he said he never married."

"Maybe it was a glitch in the app," I offered.

"Maybe, but none of that bothered me. He was just so dull. His stories didn't seem to have an end to the point where I had to actually ask 'is that it?'. I'm so fucking sick of this. I just want a spark with someone that isn't a compulsive liar or as dull as dishwater," she lamented, as she put her head down on the table.

I stroked her hair and tried to think of something encouraging to say but I had nothing. No one wants to hear about how it will take time to meet the right person, or that they'll show up when they're not expecting it. I hated hearing that shit when I was single. Instead, I picked her up and told her I was taking her home.

"You'll get a nice lie in while I look after your horrible children, my horrible children, my horrible husband and my extra horrible mother-in-law," I said, as way of consolation.

"I suppose that's something," she conceded.

We walked arm-in-arm to the car and she continued to tell me about Alexander the not-so Great. She was describing the way he burped into his drink and sniffed it in, after every sip of beer when I started the engine and took off in the direction of home. I was busy looking at Elle act out the motion that I didn't see the cyclist to my right and I pulled out right in front of him.

The bike hit the side of the car with a huge 'bang' and the collision sent the body onto my bonnet, with some part of it cracking the screen. The mass slumped off the bonnet and fell in front of the car.

"What have you done?" cried Elle.

"I..I...I didn't see him," I stammered.

"Don't just sit there! Phone an ambulance! Now!"

I frantically searched for my phone while she struggled to get her seatbelt off and get out of the car.

Tears sprung from my eyes and my hands shook as I tried to dial the three numbers no one ever wants to call.

The emergency operator answered within seconds and I didn't have time to compose myself before I tried to speak.

"Please hurry. I've just hit a man with my car and he needs help," I choked.

The rest of the conversation went by in a blur. I answered the operator's questions like a robot and after she reassured me help was on the way I hung up and sat in the car, immobile. I looked at the kidney-shaped crack on the windscreen trying to process what had just happened.

I watched Elle as she frantically tried to call to the stranger and rouse him. She looked up to the car and saw me sitting like a statue, staring at the scene unfolding in front of me.

"Get the fuck out here!" she screamed.

I slowly unbuckled my belt and got out of the car to walk towards the motionless man. I was aware that Elle was saying something in the distance but I kept looking at the blood that trickled from his ear.

"Amy? Amy? Don't you go into fucking shock here," she said, as she grabbed both my arms and physically shook me back into the present moment.

"Did you hear what I said?" she asked.

"No," was all the reply I could manage.

"Amy, I can't find a pulse. I think he's dead."

As soon as she said those words the ground fell away from beneath my feet. I fell to the ground and started to sob. Throaty, heart-breaking sobs. I was going to jail for killing some poor man. I was going to miss my children growing up and all because I didn't bother to check properly before I pulled out onto the road.

I've killed a man

As soon as the thought came to my mind I felt the vomit coming up my throat. I bent over and wretched as hard as I could, emptying the contents of my stomach onto the road. I could feel Elle rub my back as she stifled her crying. She knew what was coming, she knew the trouble I was going to be in.

I hope she can be a comfort to Ben. I'm truly lucky to have her in my life

"Ah, man, are you ok?" said a voice from behind us.

"Great, here come the gossip vultures here to have a look. Can you all just back off, this is a crime scene and the emergency services are on their way," said Elle, with as much authority as her emotional state would allow.

"Really? What happened? Can I help?" he asked again.

"Can you just fuck off, mate? You're doing my tits in and I'm trying to help my friend."

"I'm sorry, I don't mean to bother anyone it's just -"

"What? What the fuck could you possibly fucking need right now?"

"I think I need to see a doctor because you just hit me with your car."

Elle stopped rubbing my back and I stopped heaving up my insides in order for us both to turn and look at him. There stood the cyclist, very much alive and holding the side of his head.

"JESUS CHRIST, ELLE! YOU SAID HE WAS DEAD! I THOUGHT I WAS GOING TO JAIL!"

"CALM DOWN, HE DIDN'T HAVE A PULSE. I THOUGHT HE *WAS* FUCKING DEAD."

"Am I dead?" he asked.

We both stopped shouting at each other and realised we should probably help the zombie cyclist instead of screaming in the middle of a car park. We went to either side of him and helped him to sit down.

"I'm so sorry, I'm so, so sorry," I said, repeatedly, "I didn't look properly and then you went smack into the car."

"No worries, these things happen," he said, staring into space.

"Your ear was bleeding," I continued.

"Ah, fuck. I just got that pierced today. I bet I've pulled it out on something. Yeah, the stud is gone and my ear lobe seems pretty weird."

I looked at the ear and there was some blood coming from the lobe. The rest of the blood that I'd spotted must have been coming from that because he seemed lucid enough. Dazed and confused, but very much alive.

"The ambulance should be here any second," said Elle, eagerly, "We'll be with you the whole time unless there's someone else we can call."

"Nah, lone wolf, me. I'll be fine, it's not the first time I've gone into a car. I used to do these stunt videos online. I was rubbish at the stunts but the fails kept raking up the views," he said, proudly.

I wasn't sure if I should be grateful that he was being so blasé about being in a road accident or concerned that he doesn't seem to care very much.

The ambulance crew arrived within 15 minutes of the call and the paramedics began to check him over.

"He's cute," said Elle.

"Please don't take this as a dating opportunity. The man is concussed."

"I'm just saying if they take him to the hospital, I'll jump into the ambo with him and you can head home. You've had a stressful night."

Is she being serious? Is she hitting on the victim?

"Hey, Elle, they're taking me in as a precaution. Fancy coming? I could tell you more about my videos?"

"Sounds great! I'll be right with you, River. Can you shove the bike into your boot and I'll get it to him after the hospital?"

"Did you just call that grown man 'River'?"

"Yes, it's such a beautiful name isn't it?"

"No."

"Stop being so crabby! You didn't kill someone, I met a nice guy. It worked out."

"It worked out? I hit a man with my car and thought I had killed him because my best friend doesn't know that when they feel a little rhythm underneath the skin, that actually means there *is* a pulse," I said.

"I know that, I must have just been feeling the wrong part."

"Where? The fucking elbow?"

"Are you going to take the bike or not? He could be my future husband and if he's not, I'll be there to butter him up so he doesn't fucking sue you."

She has a point

"Push your boobs out more, I'm not spending my holiday money to settle out of court."

"I'm on it, princess."

She skipped into the back of the ambulance and was greeted with a very warm smile from River.

What kind of fucking name is 'River'? Forget about it, Amy. Get the mangled wreck of a bike into your car and thank the universe that this was the biggest disaster you're facing tonight

As I drove home at the speed of a snail, I could feel myself relax and even become a bit giddy. It was as if I had a death row reprieve and all of a sudden my husband being a fat-shaming jerk, or my mother-in-law being around for a few days, seemed to pale in significance as to what I could have been facing this evening. I was able to go home and climb into my bed and not worry that I ended another person's life.

I can go home and kiss Ben, deeply, knowing I wasn't going to be leaving him behind to raise our children. I mean I could, but I wouldn't – he can't win the argument. I might be on a death row reprieve but I wasn't going to change my stubbornness now. That's just ridiculous.

Chapter 9

When I got into the house, Ben was waiting up for me, looking anxious.

"Where have you been? Why would you need to buy pineapples at this time of night? Why didn't you answer your phone?"

"What?"

"Pineapples, you said Elle needed you to get pineapples."

I was drawing a blank as to what he was talking about or what I had said before I'd run out the door, trying to save my best friend from a murderer. So much had happened - and not happened - in the hour I'd been gone. I told him to sit down so I could recall my sorry tale.

When I finished he gave me a massive hug and I felt him finally start to breathe again for the first time since I'd come home.

"Is he ok?" he asked, after letting me go from his embrace.

"I think so, I mean he seemed it when he was leaving. The pair of them were too busy flirting to notice trivial things like being in an ambulance."

"He could be in delayed shock or be one of those people that seem fine and then the next day they suddenly die from undetected internal bleeding," said Ben.

"Really? Do you think that information was helpful? I'm never going to sleep tonight."

"I'm sorry, I was sort of thinking out loud. That was stupid of me."

"Yes, you seem to be saying quite a few stupid things this evening," I said, steering the conversation back to the giant elephant-in-law in the room.

"I didn't mean to remark on the food thing, I didn't realise there were more people here. It just sort of popped out before I even thought about what I was saying."

"So you do think I'm eating my feelings?"

"No, not at all."

There was something about this denial which fell flat and gave a little sting to my heart.

"I'm going up to bed, I've had a long and trying evening," I said, eventually.

"I think that's a great idea, we can cuddle up and put this evening behind us."

"Cuddle up? Oh no, you'll be sleeping on the sofa tonight. Your fat wife will need the extra room after eating her feelings all evening. I wouldn't want to smother you to death under my rolls and properly kill someone. Getting away with murder once tonight was lucky, twice would be tempting fate."

I saw his little sad lip pout out at the unfairness of the turn of events, but he also knew well enough not to try and engage me more. He let me go up the stairs without an argument and I heard him pull the extra duvet in from the airing cupboard and close the living room door behind him.

No doubt Althea would have a field day at finding him on the sofa and think a reconciliation with Saint

Kate was soon on the cards. At this particular moment I didn't really care. I wanted my bed in the hope that I could grab some sleep without worrying about undetected internal bleeding or lawsuits.

***

When I woke the next morning I didn't feel refreshed. I had a fitful sleep and there was no Ben to reach out to for comfort. I doubt he had a much better sleep than I did but I hated waking up without him.

It was after 10 when I woke and I knew the four children would already be down in the living room using Ben as a human trampoline. I smiled to myself knowing he was in further discomfort. I checked my phone to see if there was word from the hospital – nothing.

She really is ridiculous at keeping in touch; I mean her children are here

I knew I sounded like my mother, but this was getting a bit much. I decided to face the carnage downstairs and hoped that Althea was sleeping later. She was on her holidays, after all. I should have realised that I didn't have a chance of this. By the time I reached the bottom of the stairs she was coming out of the kitchen carrying a tray, laden with cereal for the children and Ben, no doubt.

"Oh, little miss sunshine is awake!" she said, with mock surprise, "Are you coming to join us for breakfast or do you have to go dashing out of the house again in search of exotic fruit?"

I rolled my eyes and mutely followed her into the room to see what mess awaited me. To my absolute joy everything was immaculate. The rubbish from last night was gone, the kids were dressed – all of them – and they were sitting in front of the television, eating cereal.

I could kiss him

I looked around for my wonderful husband to give him a hug and put the bad feelings behind us, but there was no sign.

"Are you looking for Benjamin?" she asked.

"Obviously," was all the civility I could muster.

"Well, after you callously kicked him out of your marital bed I found him shivering on that thing you call a sofa at 7am. I told him to go straight up to bed and get some proper rest. He needs his rest and a proper mattress for his back if he's going to be working hard all week while you're doing whatever it is you claim to do," she replied, "Things are far worse here than I first thought. You and I are in need of a little talk, missy."

Did she just call me 'missy'?

"Now, I'm going to get things squared up in the kitchen while you put something presentable on and we will take the children out of the house so Benjamin can properly catch up on some more rest."

"Are you fucking serious?"

As soon as the words left my mouth a deathly silence fell across the living room. Cereal spoons were suspended mid-chew, as all four children waited nervously to see what would happen next.

"Yes, I'm as serious as a hippopotamus. Now get up stairs, wash your mouth out with water and put something on that doesn't make you look like a hobo."

I'm not even sure if hippos are known for being serious? Is that even a saying? What's going on here?

Somehow, I found myself back in my bedroom trying to find something that would pass the Althea Sunday-best test. I knew before I even tried to search in my dire wardrobe that it was going to be a lost cause.

I could see if my wedding dress still fits. That will really wind her up. Yeah, you're so brave when you're in another room. At what point are you going to stand up to this woman?

I found a green tea dress that was passable and threw my hair up in a messy bun – I even bothered to put on mascara. I didn't quite understand why I was appeasing this woman. I should be walking into the spare room right now and throwing a jug of water round Ben and demanding that he kick this woman out of our home and our lives.

What's the likelihood of him doing either of those things? Zero? Or less than zero?

With a heavy heart I went back down the stairs and saw as the kids were all lined up and ready for the car.

"Why can't you do this sort of stuff for me?" I asked, hurt that I was being betrayed by everyone in my family.

They all just shrugged and waited for me to get my keys.

"We won't all fit in the car," I called to Althea, who was still busying herself in the kitchen.

"Then we'll walk, maybe you could burn off some of that pizza."

"And where are we walking to?"

"What about that *Joseph's* place that Ben tells me you're fond of."

"It's not open this early on a Sunday. Nowhere is. Most people are having a nice lie in or not being marched out of their homes."

"I know you feel hard done by Aimsy, but if we're going to survive the next few days together then we really need to have a chat and clear the air."

It was the first sensible thing she'd said since she got here.

"Agreed," I replied, tersely.

"We'll just go for a walk then. At least that will get you some exercise," she said.

Great start

It was a mild morning, at least, and we let the kids lead the way up the road. There was a play park not far from the café and if it stayed dry we would be in business. The kids chatted, happily, as they walked ahead and I awaited the next insult.

I don't know what it was about me that really just annoyed her so wildly. My explanation for my behaviour was pure self-defence and I was certain that it would hold up in a court of law.

I seemed to be having quite a few of these murderess fantasies coming up over the last 24 hours – and only one out of three resulted in someone being hospitalised. I think that's good going.

We sat down on the bench and faced each other, neither wanting to be the first to speak. She had no idea who she was coming up against. I once gave my mother the silent treatment for a solid week after she answered the phone to my school crush and told him I 'couldn't come to the phone right now because I was menstruating'.

Who does that? My mother, that's who fucking does that.

"Aimsy," she began.

Ha! She caved. I've basically won, now.

"We need to sort out this resentment you're harbouring towards me and my son. Now, Aimsy, hear me out before you get all tense and start using that foul language in front of the children again.

"There's always been this block between us and I really wanted this trip to address all of that so we could start afresh. Unfortunately, it was obvious that there was much more going on in your home and I was genuinely worried about Ben and how he's coping with all of this."

"All of what, Althea?"

"Your bullying," she stated, matter-of-factly.

If this is one of her weird jokes that she laughs manically to I'm really not understanding it

"Come again?"

"When I first arrived, the place was a mess, you looked dreadful – like you'd been out all night drinking – and poor Ben had to pick up the slack. He had to run to the shop because there was no food in the house and then he was being forced to stay home and eat that dreadful junk food. No wonder he's putting on a bit of weight around the midriff."

I don't even know where to start with this. What if I just sigh really heavily, do you think she will leave me alone? Nope, didn't think so.

"Althea, the house wasn't a mess," I replied in a tone I reserved for only the most moronic of individuals, "I had been out on Friday night for one sociable drink with my mother and was only informed of your visit two hours before you arrived. Ben went out to buy biscuits for your tea because he'd eaten them all the night before while he was parenting – not 'picking up the slack' – and as for the junk food? It's pizza, it's heavenly and you're just wrong. I hadn't particularly noticed my husband's midriff expanding but perhaps he's eating his feelings because of his overbearing and, quite frankly, ridiculous mother."

"Now really, Aimsy; is there need to resort to hurtful insults?"

"Apparently there is," I bit back, "You have been nothing but rude, obnoxious, dismissive and imposing from the second you came into my home and it's genuinely surprised me that I have had this much self-control facing all of these nasty traits of yours."

At that moment, Adam came over and pointed to Arthur, who was running faster and faster as he pushed the two terrified girls on the roundabout while they cried for their mother. I ran over to stop his hostage situation and told him to go and sit with his grandmother.

"You mean, Nana?"

I hate that name

"Yes, her! Go!"

I comforted the crying children and checked my phone to see if I had any word from their mother.

Still nothing

Saying as I was on a roll and facing people who were disturbing my zen-like calm I decided to video call Elle and find out if she planned to pick up her children - or at the very least contact me at some stage, today.

She picked up after three rings and by the looks of things she was in her own bed.

"Good of you to pick up," I said briskly, "How's stream?"

"You mean River?" she said, whispering.

"Yes, I mean that babbling brook you followed to the hospital. Have you prevented a lawsuit? Why are you whispering? I get nervous when you whisper."

"I took River back to my house, I didn't think it was wise for him to be on his own just in case he had any problems. It was the least we could do."

"Is he in the bed with you?"

"What? No! What do you take me for?"

"Sorry. Where is he then?"

"He's in the bathroom, cleaning up. We did it like four times."

"Can we circle back to 'what do you take me for?' Or what did you mean by that?"

"I meant I wouldn't pick up the phone if he was in bed, not that I wasn't going to spend the night with the most amazing man I've ever met. It would be crazy *not* to sleep with him."

I wanted to remind her that over the last 48 hours she had been enamoured with two other men – even if only for a couple of hours each – but I didn't think it would be helpful at this particular moment.

"I'm sorry to burst your love bubble, but your children need their mother so get your arse out of bed and be at mine in the next hour to pick them up."

"Roger that, princess. You're a saint for having them, I knew there was a reason I was meant to go out last night and it definitely wasn't for that boring bollox I went on a date with. River thinks so too, he's so in touch with the universe, such a pure soul."

It's far too early in the morning for talk of souls

"I'm going to stop you there," I interrupted, "One hour, my house."

I hung up before she had the chance to gush anymore about her latest conquest. I made a mental note to remind Ben not to give advice to my best friend anymore; I

112

wasn't sure how many more of these 'amazing' men I could be bothered to hear about.

Returning to Althea on the bench I told her I was going home. I didn't add what I wanted to, which was: "So you can pack your bags and get out of my life."

"I don't feel we have resolved anything here. I want to know what's going on with you and my son?" she asked.

"Your son and I are fine, you're out of line and if you want to stay in my home for the next few days I suggest you wind your neck in. Now, let's play nice so we can get through the next few days, you can go home and we can stay out of each other's way for another while, got it?"

"You really need to be more mature about this, Aimsy."

"All I need to do is get through the next few days. I do not need to dissect this relationship right now. I don't know when I'll get round to that, probably after my next lobotomy."

She screwed up her lips into a tight line and clutched her bag close to her chest. I assumed this was a show of defiance but I was too busy wrangling children away from the slide with promises of crisps at home.

I don't care what anyone says, bribery works

I could feel Althea's usual disapproving glare at my tactics but I just didn't care. My head spin began to spin and pressure was building up in my chest. It wasn't a totally unfamiliar feeling, and not in a good way.

Anxiety attack

I hadn't had one in well over a year and this was a huge achievement for me, this woman was not going to derail me. She was not going to see me fail and crumble.

I was always thankful for Ben not giving her the full details about the shambles my mental health had been in. I knew she would be the kind to lord it over me until the day I died.

I bent down to my shoes to pretend to tie my laces. This wasn't a very convincing ploy because I didn't actually have any laces. I tried to slow my breathing down so my heart would stop thumping wildly. My palms were sweating and I had the urge to run and never stop.

Fight or flight

I knew I couldn't run, for two reasons:

Firstly: I can't run. Not in the 'I can jog a bit but I'm unfit' way but more in the 'I would vomit after ten seconds and probably have a heart attack' way. For some reason, whenever I attempt to run I forget how to breathe. I genuinely forget how to do the most basic human function.

Secondly: I don't think I could reasonably explain why I suddenly decided to do a runner from her and four children without having to go into details about the complexities of an anxiety attack.

Hannah walked over to me and rested her hand on my shoulder.

"Are you ok, Amy?"

"Yes, love, just trying to tie my laces."

"You should have *Velcro* shoes like mine, they're really simple to do. Mum says we should keep things simple."

"I think you're right, sweetheart. I should start to make things simple."

I stood up and lifted her into a hug as I did.

"You're a very intelligent, girl."

"I know."

Her surety made me smile and my heart swell. She placed her little hand on my chest, over my heart and the feeling started to calm the tightness in my chest. I could feel the tears starting to form in my eyes so I gave her a kiss on the forehead and placed her down to run after her sister.

I took a long breath and counted the seconds as I slowly let the air exhale from my lungs.

I can do this

I walked behind Althea and the kids, mostly to compose myself a little further before I had to pretend to be perfectly fine but also because I didn't want to have another argument with her. I couldn't stomach it.

I knew, in her mind, she was trying to protect her son from his tyrannical wife, but she really had no idea what was going on in our relationship. The dynamic was a partnership and always had been. We were stronger than we'd ever been, yet, as soon as she was entered into the equation I couldn't stand the sight of him. My strong-willed, dependable husband turned into a snivelling 'mama's boy'. That was a phrase I hated, but I really couldn't think of any other way to describe him when she was around.

I argued with myself the whole way back the house. I couldn't decide if I was right in my irritation at how Ben was acting, or if my nose was just out of joint because Althea made every situation tense by just breathing in my general direction.

We were walking past *Joseph's* when I noticed Michael opening up for the Sunday brunch crowd. The café had become well known for its tapas style brunches and, after much convincing from Elle, there was even live acoustic music from local artists to accompany the food. I seized the opportunity to get away from the real world, even if for ten minutes.

"Althea," I called.

She turned without answering and just stared at me.

I'll take that as a 'Yes, Aimsy, how can I help you?'

"I just have to pop into work for a bit, I have to check something. I'll catch up in a few minutes."

As far as lies went it wasn't exactly my best work.

"You work in a coffee shop?" she asked, with an air of snobbery.

"I work above it, I run my own business."

I tried not to sound too boastful but also I really wanted to show her how proud I was of my achievement.

"Fine."

Well, that sure told her

I pushed open the coffee shop door and smiled at the young woman who was setting up her speaker and guitar in the corner. There were already people trying to come in but Michael refused to let them place their orders until he was 'in the zone'. They seemed satisfied with this delay and chose their seats to try and get the best view of the singer.

"Hey, Michael," I said, limply.

"Hi, Amy, hungover?"

"Why is this your go-to question for me? No, I'm not."

"Then why are you eyeing up those tray bakes like you're on a carbo-loading mission?"

"Because it's been brought to my attention that I eat my feelings and I'm having feelings."

"Ok. You're scaring me so I'm just gonna let you eat the cream bun while I go hide out in the kitchen."

"That was a wise choice, Michael."

I went behind the counter to pick which bun was the biggest and therefore the nicest. I finally decided on my chosen victim when I heard a woman speak from the other side of the counter.

"You're Anamy, aren't you?"

Just once it would be nice if someone called me by my actual name. It's not that hard of a name.

I placed my bun on the plate and reluctantly looked up to see who was mispronouncing my name this time.

"It's Amy."

"Oh, I'm sorry. I could have sworn you were someone from my fat club."

Fuck

"Eh yeah, that was probably me then. There was a mix-up with Melanie and for some reason she now thinks I'm a Scandinavian fat chick called 'Anamy'."

"Oh, cool. I was thinking your accent is different."

"Yeah, let's not talk about my accent."

Her name was Rebecca and was meeting her friends for brunch, but according to her diet plan booklet she was only allowed three sticks of celery and some clear broth on this particular occasion.

"I was coming to check if it was possible to get something like that on the menu and I spotted you."

She then noticed my cream bun which I placed, sheepishly, on the counter behind me.

"I don't think that slimming club is for me," I said, with a nervous laugh.

"Fat club."

"Sorry?"

"Melanie said we should call it what it is. It's all part of the shaming process which will make us more

117

motivated to lose weight. It's working, I blush every time I say the words and it makes me a bit queasy so I don't feel like eating."

"I don't think that's healthy."

"I'm sure it is, why would Melanie lie?"

To make a lot of money out of people with low self-esteem?

"I'll take your word for it. Enjoy your celery," I said, turning away to lift my plate and escape to the office, upstairs.

"Thanks, I will. Enjoy being fat for the rest of your life."

I closed my eyes and tried to breathe. I tried to count, I really did. I just came here to get away from every little irritating part of my life and enjoy silence, with a sugary treat. When I opened my eyes and turned to face her she was still standing there. It wasn't a smile exactly on her face, more of a smug grin.

"Have I given you food for thought concerning your poor eating choices?"

"I was really trying to just have some peace and quiet," I began.

"You mean shame eat and get fat -"

"I haven't finished speaking," I interrupted.

She blinked twice and decided to let me continue, which was her second mistake – the first was walking through the door.

"As I was saying: I came here for some peace and quiet. Not judgement about what I'm eating, what I'm wearing or what I'm 'putting my husband through'. I came here for a cream bun and some silence. Do we understand each other?"

"I'm only trying to help."

"No, you're not," I said with a laugh of derision, "You're here to judge like that psychotic bible-basher, Melanie."

"Why did you join the group if you didn't want to be faced with the truth about how hideous you look?"

This, again

"Are you being serious, right now?"

I decided to walk around to her side of the counter and with the volume in my voice rising those who were pretending not to listen to our conversation had given up all pretence and watched us intently.

"I am not hideous," I continued, "I am grumpy, tired, slightly irrational at times, I overthink, I'm petty, quite judgemental and sometimes I still think I'm a stinking hot mess of insanity, but I am not hideous.

"I am kind, I have a big heart, I'm a loyal friend and a fierce protector of those I love. I have stretch marks in abundance and a mum-tum that I'll probably never get rid of but I will be damned if I stand here and listen to some stranger judge my entire character based on whether or not I'm shoving a cream bun into my face. My weight does not equal my self-worth and I think that's something you need to have a think on before you go back to that hellhole of a class."

I was expecting a round of applause at my speech but people just shifted around uncomfortably waiting for Rebecca to speak.

"You can tell yourself whatever you want to but we both know you're better off not eating that, getting some celery into your life and maybe looking into your surgery options regarding your stretch marks. I'm here to be your mirror of truth."

I took a bite out of the cream bun and purposely left the cream on my lips as she stared in horror.

"Hmmmm you're missing something," I said as I pushed the remainder of the bun – and the overflowing cream – into her face, "*Now*, you look like a mirror of truth."

I brushed off my hands and walked out of the café, waiting until I was out of sight before I wiped my mouth. It only took thirty seconds for the reality of what I just did to sink in.

I just assaulted someone. Am I determined to get arrested this weekend? Oh, fuck. What have I done?

This record was on repeat for the remainder of the walk home and I was deathly white by the time I got in through the door. Ben and Althea were in the living room, presumably waiting to begin an intervention regarding my bullying ways. I was aware they were talking to me but I wasn't particularly interested in anything they had to say. They only finished speaking when the doorbell went and Elle came running in, dragging a bewildered River behind her.

"Hiya, guys!" she said, with all the enthusiasm you would expect from a woman who'd spent the night having sex with a stranger.

Hannah and Louise, alerted by their mother's voice, came running into the room to hug her and completely ignored the strange man at her side.

"My queens!" she exclaimed, breathing them both in, "I'd like you to meet a very special friend of mine. His name is River."

"Hi, girls."

They sized him up and glanced at each other to see if they both came to the same conclusion: this guy was a weirdo and needed to get gone.

I hear ya, ladies

"River?" said Althea, "What an interesting name."

"Yeah, I get that a lot. It's just what the universe gave me."

"So, not your parents?" asked Ben.

"No, I shed that mainstream label a long time ago."

I didn't take my eyes off Elle, willing her to hear me and realise that this was not the man for her and she should get him out of my house. Instead she was transfixed with every word coming out of his mouth.

"Get your stuff, girls, River and I are going to take you out for some lunch. Do you lot want to come?" asked Elle.

"NO!" I said, too quickly and too loudly, "Sorry, I just have stuff in for lunch already and don't want to get side-tracked. Can I have a word with you in the kitchen, Elle?"

These conferences were becoming a bit of a habit

I closed the kitchen door behind us and gave her and confused, and slightly exasperated look.

"What is going on?" I asked.

"What do you mean? We're going out for lunch. Did you hit your head when you hit my boyfriend with your car?" she laughed.

"Your what?"

"My boyfriend."

"You've known him for 12 hours, introduced him to your children and are now referring to him as your boyfriend?"

"Yes. What's your point?"

"My point is: 24 hours ago you were standing in my kitchen, drinking a smoothie made by a different man and now you've a boyfriend. Can you see where my confusion is stemming from?"

"Are you slut-shaming me? AGAIN?"

"I am a bit, yeah."

It was the truth. I felt ashamed admitting it but I had to say something.

"Well, don't. I like River. We are both children of the universe and if I want to tell the world he's my boyfriend and introduce him to my children as soon as I possibly can, then I will. I am a grown woman and I can make my own decisions."

"And what if they are bad decisions?"

"Then they are mine to make."

"So I'm just meant to say nothing and watch you get your heartbroken?"

"Who says I will?"

"I do."

She sighed and shook her head.

"Well then at least I'll have tried. Ever since you've been doing this therapy and recovery you've spent the last year being afraid to try anything in case it 'sets you back'. You might not agree with the way I'm choosing to live my life but at least I'm living it."

Her words stung and it showed in my face.

"I'm going now," she continued, "thanks for having the girls. I'll see you at work, tomorrow."

I didn't respond. I didn't even look up from the counter as she left. I wasn't sure how I felt about her accusations but If I was honest with myself then I knew there was some truth to it.

Is this is what my life had come down to? Stay safe and stay sane or live fully and risk the recovery. Neither seems appealing.

Ben came into the room with a grave expression on his face. He shuffled nervously and looked at his feet as he spoke.

"Amy, I think we need to talk."

What fresh hell is it now?

Chapter 10

"If you're here to tell me your mother is moving in to save you from your awful wife then just go right ahead. It seems to be how today is shaping up," I said, without mustering any humour in my voice.

"I've been speaking with mum about us," he said.

That's a sentence that will never end well

"And she thinks we should seriously consider counselling as a couple."

There you have it, I was right

I parked my bum down on the seat by the breakfast bar and said nothing. What was there to say? I had spent 18 months talking about my feelings and now, because his mother had come in and decided that we weren't matching up to her expectations of the perfect relationship, I was going to be forced back into an office talking about our marriage.

"I told her to shove it," he continued.

My head nearly spun off its axis when I heard those words. As I looked at him, he gave me one of his classic smiles that made my tummy feel warm and excited all at the same time.

"You did?"

"Yeah, she's upstairs packing."

Don't cry, don't cry, don't cry

"Apparently, I'm ungrateful and she is only trying to get me off the *Titanic*."

Charming woman, always has a way with words

"I'm sorry," he said.

"About what?"

"About this weekend, about everything that's happened since she's come here. I should have told you about the visit but I knew it would stress you out so I kept my head in the sand."

I appreciated the apology and for him finally sticking up for us in front of her. I was still sore about his personality change when she's around but I didn't think that was going to change anytime soon and, at the end of the day, she was leaving. I had my home and my husband back.

"I love my mum," he continued, "and I love you too. I think it's a pipedream to expect that you're ever going to get along with each other."

"I'm not going to lie, Ben, it's not looking likely. Perhaps, from now on, you and the kids can just visit her and your dad. I'll happily fend for myself here."

"That sounds awfully like a weekend off from your family?"

"Does it? Well, that's just a happy coincidence then."

I walked across the room to kiss his nose and I felt myself start to relax for the first time since her arrival. I hated that I would never have the type of relationship with her that Ben craved. I felt like I was failing him but I wasn't going to force myself to spend any more time or energy with someone as toxic as her; a woman who clearly hated me.

Maybe this was a cop out and exactly what Elle was talking about. Maybe I was hiding away from things that made me uncomfortable in case it led me down a rabbit hole and onto a dark path again.

I don't care. She's a witch and she's leaving. I've won...for now

It didn't take long for Althea to pack her belongings. Apparently 24 hours in our house wasn't long enough to quite make herself a permanent fixture. I decided it was best not to have the fake 'good-bye' conversation at the door so I hid in the kitchen as she made her excuses to the kids and said her farewells to Ben. I resisted the urge to call out anything and stood, biting my nails, in the kitchen waiting for him to come and tell me the coast was clear.

"She's gone," he shouted from the hallway.

"Oh, she is? That's a pity, I was just on my way out for a hug." I failed to hide my shameful blush that always indicated a lie but he just smiled.

"You're a terrible woman."

The rest of the day was peaceful. I felt grateful for the silence – even if that meant that Elle and I weren't on good terms – I just wanted to appreciate the calm of keeping our own company for once. In the days before therapy I would have dreaded the quiet because it meant I would turn inwards and herald the beginning of the cruel monologue about all my failings. Now, it was just about enjoying the present moment and not having to worry about anything but sitting with my family. It never lasted long, as soon as the kids could feel me relax they would usually burst this bubble by demanding snacks or drinks of juice. Sometimes, if I stayed really still or pretended I was sleeping they would annoy Ben instead, but more often than not they would walk straight past him, jump on my lap and prise open my eyes to ask me a question. Today was no exception.

"I've been thinking," said Ben, interrupting my meditative state, "We always said about going on a proper holiday, how about I organise something for us and we'll head off in the summer?"

This was unheard of. Benjamin Cole has never willingly offered to organise a dinner date, let alone a family holiday. Be very wary, Amy.

"Not to look a gift horse in the mouth or anything but: what's the catch?" I replied.

"Always so suspicious, Mrs Cole."

"So there's no catch?"

"I wouldn't say 'catch' per se…"

And there it is

"One of the suppliers keeps offering his holiday home and I keep putting him off, I'm starting to run out of excuses and I don't want to insult him by not taking it."

As far as 'catches' go, it wasn't the worst thing I could be talked into – besides a free holiday villa for the week is better than trying to find ways to entertain the children over the summer holidays that won't cost me a fortune every day; only to hear they want to go home after 15 minutes.

I hate the summer holidays. Eight long weeks of bickering, continuous rain, never-ending requests for snacks and a bank account that takes a battering equal to Christmas. It stresses me out every year, but not enough to actually get organised and have a schedule or anything, that would be far too helpful to my mental health. Not this year though, that was pre-therapy me, this was the year to put my disturbing amount of stationery to good use and organise our days so we don't murder each other.

"That sounds fantastic," I said.

"Really? I thought it would take a lot more convincing than that."

"For a free holiday villa? I know I can be a bit unpredictable but even that's a stretch."

"I wouldn't exactly call it a villa."

"I'm not expecting a beachside property or a pool, but it's all about how we make it."

"I love your positive attitude about this, I mean I really thought you'd have your heart set on a sun holiday and I'd have a lot more convincing to do. This is such a load off my mind, you're a wonderment," he smiled and gave me a brief kiss on the lips.

Why don't I learn to ask questions before assuming that my husband and I are ever on the same page?

"Eh, Ben?"

"Yes, my lovely?"

"Yeah, we're going to have to back up a bit. This property is where?"

"The west."

"West of where? Spain? Italy? France?"

"Ireland."

But of course it is

"And this non-villa is a?"

"A bungalow in a little village outside Westport. You're going to love it."

I decided to stick with the positives about the scenario. A holiday was a holiday after all and it was still a few months before I would have to actually face that particular hell.

"What's the plans for dinner then?" I asked, in a poor attempt at changing the subject.

I was always thankful that my husband never seemed to mind about my obvious avoidance techniques, I suppose they benefit him as well. I was done with the outside world for the day – mostly because I wasn't exactly certain that I wouldn't assault anyone else with a cream bun. I decided to keep that little incident to myself, for now, and send Ben out to grab takeaway roast dinners, that way I didn't have to feel too guilty about not cooking. The children would still be getting a nice Sunday lunch, but this way it would be edible and with zero clean up or preparation.

He left, taking the two miscreants with him in order for me to hunt out uniforms for the next day – as usual I had put them in the wash basket on Friday with the good intention of having it done that evening and now Monday was fast approaching with nothing done. After 15 minutes of searching all I could find were two shirts, one pair of trousers, one tie and 5 socks.

I hate Sundays

I've never really liked the day. For some it was a great day to recharge and get yourself ready for the week ahead. A Sunday well spent brings a week of content – or some other tripe you read on the internet. For me, however, it meant the end of the company of Ben at home and the school day chaos was going to start all over again. You'd think for someone who dreaded the normality of the working week I would be overjoyed about the looming summer holidays but:

A) I'm not a psychopath

B) Summer holidays bring back memories of long, boring days at home as an only child and spending a lot of time reading and counting down the minutes until I had the company of my peers again.

Now that I think of it, I don't remember the last time I didn't dread anything. I thought this sanity malarkey was meant to make every day feel like a blessing?

More and more I just feel dejected and angry with every damn thing and every damn person that bothers to come within close proximity of me.

Period? Most likely

Cusp of another mental break down? Probably

I prescribed some chocolate from my hidden stash before the children returned and I would have to share. I knew I couldn't ignore the niggling feeling that something was wrong. I was definitely in a negative mind space, for longer than I would like to admit. I was irritated by everyone – even with those that meant well – but I just couldn't put my finger on why. I knew I wasn't depressed, I had the brush with anxiety this morning, but even that had passed and I knew the reason for the stress.

The more I thought about it, the more worked up I became. I had done all this work and I couldn't answer a straight question: what is wrong with me?

In reality, I knew it wasn't a 'straight question' it's the same question I'd been asking since I was 16. A question I couldn't answer even after 18 years, a failed suicide attempt and nearly two years of intense therapy. I didn't think it would be a question I would ever have an answer for – but today, I had chocolate and that was a good enough solution for now.

***

I spent the evening lazily flicking through television channels before I admitted defeat and decided to go up to bed. I wasn't looking forward to seeing Elle tomorrow, I never knew if she was going to be her completely direct and ruthless self, or if she would clam up and pretend everything was perfectly normal. I was drained after the weekend and I didn't know if I could face another argument with someone, but there was only so much small talk I could do without snapping.

Ben had gone up to bed an hour before me so I knew I would be greeted with snores of a colossal proportion, but instead I heard music. I stopped halfway up the stairs and noticed a little flickering light at the top.

What the?

I reached the top and found more and more of the tiny tea light candles leading the way from the stairs right into our bedroom. They were arranged to form a little path and in between them were white rose petals. Instead of being moved by this over-the-top gesture of love, I tried to stifle a groan.

I'm so fucking tired, why tonight? Why?

I prayed to the universe that he was just interested in having a nice cuddle – maybe throw in a back massage – but instead I was faced with a very naked Ben standing in the middle of the room.

"What's all this?" I asked, knowing my fake enthusiasm was not working.

"I can take a hint," he said, pride beaming from his face, "You want romance, so here we go."

"Was I hinting for romance?"

"Weren't you?"

I feel like the last time I ever consciously 'hinted for romance' was about five years ago when Ben presented me with a new iron for my birthday.

"This is great," I said.

"Can you try telling your face that?"

"Why are you jiggling so much?"

"It's the heat from the candles, when I stay still for too long I'm worried that my ball hair will catch fire."

"I thought there was an unspoken rule that candles were to be kept out of any of our bedroom antics?"

"The hair grew back and I saw this on the internet. Rose petals and candles: sure fire way to get the ride."

I grimaced at the summation of whatever article that came from, but I was happy that his internet browsing was expanding from porn and football. I smiled at my naked, jogging husband and decided that I would be a complete bitch if I didn't try and put some enthusiasm into this.

"Ok, Mr Cole, would you like me on the bed? There are no thorns or anything is there?"

"No, it's just petals. Nice aren't they?"

He was so proud of the scene that I tried not to laugh when I realised there were about ten petals stuck to his bare arse as he turned round to make room for me to get passed.

"It's beautiful."

I sat on the bed, with my legs crossed and waited to find out what he planned. I always hoped it would be a back massage but I felt something more sinister was afoot. Well, not sinister, that makes him sound like a sex offender.

"Just sit back and relax," he said, "Your entertainment will begin momentarily."

He went over to his phone, that was propped up on a table, connected to speakers.

"I have to admit I did think back on the night you set me on fire, when I was looking for inspiration about what to do," he said.

"I thought we agreed not to refer to it as that?"

"Sorry, yes. Anyway, I was so inspired by your sexy dance moves that I thought I should return the favour."

Oh sweet mother of God, no. I have no alcohol in my system, he's doing some weird 'sexy' voice and he's now going to dance. Kill me now.

"Are you getting the cold?" I asked, hopefully.

"No? Why? Things are just heating up in here. Christ, Amy, can you stop making that face it's really putting me off."

"I'm sorry, you're just talking really strangely."

"I'm being sensual."

"Was this in the article as well?"

"Can you just *ssh*. Just, *ssh*."

I put my finger on my lip and literally bit my tongue, in an effort to stop my face betraying my whole body cringing.

I didn't recognise the song, it seemed to be something from the 1980's and his jogging, to avoid ball burns, had transformed into a type of rhythmic swaying and I couldn't help but move my head along with it.

Maybe he's trying to hypnotise with his testicles? There are articles for everything on the internet, these days, it really wouldn't surprise me.

"Amy?"

"Yeah," I said, as I snapped my head up and back into the present moment.

"Are you ok? You're like really staring at my stuff. It's kinda scaring me."

"For goodness sake, Ben, are you just going to criticise my every facial expression or are you going to get on with things?"

"Well, not with that attitude I'm not," he said, "I'm feeling a bit self-conscious now. It was ok for you, you were drunk."

He picked up the end of the curtains and wrapped them around his waist.

"Ben, can you please just do what you're planning. It's been a long weekend, I'm tired and I just want to get this over with."

I knew as soon as I said it I shouldn't have. He looked crushed and I felt awful.

"Don't let me keep you from your beauty sleep."

He went to walk out of the room but had forgotten that the curtains weren't budging from the wall with him, to disguise his modesty. I looked up in time just to see a sad bum, still covered in rose petals, leave the room.

Well done, Amy.

Chapter 11

I woke up with the feeling that something wasn't right. It was unsettling. I reached over to feel the warmth of Ben under my fingertips and all that I found was a cold pillow. I sat up with a start trying to piece together the night before and realised that he must have spent the night sulking downstairs.

I threw my legs out of the bed and stood on multiple tea-light candles that were still found on the floor. After I managed to blow each of them out I got lightheaded and lay down on the bed, expecting to be woken up when Ben eventually came back upstairs. Clearly I had bruised his ego more than I realised.

I shuffled downstairs, with a blanket around my shoulders, in order to track down my husband. As predicted, he was curled up on the sofa, snoring loudly. I decided tea could be used as a peace offering and retreated into the kitchen before attempting to wake him up.

Over the course of 24 hours I had managed to insult, reject and assault three separate people – that was a record, even for me. I didn't know what chaos was going to await me back at *Joseph's* but I thought the best course of action, for now, was to make sure there was peace at home.

I returned to a sleeping Ben and cleared my throat. He woke with a start and a look of confusion by his surroundings. The events of the night before clearly came back to him as soon as his eyes found mine. Suddenly the tea seemed like a pitiful attempt to make things right.

He gave a half-hearted smile and moved his legs so I could sit down, taking the tea from me instantly.

Never underestimate your husband's caffeine dependency

"My back is killing me," he said as he rubbed the base of his spine.

"You didn't need to spend the whole night down here."

"It wasn't planned, I must have run out of steam while brooding and fell asleep."

I smiled at the thought of him brooding. His eyes were permanently creased with laughter lines so the mere thought of him sitting down here with a menacing look on his face for hours was laughable.

"I'm sorry about last night, I was just tired," I said.

"I am too, just thought I would be spontaneous or something. I should know we aren't the type of people for that carry on."

"I think we could be, just as long as it's not last thing on Sunday night after a trying weekend."

"Spontaneously scheduled then?"

"Something like that," I said, relaxing more as he spoke and knowing that this wasn't going to be one of those rows that last for days.

"What are you going to do about Elle?"

"I'll cross that bridge when I come to it, I might have to sort out a potential assault charge first."

"What?"

"Nothing, well not 'nothing' but nothing to worry about right now. Ok, get upstairs and get some clothes on you, you don't want to scare the kids when they wake up."

"It seems a waste not to make the most of the quiet and your naked husband now, does it not?"

Seriously, Ben?

"Are you going to sulk if I say 'no' again?"

"I don't sulk, I brood, like those complicated alpha males all the women love."

"You need to stop reading whatever the hell you're reading online, it's getting weird."

"Just get over here and kiss me, woman."

I suppose there are worse starts to a Monday

***

Our post-coital bliss was short lived as the kids decided to come find us within seconds of them opening their eyes. Who knew small children would fly into a blind panic and think their parents had been abducted by aliens if they didn't find them in their room.

"Why are you down here?" asked Arthur.

"Did you stay up all night? Adam chimed in.

Ben helpfully pretended to be asleep so he wouldn't have to field any questions from the curious, tiny people. Thankfully my usual distraction technique of offering food did the trick and I was able to slip upstairs and get dressed before they started asking anything else.

I called them all in for breakfast and realised that Ben was still unfit to be seen downstairs and was using my favourite throw as a type of toga while he ate his cereal.

"I like your dress, dad," said Adam.

"Thank you, son, it's casual Monday at work."

137

Both children didn't know what to do with this information and weren't entirely sure if he was kidding or not.

"Don't listen to him, he's just trying new pyjamas and I think these aren't going to make the cut," I interjected.

"Oh, I don't know," Ben mused, "They're nice and airy, easy access…"

I shot him a look which made his gaze fall back down to his bowl and the table fell silent once again.

"Boys, get upstairs and start getting ready for school, I want to leave on time."

"You say that every day," said Adam.

"Yes, and I mean it every day. Get your butts upstairs and start getting ready. That goes for you too, daddy."

He did a military salute and ushered the boys out of the kitchen. I could hear Adam wailing upstairs, demanding that he too should be allowed to wear a toga to school because his uniform was too warm and he wanted to be 'airy'.

Nice one, Ben

It was the usual disorder in my attempt to get out the door with the children, and we were late as always. I don't remember a time when I left on time for anything, I don't even think this was a trait brought on by the appearance of children into my life, I was just someone who was always in a rush. Without fail, I will find some menial task that my brain convinces me I need to do at the exact moment I should be leaving the house. Ben calls this 'pottering' and it's something that I picked up from my mother.

Anytime I pick her up for something, she gets as far as the front door and turns back around to either go to the bathroom or rearrange the living room furniture – it's incredibly frustrating.

"I'm going to be late boys," I called from the bottom of the stairs

As if they care?

I wasn't in a particular rush to face what awaited me at the office and I did worry that there would be police officers at the café ready to escort me to make a statement but I still resented the fact that other people were the reason that I would be late in the first place.

"If you're not down here in the next thirty seconds, I'm leaving without you."

Ah, yet another threat I never carry out

I could hear the three of them in the bathroom, talking about superheroes, and basically ignoring the rapidly impatient woman at the bottom of the stairs.

Fuck this

And just like that, I picked up my handbag and walked out the door. I decided Ben could face the school run this morning and I could walk the ten minutes to the office and have a much more relaxing start to my day. I knew Ben would be livid but just for once, he could deal with being the shouty parent while I had a hot coffee and browsed through emails instead of trying to find a semi-safe parking spot outside the school gates.

I started to get less brave about my choice of finally following through on my threat and almost turned back three or four times. In the end I started sprinting up the road so I could get around the corner before Ben realised what was going on and managed to call me back.

By the time I pushed open the door at the café my hair was fuzzy with sweat and my hastily applied makeup was non-existent. I was faced with Michael, who didn't look very pleased to see me.

"Oh, there she is," he said, throwing his hands up in an exasperated manner.

"What's wrong?"

"What's wrong?" he repeated, "Let's see, you verbally assaulted a customer, smashed a cream bun into her face and walked out leaving me to deal with the drama by myself in the middle of the Sunday brunch rush, does that ring any bells?"

I blushed with shame and wasn't sure how on earth I could explain my actions so I let the silence continue on until he finally added:

"It was pretty badass, to be honest."

I felt relief wash over me but needed to know what kind of damage - or potential prosecutions - I was facing as a result of my temper.

"She was pretty pissed off," he explained, "she got up on her soap box and started telling people about how you were like a cancer in society and that denial wasn't body confidence it was just a quicker route to hell."

Fuck

"Most people just continued with their brunch and she soon lost steam. Her friends looked mortified to be with her but I did end up making her celery in way of an apology. I figured that would help."

"Is that all?"

"Not exactly…"

Double fuck

"She started bashing us online about how we were helping people become fat, lazy, parasites on society by eating tray bakes and putting strain on the NHS. It got a lot of traction – but fortunately for us not the kind she wanted. She got quite a lot of abuse from people for posting it at all."

"Well, that's not ideal."

"Better her than us."

Even though I was secretly glad she was getting told off by people for being such a cruel, ill-informed, ass I didn't revel in the idea that she was receiving abuse for having an opinion.

"Let it go Amy, you've caused enough trouble for us," called Michael, as he walked back into the kitchen to start breakfast preparation.

I couldn't help but feel that I was responsible for pushing this woman into expressing her views and venting online and now she was going to get sent all sorts of abuse as a response.

Just because you think it doesn't make it true. I am not responsible for the actions of others…

I kept repeating that over and over in the hope that I would actually believe it. I poured myself some coffee and skulked upstairs in order to collect my thoughts and be in a better state of mind before Elle appeared and I would have to deal with our falling out from the day before. I got as far as the top of the stairs when I heard her laugh emanating from the office.

I knew I wasn't that lucky

I pushed open the door and found her sitting at her chair, legs up on the desk and talking animatedly on the phone.

"I miss you too," she gushed, "Amy has just walked in now, I'll phone you back when I tell her the news. Love you, babe."

Did she just say 'love you'? She's obviously talking to one the kids. Fuck, please don't let her have gotten back together with Keith. That's all I need.

"Hiya," she waved, brightly from her side of the room.

"Hi," I replied, more tentatively and completely unsure as to how I was going to talk her out of getting back together with her horrible ex, "listen, I just want to get things out of the way about yesterday."

"Yesterday?" she asked, looking genuinely confused.

"You didn't leave under the best circumstances."

"Fuck, yeah. That was a lifetime ago, don't worry about it, I don't need an apology."

"I wasn't apologising. I'm never going to apologise for looking out for you. I'm all for you embracing your 'single and ready to mingle' persona but I don't want to see you get hurt. You seem to be bouncing quite hard and quite rapidly and when you were referring to that last one as a 'boyfriend' it just set off alarm bells in my head."

"Oh, don't worry, he's not my boyfriend any more –"

"See? This is what I mean. You were introducing him to your girls as a 'boyfriend' and now the next day he's gone. I will never judge how you want to run your romantic life, I just need to make sure you're being careful when it comes to looking after your heart and the girls. I love them like they're my own."

"Amy, stop. You don't need to worry about me or the girls. We're fine, we're never better as a matter-of-fact."

And now's the time she is going to tell me about how Keith has changed and the single life isn't for her. I'm going to kill her.

"I'm glad you think that, but if you're thinking of getting back with Keith then - "

"Keith? Why on earth would I get back with that waste of space?"

"I just thought that's where you were going with this."

"No, hell no. FUCK NO," she laughed, "Amy, I love you and I love that you're worried about me but you don't need to anymore.

"River is no longer my boyfriend - "

"Thank God, I just think at this stage in your life you don't need someone like - "

"He's my fiancé."

What the actual fuck

"I'm getting married, Amy."

Chapter 12

I felt like the floor was falling away from underneath me and I couldn't stop the room from spinning. I held onto the edge of my desk and looked completely bewildered at Elle, she had clearly lost her mind.

"Before you say anything," she said, "I just want to know if you'll be my maid-of-honour?"

I stared at her blankly and literally couldn't find any words in order to respond. I didn't know how to process this information let alone be part of the planning.

"It's a shock, I get it, but Amy this is it. I've never been so sure of anything before in my life. It's like every shitty relationship, bad date and wrong decision has resulted in me ending up in that car park on Saturday night and you hitting him with your car. This man is my soul mate."

The more she spoke the more ridiculous she sounded and I was seriously considering throwing my coffee in my face to see if all of this was some hideous hallucination.

"But…"

"No wait," she interrupted, "Please don't say anything about it just yet, I know you'll need time to get your head round it but I had to come in and tell you before I took the day off. We're going ring shopping, he'll be here any minute."

"But…"

"It's sudden, it's moving fast but like when you meet that person you want to spend the rest of your life with then you just want it to start right away. The universe has given me this blue whale of a blessing and I just want to grab it with both hands and never let him out of my sight. You know? Of course you know, you've got Ben. I'm so happy, Amy."

"But…"

"But what?"

"But you can't get married, you're still married to Keith?"

"That will be finalised in the next week and then I'm free to do whatever the fuck I want and that just happens to be marrying River in six weeks' time."

"SIX WEEKS?"

"I told you it's moving fast, but I'm not wasting another second without being Mrs Elle Wild."

"Wild?"

"Yes, it's his surname. I know I kept my maiden name the first time, but this time around I want to share everything with him."

"His name is 'River Wild'?"

"Yes."

"Like that bad Meryl Streep movie?"

"I don't know about the movie, but that's his name. Isn't it perfect? Like his wild soul and now I'm the only wildness in his life. He says it's my wild spirit that called to him across the cosmos and that's how he ended up there, he never cycles that route.

"You are marrying a man called River Wild, in six weeks?"

"Is that a question? Yes, I'm marrying a man called River Wild in six weeks and I want you to be my maid-of-honour."

My legs finally gave way and I perched myself at the edge of the desk in the hope that the change of position would stop the surroundings from rapidly spinning. It didn't.

"Elle, can we just slow down a minute here?" I pleaded.

"Princess, I know this is a lot for you to take in and that's why you can have the whole day and the office to yourself to do that. I'm going to run downstairs and meet River so we can find a ring that perfectly encapsulates our love story and we can catch up later."

Love story? They've known each other for 48 hours, it's not even a fucking post-it

She gave me a tight hug and disappeared out the door before I could say another word. I was left in the quiet and usually I would relish this opportunity but I felt like there was no way I would able to concentrate on anything other than my friend's colossal mistake.

What in the hell is she thinking?

I needed a voice of reason and opted for Ben. When I pulled out my phone from my handbag I noticed seven missed calls and one text that read:

Ben: Seriously? You actually just walked out and left me to deal with this? NOT COOL

That ruled Ben out as my confidante so I went to the next best thing: Joseph. He hated talking about personal matters with me in case it fell under the term 'gossiping'. I found this strange, saying as within five minutes of meeting him he asked me to bare my soul, but still, I tried not to bother him with unimportant things. I felt that Elle marrying a man she met two days ago constituted as an exception to this rule. I ran for the stairs, almost sliding down the final three, in order to find him. He was sat at the counter, as always, drinking an espresso and 'tutting' at his newspaper.

"Joseph?" I asked.

"Hmmm? Ah, Amy. Yes, what's wrong? You want to throw a custard pie at me?"

"Heard about that then?"

"Of course I did. These things happen," he added with a shrug.

I felt like 'these things happen' didn't really cover that particular incident but I had more pressing concerns.

"I need to talk to you; it's about Elle," I continued.

"Is this gossip, Amy? You know I won't tolerate gossip at my ears."

"It's not gossip, but it is urgent."

The look on my face must have alerted him that it was something serious so he dropped the newspaper and led me towards the battered sofas on which all our most important conversations occurred. When the café started doing better, I was tempted to suggest that they should be replaced with seating that had seen better days but I couldn't bear the thought of coming in here and not seeing the faded brown leather which was there the first time I walked into this place that changed my life.

"What is happening?" he asked, concern etched across his face.

"Elle is getting married," I replied, not sure how I could properly explain the last few days of her turbulent love-life.

"Yes, I know. To River, I just met him."

"What?"

"She just introduced me to him on her way out, he seems nice. This is the problem?"

"YES! She's only known him a couple of days, she's still married to Keith and she's acting like a crazy person."

Joseph shook his head and raised his finger up to silence me.

"No, no no, we don't like that kind of talk here. No one is crazy."

"Fine, she's being wildly irresponsible and I need you to help me convince her she's making a terrible mistake."

"I will do no such thing," he replied.

"Joseph, how can you be ok with this?"

"How could I not? She's a grown woman, she knows what a commitment marriage is and she thankfully hasn't been jaded enough by all that's happened with Keith not to believe in love at first sight."

"You can't be serious?"

"You say she's your best friend but for the last 18 months that woman has been walking around here with a broken spirit – not just heart – and now she is happy. You will not talk her out of what she wants, but you will talk her out of you being in her life. If you confront her about this and try to force her to see your way of thinking, she will cut you out of her life and carry on regardless. I suggest you be the friend that she wants and needs you to be. Be happy for her, be there for her and if - or when - it falls apart, comfort her. This is her life, Amy, you can't live it for her."

"But surely you can see this is ridiculous?"

"What does it matter what I see or what I think? I see a woman I care for happy for the first time in a long time, I hope it stays that way and I will support her. I suggest you do the same."

He got up and returned to his coffee and paper while I sat, staring out the window, wondering if I was the only sane person left in my life. I couldn't support this, it was a stupendous mistake and she needed a wake-up call before she ended up with two failed marriages and children who resented the merry-go-round of men that would be coming in and out of their lives. If that meant I needed to go down the tough love approach than so be it. I was never going to agree to be a maid-of-honour, but I would be instrumental in making sure that woman never made it down the aisle.

Chapter 13

I spent the rest of my day trying to do some recon work on the groom. It was proving more difficult than anticipated. To be honest I just typed his name into the internet search bar and went through the first page of results – which were mostly links to the Meryl Streep movie. He had no social media presence, where I get all my information from, so I opted for looking up articles on how to tell if I could legally kidnap Elle and store her somewhere until she wised up. I couldn't.

All-in-all it was a pretty fruitless fishing expedition and a wasted day in work. I wasn't feeling very pleased with myself by the time I left to pick the kids up from school.

I managed to avoid my phone for the whole time I was in the office because I couldn't handle a grumpy Ben on top of it all. I reasoned that I should make a nice dinner as a peace offering. For most people this would involve a new recipe to impress their spouse, however, for me, this meant just getting something on the table that would not result in food poisoning. I decided on fish fingers.

The kids were their normal boisterous selves and had forgotten all about their mother abandoning them this morning, which was nice but also quite insulting.

"Did you enjoy going to school this morning?" I asked, hoping to gauge how angry Ben was about the events.

"What do you mean?" asked Adam.

"Daddy took you to school, was that a nice change?"

"No he didn't"

"What are you talking about? Mummy wasn't there, so daddy had to take you?"

"Oh, yeah. No he was really sweaty and cross after you left so he just got Mrs White from next door to take us when she was leaving her grandson off. She was really nice and gave us a chocolate croissant on the way. Can she take us all the time?" he asked, hopefully.

You've got to be fucking kidding me

I had pointlessly dragged myself over the hot coals of guilt all day for expecting Ben to do his share of parenting and he hadn't even done it. My clever idea of delicious and exotic fish fingers were now scrapped, he was getting nothing.

The dinner was prepared in a flurry of rage and imaginary arguments with my deceitful husband, so it was no surprise that the potatoes were hard and needed a shocking amount of butter in order to just soften them to mash.

This would not go down well at fat club

The three of us sat down to dinner and I waited to hear Ben's keys jingle in the front door. He arrived when the boys had finally finished moving their food around the plate and got hungry enough to eat some of it.

"Hello, family," he shouted, as he came into the hallway.

I placed my knife and fork down and prepared for battle. This always started with a glare that could shrivel his testicles and put the fear of God into him.

He smiled at the boys as he came into the room but it slowly disappeared as his face moved from his children to me. He looked confused but decided it was safer to keep talking to the children about their day instead of asking what was wrong with me. It dawned on him quickly when both boys asked if we could start getting chocolate croissants for the drive to school every day 'like Mrs White'.

He chuckled nervously and told them to go watch some cartoons while the grownups talked. They didn't need to be told twice so we were left, in silence, in the kitchen. I refused to speak first because I knew he would just make it out that I was being completely unreasonable for leaving in the first place.

"Firstly, I think it was completely unreasonable for you to have left like you did this morning," he said.

Told you

"And secondly, Mrs White just happened to be leaving at the same time as we were and she offered. I had a huge conference call in the office first thing – which I told you about – and you just left. I took the kind offer and I went to work. So just remember that before you read me the riot act."

I let his final words hang in the air while I tried to figure out how to handle this. Should I read him the riot act as he predicted? Should I go with the silent treatment, because I know he hates that the most? Instead I opted to be reasonable.

"That's fine, Ben," I replied, as I picked up my plate and took it to the sink.

"It is?"

"Yes, that's fine."

"I feel like it's not fine. I feel like I'm waiting for the other shoe to drop or that you're going to hit me over the head with a frying pan."

"It's fine, Ben," I repeated, still with the even tone I began in.

"Oh. Right. Well, that's great. What's for dinner?" he asked, brightly.

"I didn't make you anything," I replied, mirroring his tone.

"I knew it wasn't fine."

"It's fine, Ben, if you count 'fine' as meaning you shirking off your parental responsibilities as soon as you can to a complete stranger while you rush off to the office on the one day I've had enough of screaming at you all so you can experience the stress of my usual start to the day, then yes: it's fine."

"She's hardly a complete stranger, she's been our next door neighbour for the last seven years."

"That's not the point. You do very little around this house, which was marginally acceptable when I was here fulltime but I'm not now, I have a job too and I have less time in the day to fit everything in before I have to leave and get them from school and you do nothing to help with that when you only bother to get yourself ready and leave. It's unfair, it's selfish and I'm sick of it."

"Again, this doesn't seem like the situation is fine."

"Then I guess it's not, but it will be. As of tomorrow the morning school run is all yours. I'm done. We are in a partnership and this partner is sick of the 80/20 split."

"But I have a meeting first thing."

"Figure it out. Perhaps Mrs White can take that meeting for you because she is certainly not going to be taking the children again."

I could see his face getting redder with every word I was saying but I was not backing down. I would not be the put-upon wife and he was a parent just as much as I was.

"I'm going to have a bath. I'm sure you can figure out the oven without me."

I closed the door behind me and heard a muffled 'fine' coming from the kitchen. I knew that wasn't going to be the end of this particular conversation but I had won the first round. Perhaps he would be more reasonable to the change after he'd had some dinner but, just in case, I would put some earphones in while I was in the tub so I couldn't hear the passive aggressive banging of pots and pans as he cooked his angry dinner.

I often find that there's very little that can't be solved by a boiling lobster bath, an impromptu nap or a really deep laugh. I didn't feel much like laughing after the last few days but I could soak away my worries – or at the very least, ignore them – for a while.

I never understood people who didn't like baths. They were wrong and clearly a dangerous person to be around. I tried my best to shut out all the things that were bothering me, even with the relaxing music and the temperature of the water rivalling that of a volcano, I couldn't shake the argument with Ben. I hated feeling guilty for wanting things to be even around here or the fact that Elle was trying to ruin her life. None of these things would stop playing on repeat so after a pitiful 15 minutes in the water I grumpily got out to lie on the bed, like a starfish, and sulk.

I knew my hair was wet and I hadn't bothered to put a towel around my head so I manoeuvred my neck so the damp would be on Ben's side of the bed. Yes, it was petty but as I listened to him bang cupboards and mumble to himself through the floorboards I didn't fancy being like the grownup today.

By the time I started to get cold and reluctantly dried myself, it was time to put the kids to bed. To my surprise, Ben came with them.

"I thought we could do it together, you know, like partners," he said.

There was no sarcasm or malice behind his gesture so I simply smiled and watched him throw them on their beds in order to make sure they were good and hyper before trying to get them to sleep. Normally I would be shouting about this but in the spirit of compromise – and a more pleasant evening – I kept my mouth shut.

When the boys eventually fell asleep, Ben helped me clean around the kitchen and sort their packed lunches for the next day. We chatted about his work and it wasn't until we were both sat on the sofa with cups of tea that I finally told him Elle's news.

"She's getting married?"

"Yep."

"To a man called 'River Wild'?"

"Indeed."

"Like that bad Meryl Streep movie?"

This is why I loved him

"That's pretty crazy," he said after a few minutes of letting it all sink in."

"What am I going to do?" I asked.

"What do you mean? I don't think there's much you can do."

155

"That's where I think you're wrong. That's just a defeatist attitude. She's not down the aisle yet and I think we can stop it."

"We? No, no, no I'm not on board with this plan. She's a big girl she knows exactly what she's getting into."

"Does she though? Maybe this whole divorce has caused a psychotic break and she's convinced herself that she's in love with this hippy. We can stop that, get her help and get her away from him. We could be the heroes of the piece."

"You think? Because right now it feels like we're being the judgemental assholes."

"She can't marry someone she doesn't know, this isn't a princess cartoon."

"I think you can give her all the advice you want but this is Elle we're talking about and she will do whatever she wants, you've enough experience to know this already."

"I bet she's already having cold feet, she just needs some proper advice from me and she'll see how ridiculous all this is. I'm going to text her now and say she needs to be in the office tomorrow so we can talk. I can fix this," I said, confidently.

I took out my phone to find there was already a text waiting for me.

Elle: Engagement party this Friday at the café. I've booked salon appointments for us both, I can't have my maid-of-honour sporting a unibrow. See you in the morning, princess xx

"Her feet seem pretty toasty to me."

"Shut up, Ben."

This was going to be harder than I thought

Chapter 14

I waved to my family as I set off on my walk to work and tried not to laugh as I looked at Ben's worried face. We didn't talk any more about the school run situation I just decided that he was on board with the change and left for work after I got myself – and the kids – ready for the day. I'm not a complete monster, I wasn't going to shove him off the deep-end on the first day, but this may change depending on if he's annoyed me the night before or not.

I said I wasn't a monster, not that I wasn't petty

When I walked into the office I flinched wildly at the sight of a fist coming towards my face. Fortunately it was just an over-excited Elle trying to show me her new engagement ring. I was expecting some type of ethically sourced piece of yarn with her birthstone on it but it was a pretty spectacular rock.

Hippy work pays well

"What do you think?" she asked, as she jumped up and down, "It's perfect, isn't it?"

"It's something," I replied, sipping my coffee and trying to make my way around her so I could hide at my desk for a few minutes before I had to start slapping some sense into her.

"Well? Have you an answer for me?" she asked.

Straight down to business then

157

"Elle," I began, "Can you please just stop jumping up and down and have a chat with me? We need to get serious right now. We are running a business and I need you here and sane. Not running around planning a wedding to a complete stranger that's going to blow up in your face."

Perhaps I could have eased in a bit more than that

Her face was unreadable. I was sure she was going to cry or scream but she walked around to her desk and sat down to face me.

"Thank you," I continued, "I'm worried that all this is some knee-jerk reaction to the divorce with Keith being finalised and you're throwing yourself into some make-believe relationship to prove that you're totally fine with everything being over with him.

"It's been a tough couple of years and I just think that instead of making a colossal mistake like this, why not just take a holiday? You and the girls book somewhere warm and amazing and figure out what you want for the next phase of your life. If that's River, great! That doesn't mean you have to marry him in a month it could mean you should just date him for a couple of years and then talk about marriage. Everything doesn't need to be 'go big or go home', you could just proceed at a normal pace. Sure it's less exciting but it also won't result in you getting another divorce and uprooting your daughters' lives."

The silence was awful. I don't think I'd ever been in her company for this long without her talking. Finally, she cleared her throat and said:

"Thank you, Dr Freud. Tell me again how proceeding at a normal pace worked out for you? Because from where I'm sitting you've done everything in your life by the book and yet I wasn't the one that threw themselves in a lake in an attempt to end my life; that doesn't exactly scream 'sane' to me."

Fuck me, that's cold

"That was a low blow, Elle."

"Perhaps, but so is implying that I'm going to fuck up my children's lives because I'm happy and in love. Have you ever considered that I might know what I'm talking about? Have you thought that maybe after three decades on this earth, a shit-ton of rubbish relationships, a failed marriage and pretty much manoeuvring through my adult life on my own would allow me to make that decision as soundly as possible?"

"I…"

"No, you don't; because, Amy, you think that you're the first person in the world to go through a shit time in your life, receive therapy and now you're the fucking expert on everyone else's problems. Stop viewing my engagement as a problem, it's a fucking blessing. He's a blessing and if you bothered to get to know him then perhaps you would know this and be fucking delighted."

"Get to know him? You've been together for twenty seconds, you don't even fucking know him."

"I know his soul."

"Oh give me a break!" I said, exasperated.

"Scoff all you want, but this wedding is happening, with or without your blessing. We are best friends and business partners so I want you to be a part of this, but I will proceed without you."

"I can't."

"Well, I don't see how I can be around you right now."

She stood up to leave and I jumped from my seat to object.

"You can't just walk out on me, on us. We're a team."

"Are we? Because right now all I see is my teammate telling me what I can't do with my own life and that is really shitty."

"Well I think it's shitty that you're putting me in this position and throwing my completely unrelated breakdown in my face as a reason that I'm not making a reasonable point."

"Fine, I'm sorry, you're entitled to your opinion on this and I know you're trying to look out for me but I'm getting married and you need to accept that."

She walked out of the office and down towards the café, leaving me to stare after her. I angrily replied to emails and chased up invoices, feeling braver about asking for overdue payments after our fight. Normally I'm awkward and apologetic about having to ask for our rightful money but today I was as persistent as a dodgy bailiff.

When she eventually came back to the room I was huffily typing an email and pointedly ignoring her. I refused to look up and ignored the scone she sat on my desk.

Fuck, it's heated. It smells so good. Don't you fucking dare eat that, Amy. You eat that and you're part of the damned bridal party.

"I'm sorry," she said, quietly, "That was a shitty thing to say. It was really shitty."

I stopped typing long enough to allow myself a sideways glance in her direction. She was looking down at her engagement ring and I felt a pang of guilt for taking away her happiness.

"I'm sorry too," I said, reluctantly, "I have your best interests at heart but I'm going about it in the wrong way."

She lifted her head and looked hopeful as to how the conversation was going.

"This doesn't mean I approve," I added quickly.

"I know. I just want you to give him a chance. He's really amazing and you're amazing so I know you're going to get on brilliantly. It's so important for me that you like each other, I don't have any family left and you know you're not just my best friend; you're my sister."

For fuck's sake, she's playing the sister card and now I'm going to be a complete bastard if I don't be part of this

"You're a torture," I said, relaxing into the inevitability of it all.

She threw her arms around my neck and added: "You're a soft touch, princess, I knew you would fall for that sister shite. Now, I have the salon booked in twenty minutes so we can sort out the brow situation."

What brow situation? Bitch

"Just out of interest, Elle, are you planning on doing any work for the next six weeks or should I just camp out here to cover everything?"

"I should expect next to none."

"Just checking."

We both laughed, but I knew she was going to be little to no help for the next while, and I made a mental note to put both our diaries together so I could make sure our business still operated while she threw her life away.

"Come on, we have to go pretty ourselves for the party," she said, pulling me to my feet and out the door, "This place is amazing, River recommended it. It's all organic produce, no chemicals and is going to make us look stunning. Although he says I don't need anything to do that, I have the glow of the universe vibrating from me."

"Of course he does."

I felt nauseated listening to her rattle on about the raving lunatic she was planning on legally binding herself to. Apparently he worked in some organic health food market – no surprise – and was teaching her all about veganism.

"You would never give up meat," I interrupted, "You once asked me if sausages were a vegetable."

"That was the old me, but I really feel like because the universe has brought River to me I should give back and not contribute to the destruction of the planet. It's really about priorities, or at least that's what River says, and I think it's definitely something I should consider."

"I think for the rest of the afternoon I should be allowed to hit you every time you say the phrase 'that's what River says' or any variants on that because we've been in the car for ten minutes and I want to throw myself into oncoming traffic just so I don't have to listen to you anymore."

"Fair enough," she replied, and mimed zipping her mouth closed.

We pulled outside the modestly called *Heaven Salon* and headed in so I could go through the ritual humiliation I experience every time I go to any beauty establishment. I hated feeling scrutinised by these polished-looking professionals for always having split-ends and chipped nails. I also couldn't stand the whale song music or panpipes they insisted on playing. It didn't soothe me and I ended up feeling as relaxed as I would be going for a smear test.

"Ladies, how can I help you?" said the freakishly neat woman behind the welcome desk.

"Hi, my name is Elle Wild I have an appointment for the eye works package for myself and my friend here."

"Of course, Mrs Wild, please take a seat and I'll just make sure your room ready."

"Mrs Wild?" I said incredulously.

"I know, I know, but I thought I could try it on for size to see if I liked the sound of it and River says it's cute that I'm so excited."

I slapped her on the face.

"What the fuck was that for?"

"I told you I would do that, it's your own fault and they will get harder."

"Jesus, fine. I'll stop."

"Eh, Mrs Wild, your room is ready," said the returned greeter. She looked nervously between Elle and I but we both smiled as if it was perfectly normal to find us slapping each other in public.

The room was dimly lit with candles and there was the unmistakable sound of wind-chimes being played from the speakers somewhere. It was toasty warm and we were asked to change into our robes and slippers and lie up on the couches to wait for the therapy guides to come.

"Therapy guides? Do they ask us about our childhood while plucking my eyebrows?" I asked, nervously.

"Just stop being so cynical and get into the lovely robes, this is meant to be a relaxing experience and you're not going to ruin it for me with your sarcasm."

"Ok, ok, this is nice; really nice, in fact."

"I know, isn't it? River says - "

I raised my hand to slap her again but she blocked my palm and added: "Sorry! I'll stop, I swear. Just stop beating me, I don't want a black eye for the party."

"Then stop being one of those unbearable people who don't have an original thought unless their partner has had it first. That is not the Elle I know."

She smiled and settled up onto her couch, waiting for the pampering to begin. I did the same and reluctantly let myself relax. It wasn't every day you got to bunk off work and be beautified by organic beauty sherpas or whatever the hell they wanted to be called.

I closed my eyes and tried to ignore the relentlessly irritating wind-chimes. Soon enough we were joined by our two guides, each carrying a tray with several lotions, potions and instruments of torture to use on us, all in the name of beauty.

"Ladies, you're here for the deluxe eye package I believe?" her voice was trying to sound calm but it was unnerving, like we were about to take part in some sort of ritual sacrifice.

"As all our products are strictly organic there's no need to worry about what's going on to your body."

Yes, she's definitely going to murder me

"Just relax and we'll begin with the eyebrows, moving on to the lash tint and we'll finish off with our signature head massage so you're ready to face the rest of the day with a calm aura."

The last time I had anything close to a head massage was when I needed a bag of peas on my head after Adam dropped the iPad on it as I slept on the sofa. At this point I didn't care if I was being indoctrinated into a coven, I really wanted the massage.

164

Elle and I barely spoke as they worked, I think if I tried to make conversation it would have inevitably got back to my wedding objections and my sherpa would have to navigate a furrowed work surface. For once, the eyebrow shaping was painless.

This organic shit might actually be ingenious

Next was the eyelash tint, something I'd never had before so wasn't entirely sure what the hell it was. My guide (or Laura as she preferred to being called) explained that it was a completely natural solution that would make my eyelashes appear like they were already curled and I was wearing mascara. This sounded like the dream, I got to pretend that I was organised enough to apply mascara every day without ever having to look in the mirror.

Organic shit is wonderful, albeit slightly uncomfortable on my eyes

I tried to ignore the uncomfortable feeling that was growing, but it was starting to get warmer with each passing second and my eyes were streaming. I assumed this was all part of the beautifying process, there's no way a solution could just work like magic without some sort of reaction.

Reaction? Is this an allergic reaction? Sweet baby Jesus

"Eh, Laura?" I asked hopefully, trying to disguise the rising panic in my voice.

"They've both left to get the stuff they need for the head massage. Do you ever pay attention?"

"I think there's something wrong with my eyes. I can't see."

"Of course you can't your eyes are closed, you moron."

165

Fuck, that's right

"And they're also getting really hot."

I could hear Elle shuffle on her table, like she was trying to sit up and look for herself.

"I don't know why I'm even trying to look, my eyes are covered in this crap as well. Hang on. LAURA!" she bellowed, instantly obliterating the calm ambiance of our room.

Laura came in within seconds to find out what the commotion was.

"Is everything ok, ladies? Oh fuck."

That's not what you want to hear

"Can you both just lie down for a second, I'm just going to get my supervisor."

I heard her footsteps run down the hall which did little to calm my nerves.

"Why the fuck is she fucking running, Elle?"

"I don't know. I'm sure everything is fine."

"Are your eyes burning?" I asked.

"No, they're fine."

"Of course, they're not, this could only happen to be. Thanks a fucking lot."

"Are you seriously blaming me?"

"You and that fucking River one."

"Don't you bring him into this."

"I may be blind but I will slap you, Elle."

We lapsed into silence and waited until we could hear two sets of footsteps bounding down the hallway and into the room.

"See?" said Laura.

"Oh fuck," replied the stranger.

"Can people stop saying that and tell me what the hell is going on!" I asked.

166

"Everything is absolutely fine, we're just going to remove the solution very quickly and get a little cooling eye mask over those beautiful eyes of yours," said Laura.

Yes, because that sounds completely normal

"You may have had a teensy allergic reaction to one of the ingredients in the solution but the swelling should go down in a few hours or in the worst case scenario, days."

"DAYS? Get this crap off me I'm going to the hospital. Wasn't there meant to be a patch test or something?"

"With all our ingredients being 100% natural we've never felt the need to offer that."

"Can I humbly suggest that maybe YOU DO FROM NOW ON?! Fuck, this is really burning."

"Here's the eye mask, you should put this on to start working on the swelling," offered Laura.

"Get.me.a.mirror," I said through gritted teeth.

I decided that I could dispense with all niceties because they may have permanently scarred me. I could barely see and it was a struggle to open my eyes any wider than a slither. I knew Elle, Laura and the supervisor were all gathered around me gauging my reaction to my reflection. Not only were my eyes puffed out like I'd gone ten rounds in the boxing ring, my eyebrows were also protruding from my face.

"It doesn't look *that* bad," said Elle, barely containing her laughter, "And the swelling will go down in a little while."

"It doesn't look that bad? Really? I look like Herman fucking Munster, Elle!"

If I could have glared at her, I would have; but I just wanted to get to a doctors. Funnily enough, neither of us were charged for our relaxing eye package and we headed over to my GP's office in the hope that I looked tragic enough for someone to take pity on me and give me an appointment. I knew this was going to be next to impossible because the receptionist at my clinic hates me – or anyone who dares to ask for an emergency appointment.

She didn't bother looking up as I asked to see someone she simply said the next available appointment wasn't until 'next week sometime'. As she was about to shoot me a condescending smile she finally looked up to see my face.

I was seen four minutes later.

I had visions of a high-speed ambulance drive to the hospital to fix my watery eyes and dodgy face but I was handed a prescription for some eye drops and told to get a cooling eye mask. I resisted the urge to tell her where to shove her cooling eye mask and didn't demand pain relief. I simply handed the paper to Elle and asked her to bring me home.

There wasn't a hope in hell I would be leaving the house for the rest of the week, or being seen without sunglasses until my face stopped looking like I had undergone a bad facelift.

I wasn't ready to laugh about this particular disaster and, to her credit, Elle sensed this – for once. She spent the rest of the morning getting me set up on the sofa with pillows, blankets and endless cups of tea. She put in my first dose of eye drops and left me (with the aforementioned eye mask) while she picked up all the kids and took them to her house so I could rest.

I slept for hours and when I woke up I was happy to find that the burning sensation was subsiding but I had decided that I would be milking this injury for all it was worth (especially if it meant naps and no school runs for a few days).

Ben returned with the kids after work and I looked suitably miserable on the sofa. I could open my eyes a little more which wasn't as much of a blessing as I thought it would be. This way I could see Ben's poor attempt at hiding his reaction to his deformed wife. It didn't help that Arthur kept saying: "Mummy, your face is really scary."

After that I decided to hide upstairs and practise my ghoul noises so I could really commit to my role as the resident freak show.

I wasn't left alone for long before Ben tentatively came into the room with a cup of tea and my eye drops.

"Elle says you need these three times a day for the next six days," he explained, "I know you hate anyone going near your eyes - "

"Can you blame me now?"

"But I can do it for you," he finished.

"Fine."

"Does it still hurt?"

"A bit," I offered, "Do you think I'm cursed?"

"Because you had an allergic reaction?"

"No, because I'm a walking disaster. There's always something that goes wrong. I thought after therapy everything was just going to be easy street, but now I'm just grumpy about everything and now I'm going to be permanently disfigured."

"Can we dial down the dramatics?"

I threw the duvet over my head and decided that this was where I lived now. The outside world was a turd anyway.

"Amy, therapy was never going to wave a magic wand and fix your life and turn it into some completely sterile existence, it was giving you the tools to help you navigate the mess. The mess is life. It's our life and it's pretty great, you just need to roll your sleeves up and get on with it. The swelling will go down, you will help Elle with this wedding because she's your best friend and you're not a complete tool and then we can go on holiday and relax when all that madness ends.

"Everything is going to be just fine. Just have a little faith."

"It's hard to have faith when I have the face of a blowfish," I replied from under duvet.

"You still look beautiful. I can prove it by having sex with you right here, right now – just give me a few seconds to find a paper bag for your head."

I gave him a kick so hard it knocked him off the side of the bed, but I could hear his laugh from the floor.

"Think of it this way: you've always wanted to seem mysterious, so now you get to wear sunglasses indoors like a celebrity."

This idea did appeal to me slightly but I refused to come out from under the blankets. He soon gave up and headed back to the kids while I eventually fell asleep in my cocoon of shame.

Have a little faith? The only thing I had faith in was that this River bloke was going to be a complete waste of time and I was the one that would have to pick up the pieces. I may be the one who couldn't see, but she was completely blinded

Chapter 15

It was the day of the engagement party and I had woken up to fourteen texts from Elle in various states of emotion. They ranged from nauseating love for her fiancé to complete panic over fairy light placement. My eyes were slowly returning to normal but I still refused to be seen anywhere without my sunglasses.

"You're not wearing them to the party are you?" asked Ben.

"You're damn right I am, you're lucky I'm not sporting a black veil too."

"I know you're joking but I feel like I should make sure you're not going to show up at this party like you're dressed for funeral?"

"Maybe I will…"

He left with the boys for school while I clicked on the laptop to make my way through some neglected emails and set up the business diary for next week. I had meetings that I couldn't rearrange so I would just have to hope that the weekend and some heavy makeup would work wonders when I finally faced the outside world again.

After my fifteenth text from Elle I finally relented and rang her to see what I could do to help.

"I've pretty much everything under control," she said, sounding calmer than I expected, "I'm getting my hair done later and then I'll be heading over to *Joseph's* at 7 to make sure everything is looking great."

"Are you expecting many people?" I asked.

"Not on my side, but this will be the first time I'll be meeting his friends and family."

"Are they getting a bus in from their weirdo commune?"

"Shut up, Amy, I'm nervous."

"You've nothing to be nervous about, you're Elle De Bruyn, you basically force everyone to love you whether they want to or not."

"I needed to hear that."

I left her to get on with her day of worry and flap about while I pulled apart my wardrobe in an attempt to find something that would take attention away from my indoor-sunglasses look. The answer was: nothing. Unless I decided on rocking up to this party in my underwear people were going to think that I was a pretentious ass who wears sunglasses indoors, think I'd had some bad botox or I was a battered wife. None of these snap judgements would do me any favours but I would just have to get on with it. I settled on a navy and white spotted dress which was the only thing in my possession that I didn't hate.

It didn't take long for Elle to start texting in a panic again. I ignored them while I was hunting for an outfit but when I eventually read the litany of messages I realised things had taken a nosedive at the café.

Elle: Amy, you've got to get here there's something going on outside
Elle: It's like a protest or something
Elle: They're chanting something about a diet
Elle: ANSWER ME

172

Elle: I've just been called an 'obesity enabler'.
Elle: Did you try to force feed someone with a cream bun?
Well, that's just wonderful.

I knew it was too good to be true that I would get away with the bun incident but now I would have to go deal with these lunatics while I had a face like a slapped arse.

I pulled on a dark jacket with a hood and ran out the door in order to find out if there was some way to calm things down before the start of the party. By the time I arrived I found seven people standing outside the café with signs ranging from plain insults about the food to the ridiculous. I glimpsed one that said: '78% of people in the UK die from cream bun consumption'

How would even the most stupid of people think that this was true?

Elle grabbed me as soon as I got through the door with a wild look in her eyes and the air of someone about to lose her cool.

"This is a fucking disaster, Amy. I can't have River's family and friends turn up here and be heckled by these arseholes. You've got to do something."

"They're scaring away our lunchtime customers," called Joseph, from the counter.

We all jumped at the sound of a loud thud at the window.

"Fuck me, they're throwing cream buns now. Who the fuck is that?" asked Elle.

I looked out into the crowd and saw that Melanie had decided to stand on one of the tables outside in order for people to hear her better.

"People, I thank you for coming here today to show solidarity to our faithful sister, Rebecca, who was so cruelly assaulted here for trying to help the deceitful and ungrateful Anamy."

"Who the fuck is Anamy?" said Elle.

"That would be me," I replied, rolling my eyes.

"We, the faithful, will not be silenced into the night by these obesity peddlers and we will make it our mission to stop those who have not yet seen the light. We will make an example of this place of debauchery and spread our message wide."

Debauchery? It's a coffee shop, hardly a swingers club

"That's it, I'm phoning the police," said Joseph.

"Perhaps I should go out and talk to them, this is my fault after all," I offered, hoping that someone would stop me and tell me to stay safe inside until the police came. They didn't.

I pushed open the door and pulled down my hood in order for them to recognise the enemy.

"Anamy," said Melanie, "It's mighty nice of you to join us."

"Pleasure is all mine, Mel. Now, do kindly fuck off or we're phoning the police."

There were a few nervous murmurs in the crowd so Melanie returned her attention to the flock.

"Be strong, people. This is just another test from Satan," she said.

"It's not a test, it's a promise and I'm not Satan, I'm a chubby atheist."

Rebecca pushed through the crowd to face me and I braced myself in case she decided to hurl a bun in my face as revenge. She kept a couple of feet away and started to cry.

"This woman," she said, pointing at my face, "Tried to force feed me and lead me down the path to hell with her cream bun."

This is fucking ridiculous

"I resisted the temptation and I rewarded with a 5lb loss, this week."

"You lost 5lb because you've been surviving off celery, you daft bint."

Probably shouldn't antagonise the mob, Amy

"Look, Rebecca, I'm so sorry for the bun thing. I had a horrible day and you were just at the wrong place at the wrong time. I'm so ashamed of my behaviour and I honestly can't apologise enough."

She wiped away her tears and threw her arms around my neck wailing:

"The power of our message has moved this blubbery carbo-loader to accept that we are the true leaders to a lighter life. Are you willing to return to class and renounce your fatty ways?"

"Wow, no, not at all."

"Oh. Well, I guess we will just continue to protest here until you see the light."

"Well, I guess then you can explain yourself to the police. They've just pulled up."

There was nervous murmuring in the crowd as two police officers made their way through the crowd and faced me. At that moment Joseph came out and asked them to come inside to explain the situation.

I noticed a few straggler members of the protest had slunk off and were heading down the road in the opposite direction, before the police came out to address

Melanie. She didn't notice that her numbers were dwindling, she just kept her head down and eyes closed in silent prayer.

I wanted to go inside and see what was being said but I also didn't want to put my foot in it and admit to assaulting anyone.

Just stay where you are, Joseph will sort this. Maybe I should pray too? Make it look like I'm a good egg?

"Melanie?" said a tall man, disturbing her from her connection to the Almighty.

"Yes, Bob?"

"Sandra and I are going to head on. This whole protest thing isn't worth the two free classes you promised. I don't want to get a police record. It's just a café after all."

"*Just* a café? I suppose Hell is just a sauna then, Bob?"

She got back up on the table and, judging by the shock on her face, had only realised she was down to her last few protesters.

"Brothers and sisters, this is a test. Are you going to be one of the faithful that makes sure people know our message about the fatty's of this world? Those gluttonous parasites do not deserve equal rights or anything good in this world. Remember our mission: Fat Shame, Life Gain!"

I think she was expecting a round of applause or for them to start chanting but the rest of the crowd dispersed within a few seconds until all that was left were Melanie, Rebecca and I.

"Melanie?" said Rebecca, "I'm actually going to leave too."

"No! You can't! This is all in the name of the injustice you suffered here, just days ago."

"I know that and I really appreciate it, it's just that I'm on probation and I have a month left so..."

"So, you're going to leave me too. I'm like Christ at Gethsemane, all of you asleep and only me here to serve the real purpose of my mission."

"Yeah, I guess," she replied, nervously looking at the police officers in the café. Turning to me she said: "Don't force feed anymore of your customers, you fat mess, and we won't have a problem."

With that, she walked away leaving Melanie and I to face each other.

"You haven't won this," Melanie said, "Satan never wins. I will pray on this and see what the good Lord needs me to do in order to stop here – and places like it – from being a gateway drug dealer to the virtuous of this town."

"Bye Melanie," I replied brightly, and retreated into the comfort of the café to explain to Joseph that I wasn't the cause of bringing the apocalypse to his door. When I came in I noticed that one of the officers was wiping away a tear.

"I haven't thought about that memory in a long time," she said, "Thank you, Joseph."

She shook his hand and they both left, carrying take-out tea.

"You got the mob under control, I see?" he said.

"And you were asking people too many personal questions, I see?"

He shrugged, as if this was a perfectly reasonable thing to do.

"I'll clean the cream buns off the glass," I said, as I walked out towards the back of the café in search of cleaning supplies.

"Leave it, Amy, go help Elle - she's being fussy about fairy lights. I don't want to listen to that. I just want my lunch and some quiet."

I found her in the patio area at the back of the café on a ladder.

"Don't fall and break anything, I don't think a bejewelled neck brace will be a good look on anyone."

She jumped down from the chair and glared at me.

"Have the crazy people gone?" she asked.

"Yep, it's just us crazy people left."

"That's fine, I can deal with that level of insanity."

"What do you need me to do?"

"Just keep me calm. I don't think I've sweated this much in my life. I think I'm cursed."

"I wouldn't say 'cursed', hugely unorganised, bossy, overbearing and crass but not cursed."

My attempt at a joke wasn't well received but I decided to sit down and start untangling another ball of fairy lights in order to look busy.

Elle sat across from me and gave a heavy sigh.

"Did I ever tell you about my first wedding?" she said, without looking up from her hands in her lap.

"Yes, you said it was in a registry office somewhere."

"I should have known then it was doomed."

"You're not cursed, Elle, you're just nervous about meeting his family. That's perfectly normal."

"When Keith and I got married I just wanted a small, quickie ceremony because I didn't really care about the wedding I just wanted the stability of a marriage.

"The only thing I did want was some confetti and some doves when we left. I thought it would be cute. I made sure no one had rice to throw so the birds wouldn't die and I was so happy when we were leaving that I didn't care that people were being overly-generous with the confetti throwing.

"When they released the doves, one didn't move at first. It eventually got up off its lazy arse to fly above our heads; it shit all over my hair and dress and then went back into the basket. The other got caught up in the confetti tornado, choked to death and fell out of the sky, landing stone dead in front of us. If that wasn't a foreshadowing of the misery to come then I don't know what is. Oh, I know, a fucking protest outside the venue of my engagement party is a pretty big sign from the universe that this whole thing is doomed."

I felt so sorry for her.

"The only thing the universe is telling you, is to be pickier about who you chose as your maid-of-honour," I said gently, "I'm the one who looks like she's had botched botox and I caused the protest outside. You've just fallen in love. Don't take this as my coming around to your way of thinking, I still think this is a ridiculous idea but you're not cursed. Come on, these bastarding fairy lights won't put themselves up, so stop this pity party and get to work."

Her smile was filled with relief and she transformed back into her bossy self, telling me I wasn't untangling them right or my side was put up crooked. It took most of the afternoon to have the place just as she wanted but, as usual, she made it look spectacular.

"Are they going to like it?" she asked.

"They are going to love it, and they're going to love you," I replied, giving her a reassuring hug, "Now, go get ready. I'll make sure Michael and Joseph know what you want the front set up like and I'll see you here at 7."

I didn't have much to do in the way of getting ready. It didn't matter what way I did my hair or makeup I was still going to look like a puffy weirdo anyway. I did manage to grab two bottles of fizzy wine from the kitchen on my way out. Someone had foolishly left them sitting out, so I reasoned they were asking to be liberated from the building.

If I'm going to be part of this farce, I can at least be merry

I popped open the first bottle, at home, as I curled my hair and sang along to nineties dance music. The more I drank, the less I cared about my protruding eyebrows and bulbous-looking eyes and I even decided to leave my sunglasses at home. I popped open the second as I sat on my stairs and waited for Ben to get home from leaving the kids at my parents' house for their sleepover.

"Hello, gorgeous," he said.

"I look ridiculous."

"You look beautiful," he countered, "Now, give me ten minutes to have a shower and then I will help you with that fizzy stuff. Are you drinking that from a mug?"

"Yes, it holds more than the stupid champagne clarinets."

"Champagne flutes," he corrected.

"Alright, *Downton Abbey*, hurry up and get ready."

I don't know if he took record time to get dressed or if it was because I had lost all concept of time since opening the second bottle, but he was soon beside me on the stairs with his mug of fizzy wine and saying 'cheers'.

"We haven't been out together in ages," he said.

"Too bad it's going to a funeral."

"Are you going to be melodramatic all evening? Should I get you that black veil?"

"No, I'll behave."

We decided to walk to the café, slowly. I was having a tough time in heels but it was a cool night and he didn't mind me dragging at his arm the whole way.

"You're a good walking aid. Cane? Zimmer frame? What's the word I'm looking for here?"

"Husband?"

"Yeah, that will do," I said, instantly forgetting what we were talking about.

The place was already lit up and I could hear people chatting animatedly.

"Are we late?" I asked, "We had to be here for 7."

"It's 8:15."

"Fuck. Strike one for the maid-of-dishonour."

"I think, because you're married, you're technically meant to be called 'matron' not maid."

"I think, if you call me 'matron' like some dowdy old woman, I'm technically meant to staple a napkin to your head."

"That threat was oddly specific. I feel like you've thought about that before."

I hiccupped as way of reply and pulled him into the party. The place was already full and I barely recognised anyone. I scanned the room and found Elle talking heatedly to Michael at the kitchen.

Ben and I made our way through the crowd in order to make our apologies for being so late.

181

"Michael, I told you his whole family was vegan," said Elle, "His mother is in the bathroom trying to vomit up the duck spring rolls you served."

"You didn't tell me anything about a vegan option, Elle, besides duck doesn't even really count as a meat. It's practically a fish and they're definitely not meat."

She rolled her eyes and came face-to-face with her swaying best friend.

"Sorry, I'm late," I said, letting another hiccup escape, "Ben had the shits."

"What? No I didn't! Amy, don't say that to people."

"It's fine, Ben, judging by the smell of her it looks like Amy had a little pre-party, party. Amy, get some water and try not to set anything on fire."

I gave her a salute and tottered, ungracefully, into the kitchen to search for water. I decided that my heels were just going to hold me back for the rest of the evening so I kicked them off and found myself feeling instantly better, although I felt about a foot shorter.

When I returned to Elle and Ben, they were both laughing and clinking glasses. He had obviously made her feel more relaxed about the evening and I couldn't help but feel a pang of jealousy that he was better at doing this than I was these days.

I shook that destructive train of thought out of my head and joined the two of them, with my very sensible glass of water.

"You've shrunk," noticed Ben.

"Yes, I decided that fizzy wine and heels were a bad combination and I didn't want to fall head-first into a wall."

"Solid plan," he replied, nodding approvingly.

"I better go check on River's mother. Hopefully she's stopped vomiting."

She drained her glass and went off in search of her future mother-in-law while I tried to see if I could find River in order to have an actual conversation with him. Unfortunately my eyes were still tiny and the copious amount of alcohol in my system was not helping my search.

I spotted him across the room, talking with Joseph and I dragged Ben with me, so he could help me interrogate this so-called blessing from the universe.

"Don't do it, Amy," warned Ben, holding my arm and stopping me from marching over towards River.

"Do what? It's my duty as maid-of-honour to get to know the groom."

"Matr – never mind. Fine, we can go over there but you better behave. This is important for Elle."

Behave? Like I'm some mischievous child, he doesn't know what he's talking about

I cleared my throat to get their attention and they both stopped their conversation to smile at Ben and I.

"River, I thought we should get to know each other properly. No time like the present," I said.

I realised, in my efforts to sound more sober than I was, I had adopted a strange posh accent which would explain why Joseph and Ben were both staring at me with confused expressions.

"Of course, Amy, I'm really excited about getting to know you."

God, he's such a phony

"So, you've got a stupid name," I began.

Ben spat out his drink and tried to make it sound like a cough. Joseph patted him on the back, in an attempt to escape an awkward situation but River simply smiled.

"I get that a lot, but the universe gave me this name and if anything, it's an icebreaker."

"I didn't realise the universe was such a big Meryl Streep fan."

"I'm not following," replied River.

"Your name, 'River Wild' it's a Meryl Streep movie," I said.

"I didn't know that."

"Of course you did. It's the one with Kevin Bacon in it."

"I don't know what you're talking about," he answered, looking more uncomfortable by the second.

"The one with the river rafting and they're kidnapped. Of course you know it, you picked your name after it," I continued.

River was looking more nervous as my rant about the movie continued.

"I don't think he knows the movie, Amy, let's move on," suggested Ben, poorly disguising his nervous laughter.

"Fine," I conceded, "so, are you like some sort of sexual deviant who tries to con single mothers into relationships with your penis wizardry?"

With the words 'penis wizardry', Joseph took his leave and decided to hide in the kitchen to get as far away from this conversation as possible.

"I don't really know where to start with that one," he said, sounding slightly dumbfounded, "I know this is all happening really fast but I love Elle, I honestly believe we're soul mates and the universe has brought us together. I don't know about the penis magic though."

He took a long sip of his drink and l noticed that his eyes were darting all over the room in order to spot someone that could possibly save him from this mad woman.

"Don't get me wrong, River, sex is important in any relationship but I just think it shouldn't be the most important thing," I continued.

Why am I still talking?

"Take Ben for example," I said.

"Let's not," Ben pleaded.

"Ben and I have been together for a long time and sure, the passion has waned a bit, but I still fancy the pants off him. I mean this man's thighs are just lovely. Summer is wonderful because he gets his legs out a lot."

"Please stop talking, Amy," said Ben, with his face in his hands.

"Shut up, Ben. You do have lovely thighs. Show River your thighs."

"No."

"Anyway, my point is…well, now I can't remember my point. Was it something about objectifying women?"

"Amy," interrupted River, "I get what you're trying to say. This isn't just some sex thing that will fizzle out. I love her, you don't need to worry. I'm just going to see if I can find my mum, she wasn't feeling well."

Was I talking to that man about Ben's thighs?

"Well that didn't go as badly as I thought," said Ben, "Maybe next we could find his grandmother and we could tell her about us having sex on the sofa the other week so we could be spontaneous."

"I think that would be really inappropriate, Ben."

"Oh, really? Well, now I know where the line is. I'm going to get another drink."

I was left on my own, swaying to the music and hoping that someone would take pity on me and hand me a drink, or some food.

Water is so boring; this is meant to be a party

I decided to try and find Elle, perhaps she needed help bonding with her mother-in-law; after all I got on so well with mine that any advice I had on the matter would be very helpful.

Instead I found the happy couple stealing a moment together in the hallway. River was no doubt telling her what a fool I'd made of myself and I would have to try and do some damage control tomorrow.

That's sober Amy's problem

I kept myself hidden so I could hear what accusations he was poisoning her with about me.

"Do you think people are having a good time?" she asked.

"They're all having a wonderful time, even mum."

"Was that before or after the vomiting?"

"She really likes you, she told me so. All of them do."

"I hope so, I just want all of this to be perfect. Have you seen Amy?"

"Yes, we just spoke there now."

Here we go

"It's really important that she gets to know you, I think she'll finally get on board with the whole wedding if she sees how amazing you are."

"She's really funny and she loves you. I think we are going to get on great. Stop worrying about everything, I keep telling you we are exactly where we are meant to be. The universe wants this and we are going to be so happy for the rest of our lives. Just you wait and see."

They kissed and I returned to the party. I didn't want to get the reputation of a creep who spies on couples from around corners.

Is that what dogging is? I must remember to ask Ben

I was caught off guard by the fact that River could have sold me out to Elle and wedge a barrier between us. If he had done there would be one less objection to the wedding. Instead he was kind about me.

I don't know if this was some sort of psychological mind game of his or worse: he was a genuinely nice person and this relationship was a good thing.

I hadn't remotely considered this as a possibility, I'd spent this whole time convinced that she was making a huge mistake and wasn't open to the fact that he could be a decent person. If that was the case then there was only one more question to answer about all this: What if the only ass around here was me?

Chapter 16

It was unsettling to think I could be so wrong about someone. Not because I'm always right about these things – let's be honest, that's a rarity – but because I was so certain that I was the only voice of reason in this situation. When Ben found me, distracted and back to drinking fizzy wine, he was worried by my expression.

"What have you done?" he asked, urgently.

"What? Nothing."

"Then why do you look so guilty? Did you talk to his grandmother about my thighs? Amy, I swear if you did we are leaving."

"No, I didn't tell anyone else about your thighs, you paranoid wreck. I was just wondering if I had possibly been a bit too quick to judge River. Maybe he's ok."

"Is that the alcohol talking?"

"Probably," I shrugged, as I took another sip of my drink.

A hush was called over the crowd and I could see River and Elle at the top of the room about to make a toast. If it went anyway like the last toast she made here, it would be safer for me to leave the building now.

River took the lead but held his fiancée's hand the whole time he spoke.

"I just want to thank you all for being here, this evening, to celebrate," he said, "It's been a crazy six days and the next six weeks are going to be even crazier but I couldn't be more certain about this path, this wedding and most importantly: this woman."

Gimme a break

"I know I talk a lot about the energy force that surrounds us all, connecting us to the universe; and I know a lot of you roll your eyes when I start to talk about it, but it means a lot that you turned up here to celebrate with us. Maybe some of my message is getting through.

"I just want to finish off by saying 'thank you' to Joseph for pulling this together in such a short space of time and also to Elle's best friend, Amy. I look forward to getting to know you both better. You're both so important to Elle and I hope to share that connection with you too."

To his credit, it was a nice speech. People clapped, he and Elle kissed and the crowd made the obligatory 'aww' noises, but I thought it would be remiss of me not to add something to the proceedings.

I grabbed a knife from the counter to tap against my glass in order to get the room's attention. Unfortunately, it was only now I noticed that they were both plastic so it was completely useless. By the time Ben noticed what I was trying to do, he was too late to stop me.

"OI!" I bellowed.

The crowd stopped in a stunned silence and Elle's eyes widened in fear as she spotted her intoxicated friend walking, barefoot, towards the microphone.

"What are you doing?" she hissed, through a strained smile.

"Toasting the happy couple," I said, before turning my attention back to the party-goers.

"Hello, everyone," my voice cracked a little and my palms were sweating. It turns out that no amount of alcohol in my system would curb my fear of public speaking.

"I'm Amy, the MAID-of-honour," making sure to glare towards Ben as I emphasised 'maid', "I just wanted to have the chance to speak about the happy couple and their special relationship.

"When Elle first told me she was getting married to the man I almost murdered, I thought 'fuck, she must really love me or she wouldn't be shacking up with this guy to stop him pressing charges'."

I laughed at my own excellent joke, however I was the only one to do so. Undeterred, I carried on:

"I mean, has anyone checked that River isn't just concussed? And don't get me started on that name. How anyone can take this man seriously is beyond me."

I could feel the atmosphere getting prickly around me and realised that maybe this attempt at a roast wasn't best performed at an engagement party – or anywhere.

"All joking aside, Elle is extremely important to me. I love her like a sister and it's my sisterly duty to make sure she's making good choices. I was nervous about this union, but tonight I can see there's a lot of love in the room and although Elle has been complicit in the death of a few doves in the past, she really is a catch."

People weren't sure if I was speaking in code or having a stroke and by this stage of the speech Elle decided she would wrestle the microphone from me and free the crowd from the obligation of listening to my rants.

"I wasn't finished," I protested.

"Yes, you were. It was lovely, just lovely," she said, with a condescending rub on my shoulder.

"What's this about doves?" asked River.

"I'll tell you later, Amy is going to go home now and have a little lie down."

"I am?"

"Yes," she said firmly, "Here's Ben and he wants to go home too."

I was directed towards the door and plonked down on the table outside so Ben could put my shoes back on.

"Did I do a good job?" I asked, stretching out my foot and feeling like a princess.

"It was certainly unique," he replied, pulling me to my feet and practically dragging me down the road towards home.

"You really do have lovely thighs."

"Thank you, sweety, I grew them myself."

Chapter 17

All hope of a lie-in, so I could sleep off my hangover before the children returned, was soon dashed as Elle landed at my door at the crack of dawn.

"Morning, sunshine! We've got work to do," she beamed.

I had put my indoor sunglasses back on, however it was because of the thumping headache and not because of my misshapen face.

"What?" I said.

"I have chosen the perfect venue and you're coming with me to view it."

"What about the groom?"

"He's working and you're maid-of-honour so basically you don't have a choice. Go get ready and I'll make coffee because honestly, you look dreadful."

"I can hear colour."

"Eh, great... go get ready."

I pulled on whatever clean clothes I could find and left without waking Ben. At least one of us should make the most of the lie-in while the kids were away. I left a note, explaining that I was being kidnapped and would bring home some sort of deep-fried beige food to help soak up any remaining alcohol in our systems.

I'm an excellent wife

It didn't take long to work out where we were going. We headed straight out of the city and down the motorway towards the newly refurbished – and therefore high in demand – *Hotel Redenzione*.

When we walked inside, I was faced with white surfaces, floors and walls in every direction. I instantly felt out of place, standing in my black leggings and ripped hoody.

"Isn't it beautiful," said Elle.

"Could you have possibly brought me somewhere slightly less bright for my hangover, like the surface of the sun?"

"Just try not to vomit or touch anything, I really want this place."

"It's going to cost a fortune."

"River says - " she flinched and stopped herself from finishing the sentence.

"I've decided to stop slapping you, I don't think it screams 'healthy friendship'."

"Oh, thank fuck for that. Well, anyway, River said there was to be no expense spared and I was just to plan my dream day."

"I didn't realise health food shops paid quite so well, are you sure he's not in a massive amount of debt and has a hidden shopping addict?"

"He owns 17 shops across the country, actually."

I was genuinely gobsmacked. I assumed he was some lazy twat who just about showed up for work, a few hours a week, and was leaching onto Elle for a roof over his head.

Am I ready to admit he might actually be a 'blessing'? No, no I'm not

"We're waiting for a guy called Chris, he's going to show us the room for the ceremony."

"I really wish I didn't look like death, people are staring."

"There's no one even thinking of you. I think this is the guy."

Chris walked towards us looking impeccably dressed and thoroughly unimpressed with 50% of the people he was meeting. His initial disgust at the state of me was hidden almost instantly when he turned on the salesman charm and directed all his energy towards Elle.

He did the usual spiel about all the amenities in the newly refurbished hotel but was waiting to blow his perspective client away by leaving the ballroom for last.

It was huge. There was glass for walls and a huge dome in the centre of the ceiling. It truly was spectacular and I knew Elle was sold.

"The ceremony can take place in the very centre of the room with the chairs set around you both in a circular setting, that way no one can miss a beat of this blessed day," he said, "Then while we are getting the room set up for the dinner and dancing you can all have a drinks reception in the bar area or for £5,000 extra we can arrange a marquee outside.

"Are you kidding me," I said, my voice echoing everywhere around the huge room.

"Is there a problem?" he asked.

"An extra £5,000 for a poxy tent outside, are you mad?"

"I can assure you, madam, it's not a tent. It's a marquee," he laughed, as if changing the word suddenly made this price completely acceptable.

"Elle? Are you seriously considering this?"

"If that's the price, then I guess I can ask River."

Chris smiled at me, happy with his victory.

"I could pitch a tent in my back garden for free."

"Well, you do get what you pay for so if you'd prefer that to the opulence of *Hotel Redenzione* then I can easily give away your dates to someone else. The marquee isn't in everyone's budget and that's completely fine."

"Well, if Chris says you can do without the poxy tent then that makes it acceptable," I replied.

"Chris, can you give me a few minutes with my friend so we can have another look around? I'll be out with my decision shortly."

"Of course, Ms De Bruyn."

As soon as he closed the door behind him, Elle spun on her heel and was in my face, her cheeks flushed with anger.

"What is your problem *now*?" she said.

"This all just seems a bit much."

"A bit much? How could wanting to make my wedding day perfect be 'a bit much'?"

"Because it's a lot of money to be throwing at some party to a guy - " I managed to stop myself but it was too late, she could connect the dots herself and see that I was still not sold on her crackpot plan.

"To a guy I barely know? Was that what you were going to say? Well, you know what? It seems like I know River a hell of a lot better than I know you these days. He makes me happy, we are getting married and that's all I should have to say on the matter, but saying as you seem determined to be completely fucking miserable about this, I will break it down for you one final time:

"For the last two years I have been fucking miserable and now I have met someone that makes me happy, makes me feel whole and he wants to spend the rest of his life with me. Yes, it's fucking fast and maybe it won't last – hell, maybe I won't even make it down the aisle – but I will jump two feet in and see where this goes.

"He loves me, Amy. The girls like him and, in time, they will love him too. I haven't lost my mind nor am I trying to put together some mess of a happily-ever-after because my divorce is getting finalised, this is real. I won't say this again, I won't explain myself or try and convince you of anything. If you want to be my best friend and support me then please do; but you've got to stop this constant sarcasm and eye-rolling.

"Be here or get out of the way, because this wedding is fucking happening."

She left me standing in the middle of the giant glass room and I wasn't sure what to say. I was stuck in an impossible situation. I couldn't keep my mouth shut about a ridiculous notion like this. I wasn't suggesting that they never get married, just wait until they knew each other longer than most people go on holiday for.

On the other hand, if I keep up this routine then I was in very real danger of being shut out of her life for good. It was time to pick a side. Either stick with my stubborn resolution that I was right or let her live her own life.

The garden where Chris had planned to put up the tent was beautiful and I could visualise Elle and River walking outside to take in the surroundings. Now was my chance to finally jump on board and prove that I was on her side. If she was going to make a stupid, bloody

196

mistake then I would be right beside her, holding the veil.

I ran towards the open door and waved to show my enthusiasm in my new role as the world's best bridesmaid. Unfortunately, the door wasn't open. I ran full speed into a glass door, smashing my face into it and falling back onto my ass.

By the time I removed my sunglasses and opened my eyes I could see stars as well as Chris and Elle standing over me.

"The door was closed, Amy," she said, smiling warmly.

"I'll just go get some ice and someone to clean the face residue off the glass," added Chris.

What the fuck is 'face residue'?

"Have you run out of arguments against the wedding, so you decided just to wreck the place?"

"I was trying to tell you something important."

"Yes? What is it this time? I'm making a huge mistake?"

"Yes, you are."

"You've made that perfectly clear already," said Elle, standing up and leaving me to struggle to get on my feet, like a tortoise stuck on its shell.

"I mean don't sign anything with that joker, Chris. We can talk him down, that marquee should be thrown in with the drinks package and he knows it."

"Does that mean you're going to be helpful?"

"No, it means I'm going to be the best fucking maid-of-honour in the world. Now, help me up Elle De Bruyn, we've got a wedding to plan."

Chapter 18

I had forgotten just how much planning went into a wedding, especially one that was a little over a month away. Elle was due in court this morning to finalise her divorce from Keith and wasn't being particularly helpful in making flower decisions, although it did mean she was doing actual work for our business.

She was in the middle of writing up new content for our newest client, a struggling funeral home, when she clicked off her computer and let out a big sigh.

"You should probably check that content before I send it over to Derek," she said, "It might be too bleak – even for a mortician," she said.

"I feel like this is a redundant question, but is everything ok?" I asked.

"I've been looking forward to this day for two years but at the same time it's pretty sad to get a divorce. He's the father of my children and I never thought I'd be heading to court to finalise our marriage, let alone be in the middle of organising my second. It's all just a bit surreal."

Is that cold feet I'm sensing?

"Before you start, I'm not having cold feet or second thoughts about River."

How does she do that?

"I guess even if the chapter was painful, it was still a hugely important time of my life. I'm grieving the memories, not the person," she reflected, "You'll be busy while I'm gone, your 10:30 will be here any minute."

I scrambled through my diary, frantically trying to remember who was coming in but the day was blank.

"I don't have a meeting, this morning," I said, feeling smug that I was still more organised than her.

"Yes, you do. River is calling in so you can both have a chat while sober and you're still pretending to be behind this wedding. Have fun!" she called over her shoulder, as she left me speechless in the office.

I didn't have long to verbally admonish her before River walked through the door, carrying two cups of coffee and a scone. Elle had obviously advised him to butter me up, with butter.

"Come on in River," I said, as cheerily as I could.

"She didn't tell you I was coming, did she?"

"Oh, she did. Just about seven minutes ago."

"I'm sorry, I can come back another time."

"You're here now and maybe you can help me decide on flowers."

He shuffled awkwardly in the seat beside me and I knew he was feigning interest in looking through the images of flowers of my computer screen.

"We don't have to do this, you know?" I said.

"Thank God, I really didn't have a notion about what was the right answer."

I laughed, despite myself, and decided to tuck into my scone and coffee so he could say what he came here to say. Thankfully he took the hint and cleared his throat.

"You're very important to Elle," he began, "I knew that if there was any way I could have her in my life I would need to win you over. That's a lot harder in a short space of time."

"To be clear, River, I've no objection to the wedding."

He looked relieved by my words and I was glad that I could give him some comfort before I continued my lecture.

"I just don't see the rush."

"I know it seems like it's fast – and yes, that's because it is. I think I should just let you know a bit about me. Basically, I'm a coward."

Odd way to start

"I've spent so much of my life being told what to do and just doing what I thought I was supposed to. Everyone else seemed so certain about how their life should look and where it was going so I basically followed suit.

"I worked hard, I was in a comfortable relationship and in a job I was good at, but I was miserable. I kept looking for something, anything, that would make me feel alive. I thought the key to it all was just moving forward, buying things and doing what was expected of me.

"My family are great, my girlfriend was great but none of it felt like it was *my* life. I was turning 30 and it was coming up to Christmas. I couldn't think of what to get my girlfriend for a present so I thought 'just propose'. Isn't that awful? Proposing marriage to someone just because it was some kind of way to get out of thinking of a present?

"I got her gloves, she wasn't happy. She knew my heart wasn't in the relationship and dumped my ass the day before New Year's Eve. I just knew that I had to change something about my life and, if that meant taking a whole new direction and failing, well then at least I would have tried something to shake myself out of this funk.

"Eight years later and I'm running a business that I'm so passionate about I can barely sleep for thinking of what my next move is going to be. I'm responsible for hundreds of people across the country and it's ridiculously hard work – but I love it. It's mine.

"I hadn't thought about a new relationship over this whole time but the universe decided to intervene."

That's a kind way of explaining how I almost killed him, best not to interrupt and correct him though

"There was this instant connection with Elle. I can't explain it, nor do I want to. She's magic. I feel like I can do anything because she's with me, I feel stronger when she's around and when we kiss - "

"I'm going to stop you there," I said, raising my hands to stop the oversharing.

"It's like nothing else in the world matters," he continued, "It doesn't matter that I wasted years coasting through life or that I was afraid for so long about what everyone would think of me for taking this crazy chance and starting my business. Every wasted second and past mistake was wiped away and it's because of her.

"I wasted so much time without her because of fear and I don't want to waste a second more without her being my wife. That's the long and short of it."

I tried to gulp down the lump of emotion in my throat but some scone was in the way and led to me having a coughing fit. I finally managed to splutter the remnants of the offending baked good straight into his face.

"I'm so sorry," I said, my face beaming with mortification. After a sip of coffee I managed to compose myself to put the poor man out of his misery.

"I like you River. You've a stupid name and I don't believe that you've never seen that Meryl Streep movie but I like you.

"I love her and no matter what my personal feelings on the speed this relationship is going is irrelevant. I spend a lot of my time afraid too but that shouldn't be the reason to stop two people who want to be together going on this adventure.

"I can't say I'll ever be as spontaneous or as unafraid as you've learned to be but from what I can see, you make her happy and that's all I want."

I was afraid that he'd want to hug but thankfully he left soon after and I was left to get back to my flower search.

As much as I tried not to, I was starting to come around to having River around permanently. I felt sad that he'd been afraid of living for so long and concerned that I was in danger of doing the same. The weather was uncharacteristically nice for this time of year and I felt inspired by my conversation with River to put it to good use.

I picked up my phone and jacket and sped down the stairs towards the outside world. Dialling Ben's number I felt brave and more sure of my decision that I ever was.

"Amy? Are you there? All I can hear is heavy breathing," he asked.

Jesus, I'm unfit

"Ben, get the keys off that client we're going on a mini break to that place, today."

"But the kids are at school."

"We'll say someone died."

"Eh, I don't think that's ok."

"It's fine, I'll not say it's you."

"Gee, thanks."

"The weather is great, we have this house sitting there and I'm not waiting another few months for summer when we know it's more than likely going to rain. Let's just do it."

I held my breath and thought up my next argument for doing this when Ben interrupted my train of thought with a surprising 'yes'.

We agreed to pick up the kids together and head straight for the motorway this afternoon. It gave me very little time to get everyone packed but it was only for three days and even if I had a week to prepare I would still forget half the stuff that was needed.

I was excited for the first time in ages, I was taking control and seizing happiness. I was not going to lead some sterile life in fear of the low days.

Amy Cole was going on an adventure.

Chapter 19

For future reference: four hours in a cramped car with overtired and bored children does not constitute as an adventure. It's better described as 'torture'. We didn't make it to the house – which was in the middle of bloody nowhere – until after 9pm.

The kids were exhausted, we were exhausted and we all just wanted to collapse into bed. Ben started to unload the car as I opened the door to our little haven for the next few days. I was looking forward to exploring the hidden beaches, the antiquated village and this cosy cottage. Despite my exhaustion, I was still positive that we'd made the right decision. This positivity lasted until I opened the front door.

"We've made a terrible decision," I groaned.

I was hit with the unmistakable and overwhelming smell of damp.

"Eugh, what's that smell?" said Adam, as he held his nose.

"Everyone into the house, I'll sort it out," I said.

I had no clue how I was going to fix it at this time of night. I could open the windows and try to air the place out but that meant we'd all be freezing.

"Fuck, what's that smell?" echoed Ben.

"Welcome to paradise, darling."

I told the kids to pick a bedroom while I helped Ben with the remaining bags. He was soon dispatched to the nearest shop for essentials like bread, milk and wine. We also found out that there was no electricity.

After some investigation we figured out that we needed coins to feed a meter in order to get things on again.

"This really is living the high life," I sulked.

"I'll be back in ten minutes, we passed a shop not-so-long ago. Tell the kids it's a game and there's a torch on your phone."

"Again, living the high life."

I managed to hunt out some candles but there were no matches so we were still huddled in a bedroom around my phone, trying to make shapes with our hands on the wall, while waiting for Ben to get back.

After a half hour, even the kids were unimpressed with my dog impression.

"It looks exactly like your cat," said Arthur.

"And your bird," agreed Adam.

Jesus, kids, cut me some slack.

We all ran to the door when we heard the car pull up. He handed chocolate to the boys, a bottle of wine to me and went to put coins in the meter. The house instantly lit up.

"Our hero," I said, giving him a kiss on the cheek.

"The first shop was closed so I had to keep driving until I found a garage. Thankfully they had everything," he explained.

"I pulled apart his bag of supplies, which included breakfast for the morning, and another bottle of wine.

This is why I love him

"I don't know what I can do about the smell right now but we can sort that all out tomorrow. Why don't we watch some tele before the kids go to bed."

We all headed to the living room so we could see it properly for the first time in light.

This is a fucking nightmare

It was hideous. Chairs that weren't even fashionable (or comfortable) in the last century, a tiny television in the corner (which was never going to work), at least seven different holy statues in various crevices and a horrifying amount of doilies. They were everywhere. On the table, on the back of the chairs, on the television, fire place, shelves – everywhere I turned there were doilies.

"Does this man hate you?" I asked.

"I'm beginning to wonder that myself," Ben replied.

Adam switched on the television and managed to find one working channel which had a gritty looking crime drama on. I realised it was after 10pm and there was definitely not going to be anything remotely appropriate for them to watch.

They were sent to bed with minimal protests – mostly because they didn't particularly want to be conscious here anymore than we did.

I tried to find some sort of air freshener to mask the odour in their room but there was nothing. I promised them things would be better in the daylight, although I wasn't entirely convinced of that. When I returned to the living room I was handed a glass of wine and suddenly things didn't seem so bad.

"We can turn this around," I said, confidently, "We are going to make this a great couple of days and this part will all be a funny story to tell people."

"Is it ok to drink in here you think?" asked Ben.

"Of course it is, why wouldn't it be?"

"I don't feel right with all the Jesus' watching me. Is that right? Jesus' or it Jesusies in the plural? Jesusi?"

"I don't think that's a word, Ben. Let's just drink the wine and collapse into bed. I mean it can't get any worse, can it?"

The answer was: yes.

We opened the door to the master bedroom to find two single beds separated by a table housing a huge shrine to the Virgin Mary.

"It's fitting really," I mused.

"How do you figure that?" asked Ben, as he collapsed onto his bed.

"Well the only chance of any action occurring in this holy *Bates Motel* would be down to Divine Intervention."

I sat down on the bed, making it creak loudly and leaving me wondering if I would survive the night if I actually lay my full weight on it.

"We could pull the mattresses off and lie on the ground?" he suggested.

"We would get pneumonia from the damp on the floor."

"I'm sorry, Amy. This is all my fault."

"Yes, yes it is," I said, laughing.

I pulled him off the bed, onto his feet and out of his pity party.

"We have wine and each other. At least if we're bladdered we might not feel the cold as bad."

Within twenty minutes we were already feeling philosophical about our disastrous, spontaneous holiday. Our cheeks were rosy from the alcohol and Ben's attempt at a fire wasn't completely terrible. We talked about the kids (as usual), the third child that we never really got round to wanting, the wedding and our dreams.

I loved nights like this - I always regretted them the next morning, when the kids would wake up extra early and my head was pounding from the last glass of wine I knew I shouldn't have bothered with – but now it was exactly what I needed. Talking nonsense about our lives and slowing down a bit to connect with each other.

I always found that if we didn't have nights like this every couple of weeks our relationship would get prickly, we'd become disjointed or simply just out of rhythm with each other. Sex was always a secondary facilitator to get us on track, but what really worked was us sitting knee-to-knee and sharing secrets, dreams, complaints and talking about all the mundane stuff in between. It made us, us.

I don't remember falling asleep but I woke to the sound of a loud crash coming from the hallway. I jumped up from the sofa. Ben hadn't moved an inch.

Well there's no way I'm going out there to get murdered. What's the point in being married if you can't use them as a human shield?

"Ben!" I hissed as I kicked his leg.

He jumped out of his sleep, still clutching his empty glass of wine.

"I heard a noise," I said.

"What kind of noise?"

"Like a crash."

He looked nervously towards the door and back at me.

"You want me to go out and check?" he asked, staring at me with a look of pure terror.

"We'll go together," I compromised, mentally cursing him for inevitably getting me killed too.

He picked up the poker from the fireplace and I found the largest holy statue I could see in the room. I stood behind him, pushing him out the door first.

"It's really dark," he whispered.

"Turn on the light then. You realise this is how people are murdered in horror films don't you? They go to check out the creepy noise, in the dark, instead of turning on the lights and phoning the police."

He flicked on the switch in the hallway to find several ornaments had been knocked from the cabinet.

"There's no one here," he said, straightening up and pretending that he was brave all along.

"Oh, great, so the place is haunted."

"There's no such thing as - FUCK!" he screamed, pushing me in front of him so I was faced with the huge mouse, scuttling towards us. I pushed him back into the living room and slammed the door shut behind us.

After we got our breathing under control I realised that we couldn't be held captive in the living room for the night. For one thing: I needed to pee and secondly, the children would need their parents.

"Did you just push me in front of that thing to save yourself?" I asked, incredulous at my cowardly husband's betrayal.

"You're damn right I did."

"You're not even ashamed of it?"

"Not a chance. The kids needed one surviving parent so you had to take one for the team."

"And you think you're the one that could raise our children single-handedly?"

"Eh yes, obviously."

"Obviously? The other day you asked was it normal that Adam sneezed four times in a row and should we take him to a sneeziologist?"

"It was an honest mistake."

"Sneeziologist, Ben? SNEEZIOLOGIST."

"Ok, ok, I'm sorry for trying to feed you to the mouse but we need to work together and get out of here."

I grabbed my coat from the chair, tucking my hair under the hood and pulled on my shoes so there was no exposed skin for the evil rodent to nibble on. I took the poker from Ben and opened the door a tiny sliver to see if I could spot it.

He was back on top of the cabinet, sniffing at another ornament so I closed the door again and found Ben standing on the far side of the room.

"Are you being serious?" I asked.

"I don't like mice. If it was a snake or a tiger I would definitely be able to face that for the good of the family but those things are creepy."

"What are you planning to do with that poker? The only thing you'll hit is yourself, going by past incidences."

He was right, of course, but I felt safer with the poker than without. I didn't have a plan as such, I was hoping that my mere presence would be enough to make it scarper. I took a big breath and walked out the door to face the dreaded beast.

I walked out and started to bang my feet as heavily as I could – unfortunately it was onto soggy carpet, which provided next to no sound. I settled for thumping the poker off the wall instead and growling in a menacing way.

"Maybe you should try 'meowing'," said Ben, as he stuck his mouth through the tiny crack of door he bravely opened, "Natural predator and all that."

That could work

I started to meow and tapping the poker off the wall to try and get his attention. His ears pricked up at the sound of my cat impression but not enough to get him to stop chewing the open arms of a small Jesus statue on the cabinet.

"Your meow isn't that convincing," offered Ben.

"Yes, it is! You can't exactly do an unconvincing meow."

"I'm only saying that if it were convincing he would be more afraid."

Everyone's a critic

I decided to meow louder and bang the wall harder to get his attention but my quest for authenticity sent the poker went straight into the wall, causing a large hole.

"Oh, shit."

"What?" cried Ben, "has he got you?"

"How important is this client to you and how do you think he feels about damage to his property?"

Ben eventually braved the hallway in order to see what I was talking about but kept his back firmly pressed against the wall in order to always keep his eyes on the mouse.

"How did you manage that?"

"It's not my fault, I'm hardly the strongest person in the world. This wall is made of cardboard or fucking crackers."

The more I tried to dislodge the poker from the wall the more of it crumbled away.

"It's looking at me funny. Like it wants to kill me, why does his eyes have to be so beady and black."

"It's ok," I said, "once he gouges yours out I'm sure he'll sport those so people will think he's more approachable."

"That's not funny, Amy."

"Neither is you watching me dismantle a wall so can you pull yourself together and help me."

I handed over the responsibility of the poker dislodgement to a trembling and increasingly paranoid Ben while I decided enough was enough with our uninvited houseguest.

"Look, mouse, you have got to get out of here before you give my husband a nervous breakdown."

He looked unperturbed by my predicament and barely registered my presence. He had successfully chewed away one of Jesus' arms and was eyeing up the head.

Maybe there's some sort of addictive drug for mice in the ceramics of that thing

I knew there was no way in hell I was ever going to pick up the rodent so I settled for the statue. I started to drag it slowly across the cabinet, waiting for the mouse to follow. I sat it on the ground and he dutifully crawled down to be beside it once again. I kept going with my holy procession until I got to the front door and sat the statue on the step. Once the mouse was outside I shut the door and shoved a towel at the bottom of it in a futile attempt to keep it out.

"You should have moved it further away," said Ben, coughing on the crumbling drywall.

"Next time, you can do it."

I walked past him and into the kids' room to see if they were stirring after the commotion. They weren't.

I decided it was safer for us to all sleep together in case the mouse returned so I crawled in beside Arthur and hoped that I would manage some sleep before they woke up.

As I lay there, staring at the ceiling and noticing the fast approaching dawn, I vowed that I would never be spontaneous again. As soon as breakfast was over, I was packing up the car and going home to my dry house. I don't know how exactly, but I also decided that all of this was River's fault and I was resolved to go back to hating him for making me grab life.

Bloody hippy

Chapter 20

I worried that the kids would be furious at the prospect of returning home the next day, however, they were as miserable as we were. They did manage to extort a new toy out of us through guilt. You'd think I would be annoyed at this obvious blackmail but I was impressed with their acting skills.

I was delighted to get back into my living room which looked like a bomb had hit it. There was mess everywhere due to our rushed packing but I didn't care, it was warm, didn't smell of damp and there wasn't a holy statue or lace doilies anywhere to be found.

The four of us settled on the sofas and barely spoke for the first hour of our return. The kids were busy with their new action figures and I suspected Ben was suffering from PTSD after his run in with the mouse. I was simply exhausted.

I checked my phone and found that Elle was in full wedding mode, since she found out that I was back in the land of signal. She had numerous suggestions about her hen party, all of which I was planning to ignore. I had hoped at our age she would want to forgo the whole hen party debacle but I knew this was just wishful thinking on my part.

I put my foot down and refused to do a theme. The thought of us dressing up in leg warmers and tutus was just depressing but there was one sticking point that she was adamant on, she even played the 'I'm the bride, you have to do as I say' card. She wanted a stripper.

Thanks to my faux-pas at my mother's 70th birthday party I did have the contact details of a nice Columbian stripper named Pablo, however Elle decided that a male stripper would be 'tacky' and she preferred to have a female. Her justification was that it wouldn't be objectifying or degrading to have a female strip for money, it would be empowering and a celebration of the female form.

I wasn't remotely convinced but as maid-of-honour I did as I was told. I decided to do some research into the hen night entertainment and became so engrossed in looking through the gallery of potential strippers that I had completely forgotten that I was sitting next to Ben.

"Should I be concerned that you're on some kinky dating app? You could at least hide it better," he said.

"I'm looking for a S-T-R-I-P-P-E-R for the hen night," I replied, ensuring my children wouldn't catch on to their mother's perverted internet scrolling.

"What's a stripper?" asked Adam.

I really need to remember that Adam can spell now

"It's an exotic dancer," I replied, honestly.

"Stop talking, Amy," interrupted Ben, with his head in his hands.

"Like a French dancer?" continued Adam.

"Yes, like a French dancer."

I decided to take my sordid project out of the family room and into the kitchen so I could avoid any more awkward questioning.

It didn't take long for Ben to follow me out, looking sheepish.

"I thought I could help," he offered.

"You thought I would let you sit here and pick a stripper?"

"Well now that you've said it out loud it sounds a bit ridiculous."

"Fine, you can help."

He didn't bother to disguise his happy dance as he perched on the stool next to me.

"I could get my laptop and double our ground?" he asked, hopefully.

"Now, you're just trying to look up porn in front of me. There's a line, Ben."

I continued to scroll through the gallery and clicked on the Frequently Asked Question's section. The average price of a half hour performance was £825. It was at this point that I realised I had been in the wrong profession in my twenties.

"Is that price for real?" I asked.

"How would I know?" He replied, altogether too quickly for a man who claimed never to have been in a strip club.

I rolled my eyes and decided that although this company seemed legitimate, there was no way in hell I was dishing out anywhere near that amount of money for alleged female empowerment.

I went into a local buy-and-sell website where I usually found all my little bargains; I hadn't thought I would ever be looking to 'buy' a human though. I wasn't entirely sure what to look for so I stuck with 'exotic dancer' and crossed my fingers. There were four matches, none of which specifically contained my exact search words but I remained hopeful. Two were for a masseur that provided 'extra intimacy', a phrase that made me want to vomit in my own mouth and another was a naked cleaner for hire. I hadn't realised that there was a market for that particular vocation but I made a mental note to ask Elle about it tomorrow.

Finally, there was Angela. There was very little information on her ad but there was a picture of her looking scantily clad and a mobile number. I decided to bypass technology and just phone the woman. I reasoned that if she was an undercover police officer trying to nick local perverts looking for a prostitute then I could easily explain myself and not get a criminal record.

I left Ben and the laptop so I could talk privately with her. She picked up instantly and she sounded quite normal. I don't know what voice I was expecting, perhaps a sexy and sultry one.

"Hello?" she repeated.

"Oh, hi there," I said, sounding a little too chipper, "I saw your ad and I was hoping to rent your services."

"My services?"

"Yes, you see I'm having a hen party and the bride has specifically asked for a female -"

"Say no more, I understand. I've never had a female client before, it's quite an unusual request for a hen party to be honest."

The word 'client' rang alarm bells in my head and I felt it important to clarify exactly what I was expecting.

"I hope this doesn't offend you but you're not a prostitute are you?"

The line was deathly silent and I realised that I had said the completely wrong thing.

"No, I'm not a prostitute," she replied.

"I'm sorry, it's just there was very little information on your ad and I didn't want to get things muddled up."

"It's quite alright. To put your mind at ease would you like a preview?"

"A preview? Like a private show?"

"Something like that. I could come to a location of your choice and you could see for yourself before the big day. I want to make sure we're on the same page."

I was at a loss as to what critique I could offer on this woman's craft so I offered up Ben as the deciding vote.

"You want me to perform for your husband?" she asked.

"Is that a problem?"

"Not at all, it's just refreshing that a wife has such an open attitude towards my line of work."

I felt quite smug that the stripper thought I was liberal in my view of exotic dancing so I gave her my address and arranged for her to call over the next morning when the kids had gone to school. I couldn't wait to tell Ben that his super cool, enlightened wife had arranged a stripper for him as a morning treat.

I'm going to win serious wife points with this one

I returned, triumphantly, to the kitchen and told him the good news.

"There's a stripper coming here for me in the morning?" he repeated back to me.

I couldn't tell if he was excited or horrified. I felt it was a mixture of both.

"She offered a preview of her routine to make sure it's what Elle wants. I've no clue what I'm looking for and you seemed like the obvious choice."

"The obvious choice? Amy, I've never even been to a strip club but I don't think there's many wrong ways to take your clothes off to music."

"First of all: that's a lie. I know you were at one for your stag - don't bother denying that – and secondly there's definitely a wrong way. Remember Valentine's Day a few years ago I decided to do a strip tease to Celine Dion and I ended up sat on the floor, crying, just in a bra?"

"I think that had more to do with the wine you had beforehand."

"I just don't understand why Rose couldn't move over on the door?"

"I'm not having this conversation again, Amy."

"Fine. Just enjoy the nice stripper lady, please?" I pleaded, throwing in a hug for good measure.

"I guess I'll just have to take one for the team," he laughed.

Chapter 21

Ben was pacing the floor nervously, when I returned from the school run.

"What am I meant to wear?" he asked, panicked.

"I don't think your clothing is the important part to this, but maybe something other than your superhero pyjamas."

"I wasn't sure if I should wear my work clothes or play it casual. I don't want to give out the wrong vibes."

"Ben, we're paying a woman to take her clothes off, there are only wrong vibes."

He ran up the stairs and gave up trying to ask me for advice. Angela was due to arrive in the next ten minutes so I decided to kill the time by making some tea. I was excited about being able to ask her lots of questions about her job, the more I thought about it, the more I found the whole thing fascinating.

I bet she has hundreds of stories to tell. That would be a book I would read – confessions of a stripper.

The doorbell rang and I heard Ben give a little 'yelp' from upstairs. I rolled my eyes and went to greet our guest.

Angela was stood in the doorway with a long trench coat and a warm smile. Her dark brown hair was pulled back in a tight bun and she had a great handshake. I welcomed her inside and led her into the living room while we waited for Ben.

"I figured he would be the best judge," I said, "I'm fine admitting I'm in over my head with this."

"Well, I think it's great. Some partners would feel quite uncomfortable taking this step but it's really nice to see you so open about it."

There was something odd about the way she phrased her reply which made me panic.

"And you're definitely not a prostitute?"

Angela laughed and squeezed my hand, "No, I'm not a prostitute. Will you be watching too?"

"No, I think I'll keep it as a surprise for me too on the hen night. If Ben is happy then I'm happy. I'll just find out what's keeping him."

I went upstairs to hunt down the seemingly unwilling participant and found him sitting on the edge of our bed holding three t-shirts.

"I don't think I can do this, Amy."

He looked pale and nervous, like he was about to face a firing squad.

"Ben, you're being ridiculous. I've just had a really nice conversation with Angela, she's perfectly friendly, very pretty and definitely not a prostitute."

I felt it was important to stress this as much as possible, for both our benefits. As much as I liked to massage my ego at the thought of my liberal attitudes towards this whole scenario, I still felt uneasy about having a stripper in my living room at 10am on a weekday.

"Just pick a damn t-shirt and get downstairs. I don't want to keep her waiting, it's rude."

When I returned to the living room, Angela had her back to me and was taking things I didn't quite recognise out of her bag.

Props, probably; she's really going all out then.

I cleared my throat so she knew I was back in the room and asked if she needed anything.

"A glass of water would be nice," she smiled, "I meant to ask: is Ben comfortable with water-sports?"

What an odd question. Perhaps she's doing like a Baywatch themed dance

"Well he hasn't partaken in any since our holiday to Malta a few years ago but I think he's still a fan. He loves getting wet."

That answer seemed to keep her happy and she turned back to her bag.

Ben came up behind me and still looked as pale as he was upstairs so I gave him a hug and told him to have fun.

"I'll just get the water, Angela," I said, "Ben say 'hello' to Angela."

"Actually, it's easier to get into character now so you may call me 'Angel'."

"Awh that sounds really sweet, is this like a stage name?" I asked.

"I guess so, I'm a fan of irony so I thought this would be perfect," she explained.

Her answer confused me but I chalked it down to a 'bad girl' persona she probably puts on in order to get through the routine.

I dutifully went into the kitchen to fetch her some water and when I returned she had taken off her jacket to reveal a latex cat-suit. I was taken aback by the change of clothes but I decided it was too late to get prudish now.

"Here's the water," I said, awkwardly.

"Thanks. Now, as I know this is a little different to what we are used to so I think we should introduce a safe word so everyone feels comfortable."

This did little to calm Ben's nerves as he looked from Angela to me and back to the latex-clad woman in front of him.

"Is that really necessary? This is just a dance, right?" I asked.

"I suppose you could call this experience a dance, but a dance will only flow if both partners are in-sync."

Jesus, these performers really take their crafts seriously

"Whatever you say," I replied, holding my hands up in defeat, "Ben, why don't you just shout 'pineapple' if you feel uncomfortable by the pretty woman's dance?"

This so ridiculous. Is it normal that I've needed to implement the use of a safe word twice in recent weeks? Don't pull at that thread, Amy

I gave Ben a wink and closed the door behind me. I returned to my cold cup of tea in the kitchen and turned on the radio so I could drown out the sound of her chosen music. It was an odd feeling, sitting in my kitchen knowing that a stranger was gyrating for my husband in the next room.

Should I be jealous? Meh.

As I sat at the table I couldn't shake the feeling that there was something not quite right about the safe word. Why would he need a safe word and why on earth did she care if Ben liked to jet ski?

She didn't say jet ski though, did she?

223

I ran the conversation over in my head again and realised she said 'water sports'. I grabbed my phone and typed in the words 'water sports sex' and hoped that this growing feeling of dread was me just overreacting.

Oh, fucking fuck

I sat, dumbfounded as I read:

Water Sports: sexual activity in which urine is involved.

"PINEAPPLE! FUCKING PINE-FUCKING-APPLE!" screamed Ben.

Yeah, that sounds about right

I jumped off the seat and burst into the living room to stop the stranger from peeing on my husband. I found him sitting on the floor, blindfolded, topless and his arms tied behind his back.

Angela – or Angel – was zipping up her crotch area and looking completely confused as to what she had done wrong.

"Stop! Oh, God!" I cried, pulling the blindfold from his eyes.

Ben kept his eyes closed despite the cover being removed from his face.

"Amy?" he asked.

"Yes, Ben?"

"If I open my eyes am I going to find out that this woman has just peed on me?"

"Emmm…"

"Oh, fuck."

Angela cleared her throat to remind us that she was still in the room and in need of an explanation.

"I'm sorry about this Angela," I said, "This is a huge misunderstanding. I was basically looking for a stripper to do a bit of a sexy dance."

"Oh. Right. I'm definitely not a stripper."

"I feel like this should have come up before now," I mused.

"Yeah, there were some definite crossed wires," she smiled, "Ben, I hope there's no hard feelings. Why didn't you say something when I put on the nipple clamps and called you 'turd'?"

I looked down at Ben's chest to find the two small clamps attached to each of his nipples leaving them bright red and bulging.

"Do you want me to take them off?" I offered.

"You think?"

I pulled at them both and noted that they weren't dissimilar to clothes pegs. He let out a scream as I pulled and I realised I could have gone a bit gentler in my removal.

"I'm sorry…"

"For which part exactly?" he asked.

"All of it?"

"Can you untie me please, I'd like to have a shower."

The knot wasn't difficult but he still rubbed his wrists theatrically after he was released.

"My usual rate is £50 but saying as this wasn't exactly what you had in mind £20 will do for my time."

"That seems fair," I conceded, "Ben, pay the woman."

He looked at me, horrified.

"I don't have any cash on me," I explained.

"Let me get this straight: not only have I just been peed on, nipples ripped off and bound, I have to pay for the experience?"

"It's not my fault you didn't enjoy it, I thought It was exactly what you wanted and I've never had bad customer feedback before. I have a five-star rating on Facebook," said Angela, matter-of-factly.

"Well, that makes all the difference. I'll be sure to recommend you to my friends," he replied, his voice thick with sarcasm.

"If you just pay me my money I'll be on my way."

With a large sigh, Ben retrieved his wallet and handed her the money. He managed to shoot me a scathing look before retreating up the stairs for a shower.

I flirted with the idea of leaving the house before he came back so I could avoid the fight but I figured I should wait around in case he was emotionally damaged from the experience.

I waited, sheepishly, on our bed for him to come out of the shower. He took twice as long as normal and when he reappeared in the room the scowl hadn't left his face.

"In my defence - " I began.

"Let me stop you there, Amy. There's no defence. None."

"I really didn't know about the whole dominatrix thing, I thought she was a stripper. A nice, run-of-the-mill-takes-her-clothes-off-to-music stripper."

"Well she wasn't."

He continued getting dressed silently, while I followed him around the upstairs protesting my innocence. He finally gave into my badgering and explained he would eventually calm down once his nipples stopped throbbing.

We both left the house at the same time and went our separate ways for the day. I didn't chance my luck by asking for a kiss 'good-bye', but he did give me express instructions, that under no circumstances was I to tell Elle about anything that happened this morning.

I promised.

I was lying.

By the time I reached the office I had mentally prepared a speech about how hiring a stripper was a terrible idea but I needed have bothered. When I opened the door I found a blindfolded Elle hitting a penis-shaped piñata that was hanging from the light.

"Elle?"

She took off the blindfold and smiled, "Hiya, princess! I got this online and thought it would be fun for the party. Much better entertainment that the stripper and it's a workout."

"Shouldn't you be saving it for then?"

"Nah, I bought five."

"Five?"

"Yeah, I thought it would be fun to bash one in front of River so he knows what I'm capable of doing to his junk if he screws me over."

Sound logic

"Not like you to be this late?"

"I've had an eventful morning..."

"I'll grab us some drinks and you can tell me all about it. What would you like?"

"Anything but water."

227

Chapter 22

The day of the hen party had arrived and I was feeling sick. I couldn't quite work out if I was coming down with something or I was simply nauseated by the sheer amount of novelty penis-shaped items that were in my living room.

Ben had taken the kids out for the day and I was waiting for the hens to arrive at my house for an afternoon tea. This was misleading, there was no tea – there was a topless bartender serving sandwiches and fizzy wine though.

I thought it would be awkward to be in the house alone with a topless stranger but since my experience with Angela I felt that I would never be nervous about meeting new people again.

His name was Mark and he was in college studying business management while doing this job at the weekends. He said it paid good money and the women were always great tippers.

Within the hour my living room was filled with over-excited women who were out for the day and had no intention of behaving. Elle was beaming and I honestly had never seen her look happier. I couldn't decide if it was because of the topless server or because she was one step closer to being Mrs Wild.

We did the obligatory hen party games and everyone enjoyed bashing in the piñata - some more than others, I think that one woman used it as a therapy session while envisioning her ex-husband. Even my mother looked like she was enjoying herself, which was definitely down to the penis-shaped chocolate in front of her.

"This is a good spread, Amy," she said.

"Thanks mum, make sure to eat something other than just chocolate though; especially if you're drinking. Have some sandwiches, they can be soakage."

"Oh, stop being such a mummy. Let your hair down," she said, dismissing my concern with a wave of her hand.

"I'm the hostess; that means it's my job to make sure everyone but me is having a good time."

I was spending my time cleaning around the drunk people until I was tackled by Elle and told to put my binbag down.

"You're the maid-of-honour, stop cleaning and get a fucking drink in your hand. You're toasting me off into married life not being the hired help for the afternoon.

"Now, I would ask you to make a toast but neither of us have a good track record for that sort of shit so let's just crank up the tunes and pretend we're 15 years younger, in a night club and have a chance with the hot bartender in the corner."

I smiled and decided she was right. Not about trying it on with the bartender – he was a child – but having some fun on a hen party.

The rubbish can wait, another problem for future Amy

The rest of the afternoon passed in a blur of alcohol, cheesy dance music and laughs. My cheeks and belly hurt from the laughter and when the last of the hens left,

Elle and I collapsed on the sofa surveying the carnage around us.

"What time is it?" she asked, yawning.

"10pm."

"Are you fucking serious? Christ, we're old. Shouldn't we be partying until dawn?"

"Off you go, I'm done."

"Nah, I'm done too. I had fun though. Thanks, princess."

"You're welcome, Mrs Wild."

"That's the first time you've called me that without gagging."

"I guess I'm growing up, or I'm pissed."

"You're pissed."

In two weeks she was going to be walking down the aisle and into an uncertain future. I had managed to subdue my outward misgivings but the closer the day was getting, the more sick I felt.

She's not your daughter, stop being dramatic

I felt my stomach lurch once more and knew I needed a bathroom and fast. By the time Elle eventually came to check on me, I felt like I'd been hit by a bus.

"I hope this is an early onset hangover and not food poisoning," she said.

"Your concern is really touching."

"Sorry, babe, but I've got a dress fitting tomorrow and I don't want to look green."

"I didn't eat anything but those penis-gummies from the piñata. I'm just old and can't handle my drink."

"Good to know. I'm going to sleep."

She left me lying on the cold tiles of the bathroom and that's where I stayed until Ben came in with the kids the next morning.

230

"Good night?" he asked.

I managed a blink in response and held up my arms so he could lift me up from the floor.

"Is Elle still here?" I asked.

"No, I met her on her way out. She said she'd meet you at the dress shop after lunch."

The thought of spending the afternoon in a stuffy boutique, trying on a restrictive dress was enough to send me back to the toilet.

"Should I make you some tea?" he offered.

"No, just get a shotgun and put me out of my misery."

"If you can't handle the pace, Cole, you should stay out of the race."

Aren't smug, sober people the worst?

"Just pull me into the shower and turn on the water."

"With your clothes on?"

"Did I stutter?"

"It's your classiness that I love most, Amy."

He dragged me across the floor and into the shower. I felt the warm water hit my face as I lay in the foetal position.

"Can you try and sit up a bit, I'm worried you may drown if you keep lying down like that."

I shuffled into a sitting position and pressed my head back on the tiles.

Heavenly

I don't know how long I sat under the water but I finally decided to get out when the water started to run cold. I peeled off the soggy clothes and located a towel instead. I had less than an hour before I needed to meet Elle and I felt like death personified.

"Get your act together," I demanded as I looked at myself in the mirror.

231

It took all my strength to actually stop myself from climbing back into bed but I had the horrible feeling that if Elle was left unattended at the dress shop I would end up wearing some sort of rubber, gimp suit.

When I eventually pulled up to the arranged location, she was already waiting for me and talking animatedly to the shop assistant.

"I have a very specific vision," she said, "and I hope you're able to keep up."

The woman looked nervous, but did a cautious smile and I was certain she was already used to demanding brides.

"Are you really getting married in two weeks?" she asked.

"Yes, all very last minute but it'll all come together," she said, serenely.

"You realise that most dresses need around six months to be ordered in?"

"You're shitting me?"

"No, I'm quite serious. Sizes need to be ordered in. You might get lucky, if you try one on that fits you can buy it off the rack."

"Well, fuck me. Did you know this, Amy?"

"Sounds familiar, I guess."

"Right then, Diane, we'd better get to work. Screw the vision just get me something that makes my boobs look about ten years younger and like they weren't used as a chew toy for my twins."

This time, Diane did not hide her grimace as she went into the back in search of the perfect dress.

"You look like shit," said Elle.

"I feel it. Why don't you?"

"Maybe it's pre-wedding glow. We really didn't have that much to drink, did we? You were busy cleaning round everyone. You better not be getting sick, I'll kill you if you give it to me."

Again, her sympathy was always overwhelming

"What will I be wearing?"

"Dunno, what you fancy?"

"I take it your 'vision' didn't extend further than what you'd have on then?"

"Cut me some slack, you're fussy as fuck. Just go look at the bridesmaid dresses, pick whatever one you like and just make sure it's not white with a veil."

I was pleasantly relieved at this turn of events. I had visions of lavender gowns with puffy sleeves or even something made out of hemp so even if I did find something a bit rubbish it was still going to be better than my worst case scenarios.

I was instantly drawn to the darker colours, my hands rested on a full length navy gown. It was slinky and had the shoulders cut away with a flattering cowl neckline. It was perfect.

Please be in my size…

The wedding gods were smiling and it was. I got the nod of approval from Elle and practically ran into the fitting room in order to squeeze myself into it. As soon as the zip slid up I was in love. It fell in the right places and hid a multitude of sins surrounding my mum-pouch.

Cheaper than liposuction, I wonder if I could get away with wearing this every day?

Elle called me out and I crossed my fingers in the hope that she liked the dress but when I went out to face her I was surprised to already find her in a wedding

233

dress. It was nothing like I expected her to choose – but then again, when did she ever do the thing I expected?

It was tea length and satin with a high neck, plain and simple and dipped low in a V-shape at the back. She was spinning around like a giddy teenager and she looked stunning. I was surprised that seeing her this way made me feel emotional. I was happy that she was happy. It was a long time coming and she deserved every second of it.

"Why do you look like that? Don't you like it?" she asked, panicked.

"I love it," I replied, swallowing the lump of emotion jammed in my throat, "I really love it."

"Well, that was easy. See, Diane? Told you we'd get sorted."

Diane looked relieved and once Elle gave the 'OK' for my dress too she was gone in a flash to get them wrapped up.

"Six months? What bullshit, we barely took six minutes," she said, with a wink, "I'm telling you, this wedding is meant to be. I've never been more sure of anything in my life. Now, back to Joseph's for coffee and a gossip."

By the time we sat down on our sofa at the window, we had fully dissected the night before and relayed the highlights to Joseph, who didn't ask for them.

"A penis piñata?" he asked, horrified.

"It's all the rage, Joe," laughed Elle, "Actually while I've got you here I've a question for you."

"I will not allow a penis piñata in my shop."

"Spoilsport, but not what I was going to ask. I was wondering if you'd like to walk me down the aisle? I mean you can say 'no' and I don't want to annoy your

234

real daughter or anything I just thought it would be nice."

"I don't know what to say Elle."

"Look, I know I'm a gobby mare and I've been nothing but trouble since I walked through your doors, but I don't have a clue where my dad is and I've no inclination to find out. The truth is, you've been more of a stable father-figure to me for the last two years than he ever was. Without you, without this place, I don't know where I'd be right now but I love my life and I love you."

I felt that an intruder in their moment so I stayed as still as I could, not even allowing myself to steal a breath until Joseph gave his answer.

"I am truly honoured. You know I think of you both as family and I will be proud to walk you into your new life."

They hugged as I sat awkwardly watching on and I wished that I could leave without making it obvious. When they finally separated, they both had a glistening tear in their eyes and it made me feel even more out of place.

"Right, enough of this soppy shit," she said, clapping her hands together, I'm off to pick up my girls from Keith's."

"I don't think you need to, isn't that his car outside?" I asked.

Keith got out of the car and took the kids towards the café.

"What are you doing here? We arranged for me to pick them up at your house. This is exactly what I'm talking about, Keith, you can't just pick and choose which arrangements to listen to."

"Can you just shut up for one second," he said.

She was surprised at his reply and opened her mouth to continue her rant but decided to hear what he had to say.

"I'm here because I couldn't waste another second, I'm running out of time. Ever since the divorce finalised and you told me about this crazy idea to marry this complete stranger I've realised that this is not something I can allow."

"Allow? If you're using my wedding as some excuse to try and get more custody or something I will end you right here, right now."

"No, you daft bint, it's nothing like that. Can you just, for once, stop talking long enough for me to finish a sentence?"

"Mummy, he's trying to tell you he loves you," said Hannah, excitedly.

"He wants us to be a family again," added Louise.

Oh, fuck

"I have been the biggest fool in history for letting you go. I didn't fight for us, I lied, I cheated and I took our lives for granted. I thought I wanted a fresh start but that's so far from what I want. I've wasted so much time and I don't want to miss another second with you.

"Elle De Bryun, I want you back."

Chapter 23

I felt like I was witnessing a car crash and I couldn't look away. Keith and the girls all had the same expression of hope on their faces and I was terrified that Elle would be guilted into returning to her letch of an ex for the sake of her children.

Could I just start pointing out all his horrible traits right now, in front of the children? Is that going to cause years of psychological damage? Keep quiet, Cole.

Elle still hadn't said anything. She started to use both her hands to rub her temples and walked around to the far side of the counter in order to put some distance between herself and this whole situation.

"What do you say, Elle? Can we be a family again," he said.

"Girls, can you stand next to aunty Amy for a second?" Elle said, brightly.

They did as they were told and I stood in front of them in order to obscure their view of whatever Elle was planning to do next.

"You've been a fool then?" she asked.

"Yes, a huge one."

"Right, we can both agree on that. The thing is I don't think you're a fool at all."

He smiled, clearly happy with where the conversation was going.

"Oh, that's not a compliment. I don't think you're a fool, I think you're a manipulative, shrewd, diabolical, sociopath who uses his children as some type of emotional tool in order to make me feel sorry for him.

"How dare you. HOW FUCKING DARE YOU."

With each word, Elle started to throw whatever tray bake she could get her hands on. He raised his hands trying to shield his face from the continuous missiles, but it was no use. The more she raged the better her aim got.

I turned to the girls, who were hysterically laughing at the scene, and told them to run up to my office to find the chocolates I'd hidden in my desk. Joseph was trying to prevent anymore chocolate éclairs from being used as a weapon.

"You think you can just show up here, after two years of misery and try to derail my happiness? Use my children as a tool of guilt? You are the lowest of the low, Keith. You really fucking are."

"Well you're fucking insane," he shouted, "I can't believe I was stupid enough to think I still loved you. You've always been a maniac and I deserve to be made a damn saint for putting up with you for as long as I did!"

"Oh, no! You mean you don't really love me again? What a fucking shame. You're a devious, conniving , toxic waste of oxygen and both me and the girls are better off without you in our lives. Get out and stay out."

"You can't stop me from seeing my girls."

"I've no intention of it, just don't bother even saying 'hello' to me until you can at least pretend to act like a decent human being."

They both glared at each other, while the carnage of cream, broken sponge and mushed marzipan lay between them.

"Tell your new victim 'good luck'."

She flipped him her middle finger as he left and then she disappeared upstairs to find her children. Joseph and I looked at each other for a few seconds, wondering if we should try and go after her but instead we both felt safer clearing up the mess and apologising to the customer who had hidden behind their laptop when it all kicked off.

"You don't need to apologise," she said, "I've been sat here trying to write a scene for my screen play and this is just perfect."

After a half hour, Elle and the girls returned downstairs and they all seemed happy and relaxed.

"Are they ok?" I asked.

"They'll be fine," she said, with a shrug, "I tried to explain that their daddy was wrong to give them hope that we could be a family again because he knows we would all work better as we are now. They didn't seem too traumatised. I'd better go pay for all the buns I threw at the fucker."

She gave a sigh and went into the kitchen to locate Joseph while I decided to take the opportunity to head home. My sickness had gone, thanks to all the excitement but now I was ready to collapse onto the sofa for the evening, preferably with some form of junk food.

Ben was delighted to hear the excitement of the afternoon and was annoyed he had missed the showdown at the café. I assured him that if it was to ever happen again I would ring him instantly.

I took a look at my to-do list for the weeks ahead and realised that there wasn't very much left to organise. I couldn't believe that the wedding had come together so quickly and with relatively few snags. I chose to ignore the fact the bride was asked to call off the wedding a few hours ago and run off with her ex-husband.

I got lost in thoughts of my own wedding day and I was surprised at how little I remembered about the organisation of it. I remember it consumed my days for over a year and now I could barely remember what colour my bridesmaid dresses were. It seemed like a lifetime ago and when I looked back at pictures from the day, still on my phone, I didn't really recognise the people looking back at me. They were both full of hope and self-assured that they were going to have a lifetime of happiness ahead of them. The truth was, at that age, I didn't really think about what it meant to be married. I was caught up with the excitement of a wedding and not the reality of committing myself to one person for the rest of my life.

Thankfully it worked out. We grew with each other over the years and we figured out the rest as we went along. We muddled through the early days, buying a house, having children, the sleepless nights, the money worries, all the little mundane things that make up a life. I knew how lucky I was by having the right person by my side and I knew I could count on him for future challenges too.

I couldn't imagine having to start over again with someone new. Ben knew me, better than I knew myself at times, and I couldn't bear the thought of losing him or of us not being a team.

It was only then that I realised how brave Elle was being with all this. She was placing her trust in love after being so let down by it, and was forging a whole new life for her and the girls. Up until now I was convinced it was simply foolish but really she was daring and I envied that about her.

"Ben?" I asked, "Will you do me a favour?"

"If I can, yes."

"Don't die any time soon, I really don't want to have to date again."

"I'll try my best."

"I'll be really angry at you if you do."

"I know, Amy, I know."

He patted my hand and tried not to laugh at my ridiculous request. I felt comforted despite knowing the superficial promise meant nothing.

"I don't know what life is going to throw at us, Amy, but I can promise that I'm all in. I've been all in since our first date when you had a purple scalp from that terrible DIY dye job and you tried to hide it under that weird hat.

"I've been here for the good, the great and the not-so-great. I don't know who I am without you but I know you'll always keep things interesting.

"If I promise not to rollerblade while holding an electric drill and look after myself so I'm here on this earth for as long as I can be you have to promise never to change. I always want to wake up to the possibility of another random adventure or just a quiet day on the sofa – doesn't matter which, as long as it's with you."

What do you say to that? Think of something heartfelt too, don't do that immature deflection. You're a grown woman, open up and tell him how much he means to you. Do it!

"Well, if that speech doesn't get you lucky then nothing will," I said.

You're a fucking idiot

Chapter 24

It was the day before the wedding and Elle was uncharacteristically quiet. I put it down to last minute nerves and I had spent the morning trying to get her to eat. She managed a few bites of toast before pushing the plate away.

"What's wrong?" I said.

"I just have a bad feeling."

"About River?" I asked, trying not to sound hopeful that she was having second thoughts and would postpone the wedding for a year or ten.

"No, about the wedding itself. I'm not posh enough for a bloody ballroom in some fancy hotel. What was I thinking?"

"Stop being ridiculous! If you were posh we wouldn't remotely be friends, you would have disappeared into that click at Smug Club and left me high and dry. This is your dream venue, to your dream man and you're going to have the best day of your life."

My little pep talk must have worked because she suddenly found her appetite and started barking orders at me about getting the car packed properly. We were all driving down to the hotel today and spending the next 12 hours in blissful relaxation before the big day.

The dresses were packed while everything and everyone else had been micromanaged within an inch of their lives. Joseph had been complaining about a cold earlier in the week and Elle had sent no less than 12 different herbal remedies along with every flu medication she could get her hands on. She wasn't prepared to leave anything to chance or she would be further convinced of her wedding curse.

Ben was meeting me this evening with the kids while I went up this afternoon to keep Elle calm and make the most of the spa treatments available. By the time we were both in the car and heading up the motorway I could feel her finally start to relax and look forward to the events ahead.

Her phone hadn't stopped buzzing all day, all down to an overexcited groom counting down the time until he could see her coming down the aisle.

"You know you don't have to spend the whole day away from him? I'm pretty sure it's just the night time – and it's all a load of old bollox anyway."

"I'm not taking any chances," she said, solemnly, "I'm not giving the wedding gods any reasons to smite me."

I rolled my eyes and decided there was no point trying to reason with her while she was like this. I hoped that common sense would prevail once she had a glass of champagne in her hand and after a massage.

Traffic started to slow as got closer to the turnoff for the hotel. Elle's head perked up like a nervous meerkat sensing danger on the savanna and I tried to hide the fact that I was perturbed by the unusual hold up as well.

"It's probably an accident, there's only a hold up because nosey bastards are trying to catch a glimpse of the action," I lied.

At times I wished I was a better liar but I figured it was a good thing not to be. The kids hadn't copped on about Santa or the tooth fairy yet and that was the level of subterfuge I was comfortable with.

The minutes dragged and we were no closer to the turn off for the entrance. She was as fidgety as a rabbit in headlights and in turn this was making me more anxious. I began to catastrophize the possibilities that might lie ahead until I ended up in a zombie apocalypse scenario and I realised I'd gone too far down the list and brought myself back into the present.

Why do I always end up at 'zombie apocalypse'?

It took 35 minutes for us to get to the entrance of the long driveway up to the hotel and was met by a police officer.

"Ladies, you can't come up to the hotel," he said and began to wave us towards a diversion.

"What the fuck do you mean 'can't'? I'm getting married in that fucking place in 24 hours," said Elle, barely registering that she could be arrested if she caused more of a scene.

"Elle, calm down, we are going to find out what's going on now," I stressed with a forced smile on my face.

"I don't know what to tell you, other than you're not getting anywhere near this hotel until our investigation has finished.

"And when do you think that's likely to be, Mr Policeman, sir?" I asked.

You are an embarrassment of a grown up

"I can't say."

"What are you investigating?" asked Elle.

"I can't say."

"Is it a zombie thing? I feel like you should tell us if it's a zombie thing," I continued.

"I can't – actually, yes I can say it's not a zombie thing. Please follow the diversion I need to clear the traffic behind you."

I reluctantly put up my window and headed towards the diversion on the country road ahead.

"Don't panic, there's a little roadside café a few miles away. We will stop there and get on the phone to the hotel and find out what to do."

I tried to sound comforting but I knew my voice was far too high-pitched to be believably chilled out. Elle didn't respond, she chose to look out her window and ignore any words of encouragement I tried to offer throughout the short drive. We pulled up at *Rory's Roadhouse* and sat at the counter in order to make our battle plan.

The waitress was a friendly-looking woman, who seemed delighted at our presence. The place was nearly full so I couldn't understand why our presence would make a difference to her mood.

Perhaps she's just one of those mystical 'happy' people you hear about. I've never seen one up close before...

"Do you want to phone that guy, Chris, and find out what's going on?" I asked.

"What's the point? You heard the police, we're not getting anywhere near the place. The wedding is off."

She sounded so defeated and suddenly began to cry. I was instantly uncomfortable at the thought of having to be the responsible emotional crutch in this situation. It was up to me to shake her out of this and get our thinking caps on. The hotel was bound to be fine in a couple of hours and this would just be a funny story in the speeches tomorrow but I needed my warrior bestie not this resigned mush of a woman.

"You don't know that, this is probably just a drill of some sort and we will be sipping champagne and getting our nails done in an hour's time. *Hotel Redenzione* is the poshest place in the country, it can't be anything too sordid or in need of a lengthy investigation."

Elle stopped crying and seemed to be listening to my logical take on the situation. She rubbed her nose on her sleeve and gave me a watery smile.

"Do you really think so?" she asked.

"I know so."

Fuck, I'd better be right

"Now, let's get something to eat and get on the phone to the hotel."

"Hotel?" asked the waitress, "Are you girls here from the diversion?"

"Yes, we are just grabbing some food and waiting until it's clear to head back there," I explained.

"Oh, hunny, you won't be back there any time soon."

"Why do you say that?"

"One of my regulars over there is a delivery driver for that place. Every day, like clockwork, he's in there and he was turned away. Got talking to one of the officers and he said there was a suspicious death on the premises. Real blood bath; something about a drug deal gone bad, I heard. All very hush, hush. I reckon they'll be closing the place for a couple of days to clean it up and do all that CSI stuff you see on the tele. That's what I heard anyway."

Elle began to cry again, her wailing getting louder, while I tried to figure out the next move.

I declined the waitresses offer of coffee and bundled Elle back into the car. I figured it was better to get her as far away as possible from the scene of the crime just in case she flipped out and went on a murder spree of her own.

I didn't know where I was going but I knew I couldn't take her home. I worried if she was in her own house she would take to her bed and there would be no getting her out of her despair. It was a common coping scenario for me and I didn't want her to get anywhere near that level of dejection. I just kept my eyes on the road and let autopilot take over. She didn't look up to question why we weren't heading in the right direction, she just kept crying as she texted River to tell him the news. As soon as she sent the message he rang her but she was unable to get a full sentence out without gulping over a sob. Eventually she gave up so I shouted over the noise and told him I would call soon with information.

Before I knew it we were pulling into the one place I thought I would never take anyone. My lake. *The* lake. The scene of my lowest point: my suicide attempt. I hadn't been back there since I had gone into therapy. It wasn't that it haunted me, I had been here countless times after that day, but I felt it was place I didn't need to revisit anymore. I don't know why I brought her here, I had never even spoken about its location to her and now we were here.

She looked up from her hands and saw that we were surrounded by huge trees and a narrow, stone pathway. She silently got out of the car and started on the path up to the water. I felt like I was having an out of body experience, as if Elle was walking in my footsteps on that day. I panicked and jumped out of the car to stop her from doing anything stupid. I caught up with her easily, she was quietly sitting on a bench by the water staring at the peaceful sloshing of the water up against the stones.

"This is your lake, isn't it?" she asked.

"Yes," I replied, slightly embarrassed by the question.

"I can see why you chose this place. I can't imagine a more beautiful place to die."

"Elle, please don't talk like that, you're scaring me."

"Why?"

"I know there's a hiccup with the venue but we can reorganise the wedding for even next week. You don't have to end it all."

Elle laughed, quietly at first and then into her usual booming cackle. It echoed across the water and startled the swans going by.

"Jesus, Amy, I'm not going to fucking top myself because I have to postpone the wedding."

"You're not?"

"No, princess, this isn't the end of the world. Maybe it's the universe just telling me to slow the fuck down with River. I guess it's not meant to be, for now."

She sighed and went back to looking at the water. I thought I would feel relieved at her decision to postpone things but it didn't feel right. This woman was so certain about her future with River and even though this wasn't something I'd ever be brave enough to do I had finally come around and respected her decision to go for this crazy plan. I wasn't going to sit back and let her throw in the towel without *trying* to make it work.

"You're full of shit, De Bryun," I said.

"Excuse me?"

"You have spent weeks talking to everyone about the universe or kismet and all that other shite that I don't

248

understand and now what? Suddenly it's all become a bit too real and you have to go through with it you're ready to throw in the towel?"

"I'm not throwing in the towel, the fucking wedding venue is like something from *Breaking Bad*, I don't exactly have a choice."

"Do you want to marry him or do you want a party in a ballroom? What's the most important thing to you about tomorrow? Look, if you want to slow things down and wait to marry him then I support you, but if you're not going ahead with this because you think the thing is cursed then I'm here to tell you, you're being ridiculous and I can't be friends with a ridiculous person. There's only room for one of us to be unhinged and I believe I have the monopoly on that position."

"It's not about the venue but don't you think the universe is telling me this isn't the right move?"

"Elle, I mean this in the best way possible: the universe has more important shit to deal with than your fucking wedding. If you want to get married tomorrow, you're getting married tomorrow."

"I want to get married tomorrow. I really, really do."

"Then dry your damn eyes, we don't need you puffy for the photos and get your phone out. We need to find a venue."

I grabbed my phone from my bag and started to look up locations nearby which would be suitable. We just had to hope that they were enthusiastic about holding a wedding and reception in the next 24 hours. I didn't feel hopeful but after my pep talk I had to keep up the pretence that this was something we could pull off.

"What about here?" she said.

"What about it?"

"Look at those trees over there, it's like a little secret alcove just beside the water. It's beautiful. Why don't we have it here?"

"Well, I don't know. I mean I don't know who we would even have to ask if we could? I mean is it the local council or do we need a permit? Seems a bit complicated."

"OR we could just come here tomorrow, have the wedding and hope that no one chases us away?"

"Are you willing to take that risk?" I asked.

"As long as no one gets murdered overnight, I think we'll be fine."

I didn't know how I felt about being here for a wedding. This was a complicated place for me, at times. I kept this lake a secret from everyone and now I would be inviting them all to the scene of my darkest time. What if it made something in me snap and I had a type of relapse. I shut down that train of thought immediately. I knew that it was time to put everything I had learned in therapy and about that time in my life into use.

"I think it's a fantastic idea," I said, "It's time I rewrote the memories of this place and what better way than turning it from something horrible and dark into the scene of happiest day of your life?"

"Are you sure?" she asked, nervously.

"Yes, it's time to stop keeping here a secret. I guess I've kept it that way so if I ever fell that low again I knew I could come back here and finish what I started that day. I'm going to burn that bridge and commit to being well, here and now. This lake won't hold that power over me anymore, it's just a lake. Now it can be a symbol for something beautiful and positive – it can be my wedding gift to you."

She smiled and pulled me into a huge hug. I instantly felt a weight, that I didn't know I'd been carrying, leave my body and I knew this was the right thing to do.

"To be clear, does this mean you're not actually getting me a present?" she asked.

"If you're lucky, I'll buy you a couple of classes with the Bible bashers at fat club. They seem fun."

"Deal." She laughed, "Right, princess, let's get to work. We've got shit to do."

Chapter 25

It came to no surprise that River was on board with this crackpot plan and he vowed to do whatever he could to help. Ben had slightly more trepidations but, as usual, went along with the chaos to see where we'd end up. After getting nowhere with local hotels, pubs and a couple of questionable football clubs we decided that Joseph was going to have to get stuck with us once again.

He wasn't convinced that we could pull together the reception necessities in such a short space of time but Elle simply said that all she needed were 'fairy lights and booze' which seemed to make him feel more confident of our success.

River secured a marquee which could be erected at the back end of the café, a space usually reserved as a loading bay for surrounding shops but thankfully due to our sob story – and Elle's usual abrasive methods of persuasion – they all agreed to let us use the space for the day.

"We'll just do a buffet and buy enough drink so people can be drunk enough not to mind," said Elle.

"My family don't drink," answered River, "but if we have enough vegan chocolate profiteroles to feed a hippo then they'll be happy enough."

"Excellent, just keep finding solutions like that and we'll fine," she said.

I stood awkwardly as they began to kiss passionately. "Ahem, guys? Can you quit?"

"Sorry, yes, ok what's next?" she asked.

"Photographer is on board with the change of venue and the prospect of having to leg it if we're caught, as is the string quartet – although they said they can't exactly make a quick escape if needs be," I explained, "Joseph and Michael are away to get the buffet ingredients and Ben is with them to get the drink.

"We need to start decorating the place."

"We can't, there's going to be customers in here between now and then. We'll have to do a last minute job in the morning or something."

Her forehead began to furrow at the thought of adding another huge task to the list on the morning of her wedding. She should be relaxing in her suite not up a ladder dangling lights from the ceiling.

"Negative," I interrupted, "Joseph has agreed to close up for the rest of the day until the day after the wedding. The space is ours."

"What? I can't imagine him agreeing to losing money. This is Joseph we're talking about."

"I had a chat with him and found out the average earnings he would be losing out on if he closed," explained River, "I agreed to pay him that, and a bit extra for the trouble."

"What? That's crazy! Brilliant, but you didn't have to do that," said Elle.

"I know, but trust me, it's a lot cheaper than a ballroom in a drug den," he replied with a smile.

"What are we waiting for then? Let's get to work," she shouted.

She's really enjoying this drill sergeant routine

At that moment the door jingled and we turned to find Imelda from next door holding mounds of white fabric.

"Is everything ok, Imelda?" I asked, concerned that she was going to renege on our deal and say we couldn't put the marquee up after all.

I will wrestle you, woman, don't get in my way

"I felt so badly that you were going to have to hold your wedding in this odd little café so I thought I could help," she said.

Ok, I won't wrestle you

"I had an idea that we could use all this fabric to drape over the walls and the ceiling. We could make it like one of those fancy-looking tents that the celebrities use. I rang my friend Laura, she's the creative type she said she's only too happy to help – you both helped her flower shop a few months ago.

"She's going to bring some flowers to help make it the part too. I hope you don't mind me butting in like this," she added.

I think I might kiss her

In the end I didn't need to kiss her, Elle did instead.

"You're a fucking legend, Imelda. A FUCKING LEGEND!"

It didn't take long for Laura to arrive and for her to explain her idea. She brought roses, carnations, lilies – all of them white –and set us to work draping the white fabric from the walls to the ceiling. It swopped down from every angle and transformed the once quirky colours to a clean canvas. The white made the space look bigger and the smell from the flowers were divine.

"I can't leave these here now, they'll be wilted by the time wedding. Now I know what I'm working with you can just leave the key and I'll fix it up in the morning," said Laura, "You're in good hands."

"Thank you so much, I can't believe how different the place looks with some fabric and clever draping," I said, "I would kill to have that vision."

"Not at all, after everything you both did for my shop? There's no doubt in my mind I would be out of business if it weren't for you two and I know you charged me a fraction of what you should have. I've been hoping to find a way to repay you and now I can."

She breathed in and looked very pleased with her handy work. Elle appeared carrying bundles of fairy lights, I knew there was no hope of convincing her they weren't needed.

"Fuck me, this place looks straight up classy," she beamed, "just need to find places for this lot and I'm happy. Nothing says 'posh' like fairy lights, eh?"

Laura and I both smiled and didn't bother to correct her; she was the bride after all.

We carried on working late into the evening. People continued to come and go to help clean or move furniture and cardboard up into our office so there was more room for people to mingle. Mingle was a nice way of saying 'you're standing while you eat your cocktail sausages because we don't have enough tables and chairs'. We didn't stop until Ben appeared with sandwiches and beers for the workers. They were received gratefully and it was the first time there was quiet in the café all day.

We surveyed our work and it was all coming together nicely. River and Elle sat side-by-side feeding each other and I was so glad that they had found each other. I felt warmer as I sat beside them, as if their love gave out an actual glow (I suspect it was the heat from the pizza box, but still).

The marquee was a great addition to the yard and Ben had rolled out some artificial grass from the back door of the building to the entrance of the tent like a type of red carpet. Gnomes wrapped in fairy lights were placed either side of the grass, leading and lighting the way for guests.

There was enough room for a small make-shift dance floor (hastily bought black and white squared lino), space for the DJ and a table at the side to house the alcohol. I managed to book the waiter from the hen party to come be the bartender and he offered to bring two friends, who were strapped for cash, along to help him.

As it approached midnight we began to finish up our transformation project.

"River, you've got to get out of here," shouted Elle.

"Why? Are we going home?"

"I'm not tempting fate any more, after today," she said, "I don't want to see you after midnight until I'm walking down the aisle. I don't want to incur any more wrath from the wedding gods."

He didn't argue with her, simply kissed her on the nose and took his leave. Soon it was just Elle and I sitting in the middle of the floor of Joseph's café taking in our surroundings.

"Can you believe we pulled this off?" I said.

"No, not in the slightest; let's face it we're fucking morons at the best of times we just happen to know a lot of really bloody good people. Can we go home now? I'm fucking knackered."

I pulled her up off the ground and on to her feet, we did one last sweep to make sure everything was switched off. The last thing we wanted was to accidentally start a fire, not even I would be able to convince Elle this wedding wasn't cursed if that happened.

The hair and makeup team were due to arrive to my house at the crack of dawn but I was too queasy to sleep. It had been a monster of a day and I was sure I would collapse as soon as my head hit the pillow but instead I couldn't find a position to lie in that didn't want to make me puke. After a half an hour of tossing and turning in bed, Ben finally kicked me out.

"Can you please go sleep on the sofa? I would do it myself but it kills my back," he groaned, barely opening his eyes as he spoke.

"I might head out to the 24 hour supermarket, I feel a bit sick. I'd better see if I can get something to settle my stomach before tomorrow; I doubt Elle would be too forgiving if I throw up on her dress."

He mumbled a reply and I slipped on some comfy clothes to take the short drive down to the supermarket.

I could hear Elle snoring in the spare room and I was glad she was able to get some rest before the chaos of tomorrow. I didn't meet anyone on the road and I was only person walking through the aisles. It was strange, like I was in a dream. I picked up a few items and ran over the events of the last few weeks in my head, trying to recall dates and feeling a little panic rise in my chest.

I couldn't be…

I hurried through the self-serve check out and was relieved that, for once, I made it through the whole purchase without setting off the 'wait for someone to help' alarm. I kept my mind busy as I drove home and rushed upstairs to the bathroom with my purchase.

I sat on the floor and looked at the pregnancy test. I watched the little windows, silently, for the result until I heard a soft knock at the door.

"Amy? Is that you?" whispered Ben.

Fuck

"Yes, I'll be out in a minute. Dodgy stomach," I said.

"Ok…"

I looked at the window and saw the result. I hadn't realised I wasn't breathing until my head started to swim. I let out a long breath and threw the test away. I crawled back into bed with Ben and gave him an extra tight hug before rolling over. The panic disappeared and I was finally able to close my eyes to dream about the trouble tomorrow could bring.

Chapter 26

The hairdresser was the first to arrive. I loved getting my hair done, I felt like a doll and I could never fix it remotely close to how these hair magicians could, as far as I was concerned it was all witchcraft.

I asked for mine to be kept up and out of the way, I knew I would be running around all day so it was the most practical solution. Elle was getting vintage Hollywood curls to match her rockabilly style dress. It was perfect.

I managed to convince her to have some toast but I couldn't get her to sit down. Once her hair was done she had some time to kill before the make-up would need to go on, so she was making the most of the freedom from the chair by pacing around my living room. Every so often Ben and the kids would walk into the room asking questions about missing ties, socks that were too small and what shoes matched their suits.

"Ben, you're a smart man you can figure this out," I said, "Christ, not those shoes!"

"What's wrong with them?" he asked.

"There's a hole at the front of them, they flap when you walk, I thought I threw them out months ago!"

"You did," he said, sheepishly, "I liberated them from the bin."

I admitted defeat and realised that I had, in fact, married a moron.

By the time I got them organised and chased out the door so we could finish getting ready in peace, I was behind schedule and the lady waiting to do my make-up was getting fed up.

I dutifully sat down and let the transformation process begin. Unlike every other time I handed over money to get my make-up done I bothered to do research on this particular team. I wasn't going to risk looking like a tangerine, today of all days. Elle was already well under way with hers although she wouldn't sit still long enough for the woman to finish her eyeliner.

"Elle, will you stop moving and let the woman do her job?" I said, trying not to sound too bossy.

"Sorry, babes, you work away. I just want to get there already."

She took out her phone and looked worried.

"Five missed calls from Keith," she said with a furrowed brow.

"Are you going to call him back?"

"Fuck no, the girls are here so what on earth would I need to talk to him about on my fucking wedding day? He's probably just going to try and confess his undying love so I won't go through with the wedding."

Her tone was so matter-of-fact the woman doing her mascara stopped dead.

"Are you serious? That's so romantic, are you going to leave River at the altar and get back with him?" she asked, clearly hoping she was part of a romantic comedy.

"Fuck no, babes, my ex is the devil. He would say that type of shit to mess with my head then he would run a mile if he thought I would even consider giving our relationship another go. It's all about the control with him. He doesn't want me, but doesn't want anyone else to have me either."

"Oh," she said, deflated at the truth of the situation.

"Here," I called, "Give me the phone, that way you can't see it and get annoyed. If there's anyone important phoning I'll give it back."

She happily handed it over and went back to smiling and sipping her mimosa.

"What is it about weddings and shit that makes it perfectly acceptable for us to start boozing at 8am?" asked Elle, "If I did this before the school run people would be phoning Social Services."

"Let's not get into the way society views alcohol and double standards in general; can we just enjoy the morning and talk about shallow things like make-up and boys?" I pleaded.

"Alright, princess."

Soon it was time for us to get dressed. I matched my gown with simple diamond tear drop earrings and a sparkly bracelet and then helped the bride into her dress. She was stunning, like someone who had just walked out of a 50's inspired photo shoot. Her bold red lipstick matched the towering red heels she decided on matching with her dress. I would never have the nerve to pull something like that off, but this just screamed 'Elle'. She took my breath away. I tried not to cry mostly because I didn't want to ruin my make-up, but I was overwhelmed at how emotional seeing her in the dress was making me.

Joseph arrived, followed by the car to take us all to the lake. Elle had managed to secure a vintage Volkswagen campervan at the last minute, so we could all fit in and I didn't have to try and squeeze the whole bridal party into my tiny car. I offered to sit up front with the driver in order to give directions. Apparently my hand-drawn map was no help whatsoever so it was up to me to get us there. Joseph hooked arms with his pseudo daughter for the journey and he looked genuinely proud to be part of the day. Hannah and Louise sat across from them, chatting happily and admiring their flouncy white dresses.

"I look like a princess," announced Louise.

"You look like a butt," said Hannah.

They both fell about their seats laughing while Elle looked on, proudly. She was unnaturally quiet. I kept my eye on her in in the driver's rear view mirror and every so often she would let out a large, contented sigh. I wondered if she was nervous or if she was just eager to get the whole day started. I thought back on my own wedding day and remembered the awkward drive to the church with my father. I couldn't wait to get out of the car and down the aisle – mostly because it meant I could have champagne and calm my nerves before having to endure a whole day of small talk with our extended families.

Dad wasn't one for talking about his feelings but I could tell that he wanted to try. Emotion caught in his throat so he abandoned what he was straining to say and went back to remarking about the flow of the traffic. I didn't mind, the memory made me smile and was quintessentially him. He was with me, that's all that mattered.

I could feel Elle's phone vibrating in my bag and checked to see who it was.

Keith, again; maybe I should answer it and tell him to 'piss off'

I decided against that plan of action and with the turn off for the lake only a mile away I thought it was better just to turn the phone off.

"There's not much of a path here," remarked the driver.

"Just get us as close as you can, we can walk the rest," called Elle from the backseat.

The clouds were getting greyer but I hoped they would just stay dry for one more hour so we could get through the ceremony without being blown into the lake. When I got out of the car the wind carried the sound of the string quartet and I could hear the murmurs of the guests chatting excitedly. The photographer had started snapping as soon as we pulled up and I knew I would be spending the day avoiding this woman. I hated getting my picture taken, even when I knew I looked well, there's just something awkward about my face that never looks right no matter what way I try to pose.

I walked up ahead of Elle and Joseph to signal to the musicians and the registrar that the bride was coming. I caught a glimpse of Ben and the boys, who all started to wave manically at me. I couldn't help but laugh and waved just as stupidly in return.

As soon as the music started up again I sent the twins, hand-in-hand, up the make shift aisle to the canopy of the trees. I turned to Elle and gave her a wink: "Knock 'em dead."

She giggled and told me to 'fuck off' before I disappeared around the corner and up towards her waiting groom. River looked handsome and more nervous than I'd ever seen him. Up until now he'd always seemed so calm and relaxed, completely at one with his surroundings but now he was like every other man waiting at the top of the aisle for his bride. It was sweet.

I stood across from him and offered a small smile, but as soon as the music changed to her entrance melody his focus was going nowhere but to the top of the aisle so he could finally see Elle. As soon as he laid eyes on her he took a breath, saying 'wow' as he exhaled. Both Joseph and Elle had tears in their eyes as they walked in unison to the music. By the time they reached the top it was taking all my effort not to sob uncontrollably at the two of them. Joseph gave her a kiss on the cheek and shook hands with River before taking his seat beside his daughter and Michael.

The couple were so engrossed in the moment and looking at each other that I thought it wouldn't have mattered if there was a tornado on the horizon, they weren't moving from that spot until they were man and wife. Everyone could feel the magic they were witnessing and we were all barely breathing in order not to break the spell and the intimacy we were part of.

It was then that something in my peripheral vision caught my attention. There was someone moving at the back, whilst everyone else was seated in the white deck chairs placed at either side of the aisle.

I turned around properly and saw Keith lurking close by, but once he realised I'd spotted him he hid behind a tree.

This can't be happening

I tried to get Ben's attention but it was Adam who noticed me making strange faces first. He started to make them back at me and then began giggling. When Ben finally turned to tell him off, Adam pointed to me instead. I tried my best to psychically convey what the situation was. I hear all the time about how these couples who have been together for so long can simply just look at each other and have whole conversations. We were clearly not one of these couples.

Bloody Ben

I started to mouth 'Keith' at him but he still hadn't a clue what I was trying to say to him. He started to point at his mouth and looked more confused by the second.

Not teeth, you idiot, KEITH!

The registrar had got to the point where she was asking if anyone had any objections to the marriage.

Why is this still part of the fucking ceremony? You've just given him a damn invitation to interrupt.

I knew what I had to do. I handed my flowers to Hannah and my shoes to Louise, who both looked delighted at the free stuff. I took my dress in my hand and started to sprint as fast as I could across the grass and towards the bushes. At the same time, Keith had decided to come out of his hiding place and make his dramatic declaration of love.

Not on my watch, asshole

Before he managed to get a word out, my shoulder made contact with his stomach, winding him completely and left him staggering backwards, unsteady on his feet. I had prevented a disaster and was about to walk back up the aisle when I felt my dress being pulled backwards. In his efforts to keep standing, Keith reached out and grabbed the back of my gown hurtling us both backwards and towards the lake. I let out an almighty scream and heard a huge splash as Keith, then I, hit the water. The water smelt as bad as I remembered and it was much harder to clamber out of it with a heavy, soaking dress on. I could hear Keith shouting all sorts of insults at me but I was keeping my attention at getting through the sharp reeds and onto dry land. I looked up to see Ben's hand reaching down to help me out.

"Hi, sweety, do you think anyone noticed?" I said, laughing. I was quiet at first then I just kept getting louder and louder. The more Keith struggled to find his footing and get out of the water the louder I laughed. I turned to find Elle and River staring at me and the floundering man in front of them.

"Elle, I'm so sorry," I said, as seriously as I could between giggles, "I was trying to get rid of him without anyone noticing."

"Well, babes, you failed," she said, "But that was fucking epic. Have you thought about joining a rugby team? Keith, get the fuck out of here or I'll set my bestie on you again."

"No fucking problem," he shouted, as he eventually managed to get to the bank, "I don't know what I was thinking trying to get back into this lunacy. You two are both fucking crazy."

He stomped off towards the car park while Ben tried to get everyone calmed down and back to their seats.

"If you've finished assaulting people, can we finish getting married?" asked Elle.

"Yeah, but I'm just going to stay at the back because I smell completely revolting."

"No arguments here, princess."

I watched as they returned to the registrar to finish what they'd started. It was a mercifully short ceremony and I was counting the minutes until I could get home and into some dry clothes. Ben put his jacket around my shoulders but refused to stand too close to me for fear of getting sick.

As soon as it was official I begged Ben to take me home so I could shower and change. Despite smelling like a sewer it did get me out of having to stay around get photos taken in the forest. I agreed to meet them all at the reception after I got into dry clothes and prevented hyperthermia.

Ben drove with all the windows down and the kids held their noses as they sat in the back of the car. I shivered constantly but I knew there was no point in trying to convince them I wasn't 'that' bad and they could put up their windows. I dashed into the shower and it was a sweet release to feel the hot water burn my skin. I took much longer than normal in order to get feeling back in my toes.

Ben was waiting on me with a towel with his arms outstretched. He wrapped me up in a hug and kissed my forehead.

"You're a wonderment," he said, approvingly, "Not many people would rugby tackle someone to stop them from ruining a wedding. Even less would jump into a lake to really drive the point home."

"That's not exactly what happened."

"Oh, it will be when I tell people the story."

I laughed and sat on the bed trying to figure out if I could get away with wearing yoga bottoms and a hoody to the reception.

Probably not

Despite scrubbing myself thoroughly the smell of the water was still stuck in my nostrils and it was doing little to help my sickly stomach. I managed to find a coral coloured day dress and asked Ben to fix me some toast while I tried to do something with my make-up and hair.

*What a complete waste of time and money. I had
pretty hair and glowing skin for all of two hours and now
I'm back trying to deal with this car crash of a head
again.*

Ben returned with the toast, swimming in butter. I
would usually give out about him trying to give me a
cholesterol problems at the sight of this but I was
starving and this smelled spectacular.

"I was thinking," he began, "We're very lucky."

"Are you only noticing this now?" I asked.

"I just mean, I'm delighted that Elle is started her new
life with River, and all that, it's just I'm so relieved
we're past that bit. We've been together for long enough,
there's no big surprises in our characters, we've had the
kids and they're at a handy age for a while before the
horrible teenage stuff happens, the house is nice, we're
both happy in work. We're just very lucky."

"Yes, we are."

"Do you think Elle will want more kids now?"

"I really don't know, she hasn't mentioned it."

"God, I don't envy her if she does go down that route.
Jesus, imagine she has another set of twins. Anyway, are
you nearly ready? I don't want to miss the grub."

"Nearly," I replied, "Can I ask you something?"

"Shoot."

"So, are we done with babies then? Like we're
closing the door on the chance of another one?"

"Yes! I mean, I thought we both felt that way? Do
you want to talk about trying?"

"No, it's ok. There's no need."

"We can talk about it if you like?"

"No, you misunderstand me, there's no need to talk
about trying."

"Why's that?"
"I'm already pregnant."

Chapter 27

To say the look on Ben's face was one of 'shock' was like saying a hurricane was a bit windy. He didn't speak a word for a full five minutes, so I simply went back to eating my toast. His mouth lay open like a fish and every so often he would shake his head in disbelief. When he finally checked back into reality he walked into the bathroom and stuck his head under the tap to wet his mouth.

"Are you sure?" he asked.

"Yes, I took a test last night and another one this morning."

"But…but…but you're on birth control."

"I guess I'm one of the lucky 1% who it didn't work for this month," I said, taking another bite of the toast."

"How are you being so calm?"

"What's the alternative? Sitting dumfounded for a half hour. I'm still going to be pregnant after I snap out of it."

He went back to sitting silently on the bed while I finished getting ready.

"But, Amy, we're old," he said.

I laughed at the absurdity of his claim that 35 was 'old' and kissed him on the cheek.

"It's going to be ok, Ben, now let's go celebrate our friend's wedding."

The four of us walked to the café and could see a number of people standing outside.

I instantly panicked that there simply wasn't enough room for everyone, even with the marquee. As we came closer I noticed that they were all very casually dressed and then I caught a glimpse of a placard.

Oh for the love of God

Melanie had managed to rustle up some more deluded groupies into staging some ridiculous protest at the café.

"Do you want me to phone the police and get this sorted before Elle sees?" asked Ben.

"No, leave it with me," I said, confidently.

I pushed through the crowd that was slowly gathering. I was relieved that they hadn't become more organised and were trying to agree on what to chant in order to make an impact.

"OI!" I shouted as loudly as I could.

The crowd parted and all stopped what they were saying to look directly at me.

"Now, I am having one hell of a day – one hell of a week actually and the last bloody thing I need is to deal with a pack of fucking lunatics who think that the only way they can get into heaven is by boycotting a cream bun.

"Get your shitty signs and nonsensical philosophy the hell away from my friend's wedding or I will make it my personal mission to visit each and every one of you at your place of work or residence and hold my very own protest. I have time and no hobbies so this could really be the thing I'm missing from my life."

Melanie finally made her presence known by coughing and politely asking one of the protesters to

271

move out of her way. She had a fake smile on her face and she didn't stop walking until she was mere inches from my face.

"Now listen here - " she began.

"NO!" I raged, cutting her off before she picked up steam, "I will make your life bloody miserable if you don't all piss off or I will phone the police again and press charges for harassment."

The crowd started to murmur and I could sense that they were feeling uneasy with where this was going.

"Whatever she's told you about this place is untrue," I continued, "It's a wonderful café, run by a wonderful man who serves wonderful food. I met my best friend here and today is her wedding day. This café is so wonderful that she chose to have her reception here."

Chose is a stretch but they don't need to know that

"I have been a bit chubby my whole life and I know I make terrible decisions when it comes to food but I know, hand on heart, that this bizarre group that this woman has put together is not the answer.

"She is a twisted Bible-basher with her own agenda, and she's using you. She's been here before with others just like you and we phoned the police then too. She's taken on this crusade against me and this business for reasons beyond me but I'm pretty sure her issues go a lot deeper than the calories she consumes.

"I am asking all of you, nicely, to catch a grip of yourselves and ask yourself what you're doing here. Is protesting outside an innocent man's business going to make you thinner? Is being thinner going to make you happier? I'm going to guess a firm 'no' for both of those answers.

"I'm giving you all the chance to walk away from this toxic, troubled individual and maybe just look at your portion sizes if you want to lose a couple of pounds and not equate that to your future success. Being thin and being happy are not mutually exclusive. Now, if you really want to stay and ruin the happiest day of my friend's life because you think it will somehow make you skinny, then go right ahead BUT if you can see sense and realise that this woman is pushing her own insecurities on you and not in any way helping, then leave now with your dignity."

It was my best attempt at a rousing speech and I wasn't sure it was going to work but it was worth a shot. Ben started to clap his hands and begin a round of applause but it didn't take so he simply stopped and looked awkwardly at his feet.

Melanie didn't say anything but looked a bit uncomfortable as she waited to see what the crowd would do. It was a silent standoff but finally someone broke. The people began setting down their signs and walking away from the café.

I started to feel relief and waited for them all to see sense. At the end Melanie and two others remained.

"I'm surrounded by the faithful, they will be rewarded for their commitment," she said.

"Do what you want, I'm phoning the police and you can spout that drivel at them if you like. Come on Ben, let's leave the crazies in the cold."

I didn't bother phoning the police again, I felt guilty for wasting their time on these ridiculous people and it didn't take long for them to realise their protest wasn't going to be putting anyone off, today at least, and took their leave.

I surveyed the café and it looked even more beautiful than it did last night. Laura had come this morning and there were fresh flowers everywhere. Everywhere looked so clean and pure like the fresh start Elle was so desperate to have with River. It was perfect. It may not be the ballroom she planned on but it was much more intimate and meant more to the two of us than anywhere else in the world. This was where this crazy ride all began and I couldn't think of a more fitting place to have her celebrate the beginning of her next adventure.

The guests began to arrive in small groups and were happy to help themselves to the tray bakes, tea or something stronger in the marquee. I stuck to peppermint tea in the hope that it would prevent me from getting sick in public, while Ben quickly took the opportunity to get a stiff drink and let the news of my pregnancy sink in. I didn't bother to chase after him, I was busy trying to get my own head around it.

Is this actually happening? What if I have another miscarriage? What if I go crazy again?

My destructive train of thought was interrupted by the appearance of my parents. It was always unsettling to me how much Elle had taken to my parents – especially my mother – but she loved them both and never missed an opportunity to invite them places.

"Hello, darling, I see you've changed," said my mother with a wry smile.

"Yes, mother, I was a bit damp."

"I thought you were fantastic," beamed dad, "I'm really glad we got you those swimming lessons. Where's the beer?"

"Out the back, Ben's already out there."

Dad disappeared instantly, with Adam and Arthur in hot pursuit in order to see what all the fuss was about in the tent.

"Your face looks puffy," remarked mum, "You should cut down on the carbs."

I couldn't be more than 8 weeks pregnant and I was already bloating out. I'm going to be a fucking hippo by the end of this

"Will do, mum," was all I could manage, "how about you find dad and see if there's anything you'd like to drink."

"Are you getting rid of me, Amy?"

"Not at all, I'm just playing hostess and I don't want you to be here on your own."

"Fine, fine, I can take a hint. Never let it be said that Eloise Galbraith outstays her welcome."

I live in hope of the day when I can say 'Eloise Galbraith always says 'no' to an invitation'

Eventually the happy couple and the twins arrived to the celebration. They had taken two hours to get all the photos and Elle's teeth hadn't stopped chattering since she walked into the place.

"I think my tits are blue," she hissed in my ear, "I can't feel my toes."

I led her into the bathroom and got her to sit down on a stool as she kicked off her shoes and I turned the hand dryer on in an attempt to get some feeling back into her feet. Her make up still looked flawless, except for a little rosy nose due to prolonged time outside. Once she'd achieved enough feeling back in her extremities and powdered her nose we returned to the guests and began the arduous task of small talk with all of them.

I was still rubbish at small talk and often had to make a swift exit when things turned awkward – usually after I asked an inappropriate and hugely invasive personal question when I got bored of remarking about the weather. I made my excuses and left River's uncle slightly bemused after I asked him what his view on euthanasia was. This was usually the point in which I would drown my discomfort with alcohol but no such luck on this occasion.

Damn you, baby!

The buffet was a hit and people became quite inventive in their search for tables and chairs. Plates and legs were balanced on counters, shelves and steps. People were dotted in every corner, inside and out, but, most importantly, they were all smiling and completely unfazed by the haphazard set-up of the place.

Everyone crushed themselves into the front of the café when it was time for the speeches and a hush came over the room when Elle was first to take the microphone.

"Hi, everyone," she called, "I just wanted to say a quick 'thank you' for all of you coming out here and taking part in this day. I know it's not exactly what we had planned but the important thing is that we got married in front of all the people we love and Amy nearly killed my ex-husband."

The crowd laughed and started to clap in appreciation, I decided it was better just to go along with it instead of burning in embarrassment, so I took a theatrical bow.

"In all seriousness, today wouldn't have been possible without that woman giving me a good talking to and reminding me about what was important about this whole day: love. I love this man more than I thought someone could love another person, and I'm so excited that we have our whole lives ahead of us to have a great big adventure.

"My girls are my world, but it turns out there's room in my heart for him as well. I guess I just didn't realise it until I found him; now I can't imagine my life without him in it. I am honoured, River, that you chose to share your life with me and take a chance. I admire your bravery for tying your horse to an unpredictable wagon.

"I may be unorthodox and gobby and I can curse like there's no tomorrow but that just means that I'll always keep things interesting and my insults will usually be unique so if we fight you can add to your own vocabulary. I fucking love you, Riv, I really fucking do."

She raised her glass and started to cry so he stood beside her and gave her a kiss until she stopped. The room clapped and clinked glasses, toasting to love and waited for River to say his piece.

"There's not much else I can say here that won't just tread on what my wife has already said. All I know is that up until this point I lived a life of 'what ifs' and 'should haves' and living in fear of what people would think. I have never been more grateful that I was hit by a car and knocked into the best decision of my life.

"I never want to live another second in fear of the future, I want to run towards it with her by my side and find out what exactly life has in store for us. If you take away anything from today simply ask yourself: what could you achieve if you weren't afraid? It's the same question I asked myself a few years ago and it turns out I could make my dreams come true. So, to quote my wife: 'Just fucking do it.'"

We all cheered and toasted the couple. After listening to them both I felt inspired about what lay ahead for me and my family. Maybe this baby wasn't planned but it doesn't have to mean it's a bad thing. I've two kids, it's not like I'm going in blind and like Ben said: we were already very lucky in our lives, adding another person into the equation won't break that.

I felt Ben's arms fold around my waist and pull me into a hug. His chin rested softly on my shoulder and his hair tickled at my ear.

"Feeling better?" I asked, without turning.

"The beer is helping," he admitted.

"Are we going to be ok, Ben?"

"No, I don't think we are."

I panicked at his words but he gave me another squeeze and continued: "We're going to be fucking epic and you're going to rock this pregnancy."

I smiled and turned to face him properly, feeling relief at his smiling face.

"You know why?" he asked.

"Why's that?"

"Because you're Amy fucking Cole and there's nothing you can't do."

I feared his optimism would be short lived once the buzz of the alcohol wore off but I was willing to roll with it for now.

"You're very wise, Mr Cole."

"I know, right?"

We spent the evening dancing and laughing with our friends and children. I ate more cake than the rest of the guests combined and I kept hugging Elle every time we crossed paths. It was approaching midnight and although my parents had taken the kids to their house hours ago, leaving me a free agent for the evening, I was ready to collapse into bed.

I helped a drunk Ben home and put him to bed. I just removed his shoes and socks and didn't bother to wake him to get undressed. I decided to get some air and clear my head before trying to sleep. It had been an eventful day and there was still a ringing in my ears from the band.

I poured myself a glass of water and decided to sit on the step outside my front door. I looked at the moon and the stars above my head, taking in the cold air and embracing the quiet. I thought about the little life steadily growing inside me and started to worry about all the things that lay ahead. I never enjoyed pregnancy, I just wanted to fast forward to the part where I was meeting the new love of my life. I was excited at the thought of meeting this little being and seeing how they would fit into our family. I wondered if it would be my long-awaited girl and how the boys would react to the news. I imagined how the new baby would look and if one would finally take after me. I lost myself in all the possibilities that lay ahead for me and felt content that this wasn't going to end in heartache and this child would make it into the world.

I looked at the stars and thought about my lost Lily. I still thought about her but that time in my life no longer burned a pain in my chest. It was what it was and now I had to live my life the best I could without hanging on to what I'd lost. She would always be a part of me but I had to stay in the present, now more than ever, and make sure I live my life fully and without fear of slipping into the depths of depression again.

I knew there would be tough days ahead but for some reason I knew everything was going to be ok.

Three months later

Chapter 28

"I'm calling bullshit on the whole pregnancy myth," I called to Ben from the bathroom, "At no time do I ever feel like I'm fucking glowing."

Ben tentatively came into the room to check his irritable wife.

"You look like you're glowing now," he said, nervously.

I lifted my head out of the toilet long enough to glare at him and say: "It's fucking sweat from the continuous vomit I'm throwing up because YOU knocked me up with the spawn of fucking Satan!"

As soon as I finished my accusation I could feel another wave of nausea hit and I returned my head to the toilet bowl. This is what it has been like, daily, since two days after Elle's wedding. I had never known sickness like it and I was losing the will to live. All my positivity about our bundle of joy had been thrown up about two weeks ago, now I was just accusing Ben of ruining my life.

The only person I could stand to be pleasant around was Elle. She was delighted by my news and had been molly-coddling me ever since she found out. I waited until she was back from honeymoon to share my news, but it didn't take her long to figure it out as I couldn't walk anywhere in the office without having the wastepaper basket in my hand at all times. My weekend mornings were spent here and it wasn't until late afternoon I would attempt to eat anything. I felt that the only silver lining to this hideousness would be that I would lose a bit of weight before the bump took over but my baby had other ideas. I was a bloated, puffy, miserable lump who had another 20 weeks of this torture to get through. To top it all off, my mother-in-law had decided to visit again.

Why does everything happen to me?

"Aimsy," she called from downstairs, "Can I get you anything?"

The sound of my retching was reverberating all over the house so there was no point in trying to keep quiet for my unwelcome guest.

"Get your mother out of my house before I kill you both," I hissed at Ben.

"She's trying to be helpful, Amy, she's been a big help with the boys these last few days," he said.

I couldn't argue. The last two days the sickness had been particularly volatile and I was little or no help around the house. The smell of any type of food would have me running to the bathroom and I knew I couldn't let the boys live on take-away food for the next five months. I was grateful for her help and at least with her here I knew there was going to be actual laundry done and the kids wouldn't be sent to school in questionable underwear.

I got Ben to help me back into the bed and I stared blankly at the laptop beside me. These days most of my work was done from my bed office while Elle held the fort by herself. My insomnia paired with the relentless vomiting meant I was most productive around 3am. Elle would regularly wake up to several emails sent overnight with pitch ideas, marketing plans and proposals for clients.

The doctor warned me if I was unable to keep anything down by today I would need to be admitted. I loathed the idea of being stuck in a hospital, but if they had some miracle cure to make me feel even halfway human I would treat it like a five-star holiday.

"I think it's time to admit defeat and see the professionals," said Ben as he pulled my legs into the bed properly.

"Do you think there's something wrong with the baby? Is that why I'm so sick?"

"Settle, petal," he soothed, "We'll get you dressed and go see what they say."

I sat like a toddler, unable to muster the energy to get changed and simply allowed Ben to dress me. He led me down the stairs and I caught a glimpse of the boys talking enthusiastically to their granddad about their latest toys. Althea came out to the hallway, concern etched across her face.

"Aimsy, you look awful," she said.

For once it didn't sound like her usual insult, but it seemed like it came from a place of actual worry.

"I'm going to take her up to the hospital," explained Ben, "We won't be long."

I was shocked to find myself caught up in an embrace from my mother-in-law and even more surprised to find that it felt lovely.

"You're a strong woman and that little baba is just fine. You just go and let them get you better, everything will be fine here," she said.

I gave her a watery smile and nodded my head in agreement, careful not to cry and lose anymore fluids from my body. We drove slowly to the hospital in Ben's attempt to knock bring on any travel sickness.

"Your mum is really nice," I said, looking out the window.

"It's a good job we're going to the hospital you've clearly had a knock to the head."

"I mean it, she's been really helpful the last few days. Maybe this child isn't the antichrist, maybe it's going to bring us all closer together."

"Ok…"

He must have thought it was easier, or safer, to turn on the radio and stop the conversation in its tracks. He had learned by now to not take what I said when pregnant as Gospel because it was more than likely my hormones talking. Once, when I was pregnant with Adam, I told him I was perfectly fine with him going on a 'lads' weekend to Scotland when the baby would be six weeks old. This permission was swiftly revoked when the sheer enormity of parenthood hit and I decided that neither of us were ever leaving the house again.

"I know our relationship has been difficult in the past but I think we're turning a corner," I continued, over the music.

"You're right, you are turning a corner – this one, into the hospital."

I gave up trying to convince my husband I was growing as a person and settled myself into just getting through this visit without getting admitted.

The doctor took one look at me and told me I wasn't going anywhere. I was dehydrated and would be staying put until I could keep something down. I was instantly anxious at the thought of staying here, but once I saw the bed and the nurse was so kind to me I decided that I was in the best place possible.

Ben was sent home to get my things whilst I was taken in for a scan to see how the miscreant in my womb was doing. No matter how many times I had a scan I always held my breath until I could see the fluttering of the heart so I could feel some level of comfort.

There it was, beating away; completely oblivious to the hell it was putting me through. It was the first time I properly smiled in days and I was so relieved to see all was well. I decided that I could put up with the sickness and the hormones if this little thing would play ball and stay safe until it was ready to come out and meet us.

I love you, you little shit, now please let me eat something

By the time Ben came back I was already lying on the bed clutching the print out from the scan. He kissed my forehead and helped me get changed once again. I was under strict instructions not to eat or drink until the vomiting subsided while they hooked me up to an IV of fluids. I was perfectly relaxed in my surroundings and felt much better about the situation since I saw the scan.

"Everything is going to be ok," I said.

"I know," replied Ben, "I hate that you're having it so rough but it will all be worth it in the end."

Big words from the one who doesn't have to push out a bowling ball from his body in a few months

I decided to let him be a comfort instead of picking a fight that no one would win. I eventually sent him home so I could try and sleep – when really I was making the most of the time away from the house.

If I just pretend this is a spa I could actually enjoy this part. A spa that offers no food or drink and smells like chemicals.

It took three days for the vomiting to subside and for me to keep any food or drink down but I was finally allowed home. It was wonderful to find the house looking immaculate and I once again decided to finally bury the hatchet with Althea – not in her back as Ben guessed.

Elle was at the front door within a half hour of me arriving home, laden down with balloons and a box of buns. We sat in the living room so I could dig into the sugary treats.

"Maybe I should stick to fruit," I said, already picking up the éclair.

"Fuck it, if you can't get chunky when you're up the duff then when can you?"

"You know it's not healthy for the baby," said Althea
Don't kill her, she cleaned your house

"You're right, Althea, we will give the rest to you and you can take them home when you're going."

She smiled and took the box away into the kitchen to remove temptation.

"She's a fucking buzz kill," remarked Elle.

"She's alright," I offered, greedily stuffing the éclair into my mouth, "So what have I missed in work?"

"Ah the usual shit, but I did sign a new client yesterday."

"Really? Who?"

"River," she laughed.

"He's hardly struggling."

"No, but we are and if I can't make the most of some nepotism when I'm married to this guy then when can I?

287

He wanted a new marketing team, I offered us and threw in a blowjob so he was sold."

"Do you offer that to all our perspective clients?"

"Only the ones I fancy."

We both laughed and I was secretly relieved at the news. This was a huge deal for our little business and could attract other big clients our way.

"We still don't have a name," I reminded her.

"Two girls, one - "

"I'm going to stop you there," I hastily interrupted.

"I'm kidding, you prude. Ok, what about: Camel Toe Solutions."

"That makes no sense. It has nothing to do with our business."

"Yes, it does. We could say something like: We get you out of tight jam."

We spent the rest of the afternoon thinking of other ridiculous business names and came no closer to actually finding one that worked.

"Alright, princess, I've got to love you and leave you. My husband will be expecting dinner on the table so he can ravage me on it afterwards," said Elle.

"Please don't tell me that stuff, I have a very delicate stomach, remember?"

"Ah less of the innocence, Cole, it wasn't the Immaculate Conception that landed you in this situation, you filthy beast."

She cackled loudly at her own joke and left the house. I could still hear her by the time she got into the car.

The constant feeling of nausea had been replaced by an appetite I couldn't satisfy. One minute it was savoury, the next it was sweet, another minute later I was looking for something altogether more lurid. I remember one of my non-pregnant friends used to ask me about my sex life during this time.

"I heard you get super horny all the time," she said.

"That's a myth circulated by men so they can guilt their partners into having sex while pregnant," I clarified.

I never feel less sexy than when I'm pregnant. Most of the time I can't really stand the sight of Ben when pregnant, it's nothing personal, he just can't seem to do anything right and I daydream about murdering him. This vengeful feeling tends to subside when the baby arrives and my body is filled with so much love I think I may explode. It's a very confusing time for Ben to be around me.

That's why this sudden feeling of arousal had completely taken me by surprise. I thought I could put it out by eating a huge portion of pasta doused in creamy curry sauce. It didn't, and I vowed never to eat that disgusting concoction again.

There's no point fighting it, I'm going to have to sleep with my husband

I wandered upstairs and found him cutting his toenails on the bed. The sight of this would normally induce a relentless fury – mostly because he never remembers to clean them off the covers – but I decided to swallow the irritation and charm my way into his pants.

"Hello, there," I said, trying to sound a mix of seductive and alluring.

"Why's your voice so low? Is this another pregnancy thing?"

Ok stop talking like that

"I wondered if you'd like to have your wicked way with your sexy wife?"

289

"The kids are downstairs?"

"So? We can turn on cartoons and they'll be oblivious."

"I dunno, seems a bit weird."

"We have sex all the time with them in the house!"

"Yeah, but they're unconscious."

"Have you seen our kids watch tv? A bomb could go off and their eyes wouldn't move from the damn screen."

He seemed to be weighing up the moral implications of this and decided that them catching us and ending up in therapy was worth the risk.

"What if I hurt the baby?" he asked, with fresh concern on his face.

"With your ten foot knob?"

"HEY! There's never been a complaint about my size before now."

"I'm pointing out the ridiculousness of your concern, not complaining about little Benny."

"I've asked you not to call him that."

"What should I call him?"

"Nothing! There's doesn't need to be any name but like if you're going to it should be something like Thor or Titan."

"Duly noted," I said, "Now, go turn on the tele then get back here and drop your drawers."

I scuttled under the covers to try and keep warm. One of the perks of pregnancy (and probably the only one) was that I was rarely cold. This was fine when the weather was rubbish but a nightmare in summer time. I shivered, naked, and waited for Ben to come back. I looked at my 20 week bump that looked more like a 30 week one. I'd lost count of the amount of times people had asked if I was having twins or how many times the doctor asked me to double check my dates. It was mortifying. My boobs had seen better days too and as I continued to survey my naked body I felt more and more uncomfortable about Ben seeing me naked. I got out of bed and went to my wardrobe to fetch some pyjamas but Ben burst through the door before I managed to get any out.

"You look fantastic," he said.

I searched his face for the lie in his words but I found none. He was really looking at me as if I was the most glorious woman he had ever seen and suddenly all I wanted to do was be with him – with or without my saggy boobs on show. We both got back under the cover and began to kiss. He gingerly lay on top of me, careful not to put his full weight on my bump and we kissed, passionately. I felt little tingles of electricity all over my body that only ever appeared when I was with him. They exploded in technicolour when we shared our first kiss and now years later they still appear but have transformed into tingles burrowed into my muscle memory as if my skin remembers every touch he's ever given me.

"I love you," I said, "I just wanted you to know."

"Now's as good a time as any," he laughed.

"Daddy, why are you jumping on the bed?" asked Arthur.

"SWEET MOTHER OF GOD!" screamed Ben as he clambered off me and tucked the covers up to his chin, "Sorry, son, you scared me there."

His attempt to sound completely at ease, failed miserably, and he just sounded completely out of breath and high-pitched.

"Why were you jumping on the bed?" he repeated.

"I wasn't," said Ben.

"I heard you, there was a squeaky noise so I went to see if it was a mouse and I saw you jumping under the covers."

Please make this stop and the ground swallow me up for eternity

"Your dad and I were playing hide and seek," I offered, "He caught me and jumped on the bed to scare me."

"Oh. Well done, daddy," he said and then left to return downstairs.

"We are never having sex again," said Ben, as soon as he was confident that Arthur was out of earshot.

We both stared at the ceiling, lying side-by-side in silence. Suddenly we both burst out laughing and decided it was best to find some clothes before we did actually scar them for life. There's nothing like possibly traumatising your child to really kill a romantic moment.

Cheers, kids

Chapter 29

I regaled my tale of debauchery to Elle who couldn't contain her delight at our misfortune. It was the following day and I was finally well enough to be back in the office and I wanted to find out everything I had missed since my head had been stuck down a toilet.

"You're going to have to stop sharing your sex stories with me," she said.

"The constant over-sharer is asking *me* to keep things clean? Marriage has changed you, Elle."

"It's not that, it's just that Ben is like my brother now and I don't want to think about that sorta stuff when he's involved."

"After yesterday I can assure you there will be no sex stories to share for quite some time. Maybe when this one is at college I might be able to convince Ben to have a quickie."

"I was thinking if you're managing to keep food down these days I might have a dinner party. Are the Coles available for some lovely vegan food at our place, tonight?" she asked.

I found it hard to marry the concept of 'vegan' and 'nice' but I agreed none-the-less. It saved me cooking dinner, especially as the kids were practically living off whatever frozen meat, covered in breadcrumbs, was found in my freezer.

"It's a date," I said, "Do you want me to bring anything?"

"An appetite and fake yummy noises if the food is disgusting. River is really kind about my cooking but he's losing weight with my inedible dinners," she confessed.

"That's not exactly making me feel excited about the prospect of dinner."

"It's too late now, you've agreed."

I decided not to tell Ben about Elle's description of her food and thought he should make up his own mind. The boys were delighted at the thought of spending an evening with the twins, especially as it meant they got to stay up a bit later on a school night.

I hadn't seen much of River since the wedding. A few days after the celebration they left for their honeymoon – a three week Caribbean cruise – and since then I had more or less been a prisoner in my own home, thanks to the bump.

They were still living in Elle's house but were trying to find somewhere new that they could make their own memories in. She didn't talk about it much but I know this house still held a lot of memories of Keith and their life together before it all fell apart. I wondered if living in this shadow bothered River; if it did, he didn't let it show as he answered the door and welcomed us into the house.

There was smoke billowing from the kitchen so River ran up the hallway and closed the door before the smoke alarm went off. Before he closed it completely I was sure I had spotted an open flame coming from the hob.

"Should I check on Elle to see if she needs any help?" I offered.

"No, no, it's fine I'll go help her now. You all just go and relax in the lounge and we'll call you for the first course."

The boys disappeared upstairs to find the twins and I knew we wouldn't see them until their bellies started to rumble. The smell of smoke was starting to get a bit overpowering from where we were sitting and Elle's cursing was getting louder and more random.

"The fucking nut-gobbler of a spatula melted onto the fucking pot," she screamed, "The bastarding pasta is ruined now."

I gave a weak smile to Ben who was looking more concerned by the second.

"I think we'll be getting a take-away on the way home," he said, nudging me in the ribs.

"As long as that's all we get from this experience and not food poisoning or third degree burns."

River came into the room and announced the first course.

"I've left little nibbles up for the kids," he said, "The girls aren't big fans of a sit-down dinner so we give them a little bit of everything and call it 'tapas'. Whatever works, eh?"

He was getting the hang of this parenting subterfuge quickly

We sat down at the table and were presented with fruit salads. 'Salad' seemed a bit of an exaggeration for what was in the bowl. It was half an apple, a segment of orange and a banana.

"This looks…great," I said, keeping my end of the bargain by trying to sound enthusiastic in front of River.

"It's ok, Amy, I know it's shit," Elle replied, "I was trying to make these little veggie pastry parcels but the fucking things caught fire like kindling in that oven. I've never seen anything like it."

Ben was struggling to contain his laughter so settled for trying to shove the whole banana in his mouth to muffle the sound.

Elle glared in his direction before pointedly stabbing her apple with her fork. At that moment the toaster popped to break the tense stand-off between the two.

"Main course is ready," she said, flatly, "The pasta dish I made is currently stuck to the bottom of the pot and is that horrible smell you smell.

"Would you like butter or marmalade on your toast? Don't worry they're both vegan friendly versions."

"Is that a serious question?" I asked, unsure as what was the correct answer. Her look told me she was being completely serious.

"Butter, please."

She was onto a roll with the toast so she kept piling them onto our plates each time the toaster popped another two slices. She only stopped once we all had to tell her we couldn't possibly eat any more.

"Are my guests full? We aim to please here in my kitchen," she said.

If she brings any more toast I may vomit

"Now, what would you like for dessert?" asked are hostess.

"What are the options?" asked Ben.

"Well it's basically either more fruit or more toast – but I can put chocolate spread on it this time so it's sweet. Vegan friendly!"

She looked a bit manic as she left the table to hunt out the chocolate spread. Her head disappeared behind the door while Ben kicked my ankle to get me to stop her from putting more bread in the toaster.

"Actually, Elle, we're all good for dessert," I said, "Why don't you just sit down and have a chat. That's the best part of a dinner party anyway, not the food."

I hope she's buying this lie because I'm certainly not

When she came back to the table she looked utterly miserable. She put her head down on the table and started to cry.

River rubbed her back to try and calm her down while I started to tell her how much I enjoyed the toast and I probably wouldn't have been able to eat the pasta anyway because the baby hates it.

She lifted her head up and tried to smile but her mascara and run and she looked more like a demonic panda.

"It's not about the food," she explained, "You've always known I'm a rubbish cook. I just wanted everything to be perfect."

"Elle, you've got the rest of your life to master the perfect dinner party."

In my effort to cheer her up I managed to make her cry even more.

"What did I say?" I asked River, "I was trying to help."

"Elle wanted you both here tonight because she has some news and just wanted the food to go well," he said,

"Oh my God, you're pregnant!" I screamed, "Don't cry, I know I make it look totally fucking awful but that's just me, you're going to be brilliant."

"I'm not pregnant, Amy," she said, "I just wanted the food to be really good so the rest of the night wouldn't seem so bad."

I didn't like where this conversation was heading and all of a sudden there were loud sirens in my head whilst my body was screaming at me to run away and not hear what Elle was trying to tell me.

"Amy, I have cancer."

Chapter 30

When I was five-years-old I lost my mother when we were in a supermarket. It was terrifying. One minute I was holding her hand talking about what we were going to have for dinner the next she was gone. I had wandered off to look at the baker, who was putting out fresh doughnuts and when I turned to pester my mum into getting me one, but she was nowhere to be found.

In that moment I felt that the ground had come away from underneath me and I was freefalling into a nightmare. As I sat across from Elle at that dinner table I felt the exact same way.

I was aware she had continued talking about her cancer but none of the words were making sense to me. Only snippets of information would make it through to me.

Breast cancer. Growth removal. Operation. Radio therapy. Daily medication. Chemo…

Unsurprisingly the nausea had returned but I knew it was simply down to this news and not the bump acting up. I felt the colour drain from my face and my expression mirrored that of Elle's. Ben and River were talking about the logistics of it all, dates and timescales of treatments whereas I kept my eyes on Elle to see if I could find the words to say.

299

Instead, I took her hand in mine and kissed it. She smiled and cried at the same time. She took a big breath and tried to compose herself, putting up a façade of someone who was completely fine once again. I didn't know what to say to her so I just kept holding her hand and hoping that everything I couldn't verbalise would be transferred by my touch. I don't know how long we sat that way but eventually our husbands left the table so we could speak privately.

I had dozens of questions but none of them seemed to matter. Only one was pressing right now.

"How can I help?" I asked, "Just tell me exactly what you need and I will do it. I don't care what it is."

She pulled me into a hug and said: "I always wanted a sister. I think you're more than that though. We're like soul mates without the sex."

"So…married people?"

My poor attempt at a joke garnered a sympathetic smile from Elle but she wasn't getting away with not answering my question.

"Tell me how I can help, please?" I asked.

"I don't know, princess, I really don't. I'm going to see a consultant to get a date for the operation but for now I guess I just need you to keep me sane. I don't know what's going to happen but I know I won't be able to face it without you by my side."

"You don't have to worry about that for a second," I said, "I will be here, there, wherever you need me to be. You won't have to face a second of this by yourself, I swear to you."

We hugged for the longest time and for once I didn't think about how long it was socially acceptable to hold someone. I wanted to stay there for the night, just so I could reassure her that she was not alone, she would never have to be alone again.

We drove home in silence. The kids had instantly fallen asleep in the backseat whereas I was scrolling through my phone to look at holistic cancer remedies I can force her to do on top of the treatment. I came across statistic after statistic about the improvement in survival rates for people with breast cancer and for some reason it made me angry. I could feel the rage begin to burn in my stomach and flow into my hands making me want to squeeze the life out of something. My breathing became more pronounced the longer we were in the car and I felt like I needed to jump from the vehicle and just start running.

I thought better of this plan, mostly because I usually trip over air when trying to exit the car when it's fully stopped so the likelihood of me surviving a jump while it's moving was slim to none.

"Do you want to talk about it?" asked Ben.

"Talk about what?"

"Elle of course."

"Ok, what would you like to talk about? The fact that everything is completely pointless?"

"It's not pointless, River said the doctors are feeling very optimistic about the treatment. It's going to be tough but Elle is tougher."

"Not about the treatment, about life. What is the point in all of this when out of the blue cancer will get you anyway? You work, you have kids, you look after yourself, you fall in love and then this cancerous fucking growth decides to screw you over anyway. What's the fucking point?" I raged.

"The point is: life. Something shit is happening to your best friend but that doesn't mean it's the end of the world as we know it and you should just throw in the towel. This is when you fight even harder because when we come out the other side it's all worth it to be with the person you love."

"I don't know what I will do if I lose her," I said.

"You don't have to worry about that now. I don't know what's going to happen to Elle, none of us do, but I know she's got a hell of better chance with you fighting this thing alongside her than without."

"What can I do?"

"Just be there. Help with what she needs, whether it's having the kids for a while so she can rest after treatment or make her something to eat – cancer, or not, that woman clearly needs help in the kitchen – or just make her laugh. Help her realise that there's a reason to keep fighting. That's all we can do for now."

"What if it's not enough?"

"Amy, I've known from the second we met that you are enough, you are so much more than enough. I predict you will be the first person to cure cancer just by being in her presence."

"That's not funny," I said, smiling regardless.

"My point is, you two are a package deal and so this stupid growth has double the fight on its hands. It doesn't stand a chance."

He pulled up into our driveway and kissed my head while I cried quietly beside him. I know he was trying to build me up so I could be strong for Elle but at this minute in time I couldn't see how I was going to be any use to her. She was the strong one, she was the one that pushed me forward and the thought of cancer robbing her from me was terrifying.

"I feel so selfish," I confessed, "This is happening to her, not me. What about the girls and River? They all must be going through hell."

"It's a shock, you get to be a little selfish and scared when you're here with me, I won't tell anyone. Tomorrow? You have to knock it off, we're the cheerleaders and I can't have you cursing the sky and crying when you're supposed to be keeping her mind off things."

I cried myself to sleep that night as I ran through all the memories I had with Elle up until now. The show reel of us was one of the most special times of my life but there was so much left we needed to do. Tonight I would cry and complain about how unfair everything was, but Ben was right, tomorrow started the fight against this thing, a fight I would make damn sure she would win.

Chapter 31

I couldn't sleep. I felt like there was too much to do before tomorrow would come. If I was going to be of actual use to Elle I needed to do my research. I knew the Western medicine approach was the best way to go and River would have the know-how on the holistic side of things so I had to find a different approach.

I was lost in a sea of *Pinterest* 'cancer-beating' smoothie recipes when I had a flash of inspiration. I constantly came across people talking about the all-healing qualities of cannabis oil.

Surely there must be some truth to it?

Ben was asleep and I wasn't entirely sure he would approve of my line of thinking so I went to my usual port-of-call: the same website I found Angela.

If people start looking through my internet search history they're really going to think I'm a lot more adventurous than I am. Searching a dominatrix and drugs while 20 weeks pregnant and dressed in a unicorn onesie. This is what my life has come to.

I wasn't sure what to look for so I just typed in the obvious choice: cannabis oil.

No results came back and I wasn't entirely surprised by this. I doubted the friendly neighbourhood drug dealer would make it that easy for them to be tracked down. I knew there were suppliers in the local shopping centre so it couldn't be *that* illegal. I wasn't convinced that if they were selling it in the shops that it was strong enough for battling cancer so I kept going in my own search.

I decided to go through my online friend list to see if I was still in touch with anyone from my university days. I had the distinct impression that I hung round with plenty of stoners. I got as far as 'P' in the list and came across Paul.

Paul was a political science student who bored me half to death and always smelled of marijuana.

Why am I still friends with him on this?

His profile picture was, predictably enough, a Rastafarian flag and I made a mental note to have a clear out of my friends list after all this. I hadn't spoken to him in years but he was never the type to hold a grudge.

Probably because he was high every time you spoke to him

I decided to just bypass any small talk and come out with my request, even if he couldn't help me he could maybe put me in touch with someone that could.

Amy: Hi Paul, Amy Galbraith here from uni. Hope you're keeping well. I'm not very good at small talk so I just thought I should come right out and ask: can you get me some drugs?

I hit 'send' and waited a few minutes to see if he was online. I wasn't feeling confident as it was late at night, but then I realised it was only 10:15pm and I was, in fact, an old woman who goes to bed at 9pm on a weeknight. The three dots appeared as he began to type and I held my breath to see if I could get some help.

Paul: Who?

Well, that's a great start.

Paul: I'm kidding! Hey Amy, long time. How's suburbia?

Amy: It's great. Now, about the drugs?

Paul: Sure, I can sort that for you. What happened to your guy?

Amy: What guy?

Paul: Your own supplier. From college days?

I read and re-read his messages a few times before realising that Paul clearly thought I had been smoking the whole time he knew me at college. I wasn't sure how to process this information. Should I be insulted that he thought I was some sort of dope fiend or impressed that I managed to pull off a more interesting persona? If anything I thought most people in our circle viewed me as a bit uptight. Before I could write back, Paul had started to type again.

Paul: Was your guy just into the hard stuff?

Now, I'm completely lost

Amy: I didn't have 'a guy' in uni. I hadn't come close to even smelling the stuff until I met you.

Paul: You're kidding? You're telling me you weren't on coke?

Amy: WHAT? NO! Why on earth would you think that? Did everyone think that?

Paul: Well…yeah. I thought you knew, we called you 'Blow'.

Suddenly the penny started to drop. I was indeed called 'Blow' for a while but I figured it was because my face was so puffy and people thought I looked like a blowfish.

Paul: So you were really just like that? Sober?

Amy: like what?

Paul: like…. on. You were always just so 'on'.

306

Amy: If by 'on' you mean highly driven and intelligent then I guess I am just that type of person.
Paul: Fuck. Wow. Seriously? That's a real mind melt

I was getting more insulted with every message he was sending and I decided that this trip down memory lane to score some cannabis for my cancer-stricken friend was going to have to end.

Paul: I don't do coke, sorry.
Amy: NEITHER DO I!!!
Paul: Are you sure?
Amy: Am I sure I didn't do Class-A drugs now or during my college years? Yes I'm fucking sure.
Paul: I think you're protesting a little too much. Do you want a number for a support group if you're trying to get off that stuff? It'll kill you.
Amy: Goodbye, Paul.

I slammed the laptop closed and stomped up the stairs to bed. I did my usual bedtime routine of making a mental list of what all I needed to do in the day ahead.

Go to the shopping centre in the morning and get the oil. Maybe track down everyone in university tomorrow and send a blanket email to explain you weren't a coke addict. Maybe not.

Chapter 32

Elle and I sat at our desks pretending to read emails but I knew neither of us was remotely concentrating on work. When she walked into the office, this morning, she shot down any attempt I made to talk about the situation.

"We're here to work, use me while you've got me," she said.

I didn't bother to reply or argue, I knew there was no point in trying when she was in one of these 'fuck the world' moods. Usually I would feel anxious about the tension but today was different, today I had to be the pusher and the one in charge. She would just have to put up with it and me.

"Finish that email, we're going out," I announced.

"Where?"

"Never mind where, just finish up and meet me downstairs. I'm going to grab us hot drinks for the road."

I could hear her mumble a complaint as I was leaving but I decided to ignore her and carry on with my plan. She reluctantly followed me as we picked up our drinks and got into my car.

"Look, Amy, I know you're trying to help and everything but I'm really not feeling up to the 'kumbya', life is magical shit," she said.

"Shut up and drink your drink."

I put on the radio so we could carry on with the drive peacefully and I wouldn't be able to hear her complaints. It didn't take long for her to realise we were heading to the lake and she shot me a 'why here?' look. I didn't try to look at her or answer her questions, I just knew we had to get to the lake and start this journey together properly.

I got out of the car and waited for her to join me at the waterside. There were a few people walking their dogs and feeding the swans. I resisted the urge to tell them off for giving them bread but figured I had a more pressing issue to address first.

"Amy, what the fuck are we doing here?" she asked, exasperated.

"Cancer is shit," I said, "You're allowed to be angry about it and fed up at life knocking you down, it's all part of being human and experiencing all the ups and downs."

"So?"

"So, get angry about it."

"What do you mean?"

"Here and now, just get fucking angry about it. Scream at the water and shout about how unfair this all is and curse God or your body or just fucking bad luck for putting you through this but get it out now."

She looked at me as if I was mad but something seemed to resonate with her and she looked out to the water. I braced myself for her to start shouting but she simply turned to me and said in a quiet voice: "It's not fair."

The tears started flowing fast and freely down her face so I took her hand and turned to the water.

"MY BEST FRIEND HAS CANCER AND IT'S SHIT," I screamed.

A couple, who were walking their sausage dog, started to pick up their pace to their car to get away from the odd, screaming woman beside them. Elle laughed at their reaction and wiped her tears.

"I HAVE CANCER AND IT'S FUCKING SHIT," she screamed.

She started to laugh harder and then a genuine smile appeared on her face, she took another big breath and continued: "I HAVE CRACKING TITS AND THEY'RE TRYING TO KILL ME."

She grabbed her breasts as she shouted, causing one jogger to trip over in surprise.

"MY HUSBAND CUTS HIS TOENAILS ON THE BED AND DOESN'T CLEAN THEM UP AFTER," I added.

"What? Just because you have cancer doesn't mean you have the monopoly on suffering."

She gave me a playful punch, took another deep breath and shouted one final time.

"I DON'T WANT TO DIE."

The words hung in the air and we both stood helplessly at the edge of the water letting the enormity of what was to come sink in. I took her hand and led her over to the bench to sit down.

"You're not going to die," I said, simply, "I don't know much about the world but I know you're not going to die."

"How do you know that then?"

"Because I have a kid in my belly that needs to meet her godmother, a business that is only starting to take off, and when our husbands inevitably die first we have a few decades as a lesbian couple to embark on. Haven't you realised yet that this is all about me?"

"How could I forget?" she laughed, "I need to stop stealing your thunder like this."

"I'll tell you what: you can have the attention for a bit while you sort out this pesky cancer thing but afterwards it's straight back to me, deal?"

"Deal, I much prefer figuring out your nonsense."

We sat on the bench talking about nothing in particular and finishing our drinks. It was a warm afternoon with summer just around the corner and the trees were bursting into life with hundreds of shades of green lining the lake's edge.

"You'll never guess what I found in one of River's boxes when he was moving in," said Elle.

"What? If it's a porno magazine that's not really a surprise - old school, yes, but hardly shocking."

"No, it was a movie," she replied, smugly.

"A porno movie? Was he in it?"

"Not a fucking porno, will you get your mind out of the gutter for once?"

I rolled my eyes at the irony of that sentence coming from her of all people.

"Please, continue," I said, sweetly.

"It was a very special movie called... *The River Wild*."

I jumped up from the bench and started bouncing in my excitement.

"I KNEW IT, I FUCKING KNEW IT! You married a complete weirdo," I shouted.

"I know, right?" she laughed, "I left it out on the bed for him to see and you should have seen the look on his face when he found it."

"What did he say?"

"Not much of an explanation other than he found the film 'transformative' and his name just 'organically grew from there'. He begged me not to tell you but it's not like he can shout at me now that I've cancer."

"See? We've been thinking about this whole thing the wrong way. Think of all the stuff we can get away with now and no one can get mad at you."

"Exactly, I'll just start coughing dramatically if they give out."

We're definitely going to hell

When our bums began to numb on the bench we decided to take a short walk to the canopy where the wedding took place. I loved that the lake now reminded me of that happy day – despite me being covered in pond scum. It was a beautiful place that deserved to house beautiful memories, not ones of heartache, loss and regret. Now, it was filled with love and hope.

"You're going to beat this, Elle, I know it."

She simply smiled and said: "I love you, Amy Cole."

"I love you too."

We stayed beside the water for hours talking about everything and nothing but before we returned to the car, and went back to reality, we made a vow that whatever was coming we would face it together. Elle had changed my life and now it was my turn to save hers.

AMY COLE WILL RETURN IN 2019 IN:

**AMY COLE
HAS IT ALL
FIGURED OUT**

Elizabeth McGivern

Acknowledgements

Well, here we are again. You must be a glutton for punishment if you've come back for more, eh?

I always viewed this book as the 'difficult second album' but in reality I was just pretty great at avoiding my office and writing it.

Since the first book came out I have met and spoken with so many people I would never have had the chance to talk to and who could relate to what Amy had been through. I hope the same happens this time around – but maybe not those who enjoy water sports.

The usual gang are deserving of praise for helping me complete this book:

Betty, thank you for not disowning me after you read this. Please don't try and wash my mouth out with soap.

Dad, you have my permission never to read this book. I think it's best for our relationship if you don't know just how twisted your daughter's brain is.

Rachael, thank you for reading chapter 21 and doing your big laugh; I felt much better about putting that out into the world after that…

Lasairiona, I'm sorry the cover didn't feature a Taliban fighter in a bikini. My bad.

Sarah, thank you for being my cheerleader and I promise to listen to you talk about Palestine over lunch, but I will never join your football team.

Now for the real MVP's

Oliver, you are the most incredible little weirdo on the planet. Your imagination and creativity is awe-inspiring, never change.

Oscar, you are the most ridiculous miscreant and I couldn't love you more. You're fearless, hilarious and every day with you is an experience, never change.

Conor, absolutely none of this would be possible without you. I know you think you have Stockholm Syndrome – and you're probably right – but I don't want to know what a single day is like without you. Thank you for letting us all drive you slowly mad, never change.

Elizabeth McGivern is a former journalist turned hostage-in-her-own-home surrounded by three men and a horrible dog named Dougal.

In an effort to keep her sanity she decided to write a parenting blog after the birth of her first son so she can pinpoint the exact moment she failed as a mother.

In an unexpected turn of events, the blog helped her to find a voice and connect with parents in similar situations; namely those who were struggling with mental health issues and parenting. It was because of this encouragement – and wanting to avoid her children as much as possible – her debut novel, *Amy Cole has lost her mind*, was born.

Elizabeth lives in Northern Ireland although wishes she could relocate to Iceland on a daily basis. To witness her regular failings as a parent you can find her on:

www.mayhemandbeyond.com
Facebook.com/mayhemandbeyond
Instagram: mayhemandbeyond

12022654R00187

Printed in Great Britain
by Amazon